47/24

CW00538775

Gavin Robertson is
He studied Life Sci
and then parasitolog
cal Medicine. He took a PhD at Cambridge in Entomo
logical Population Modelling where he began to work
with computers. Afterwards he travelled extensively as a
technical advisor on tropical agriculture, did an MBA
and ended up negotiating US aid in Washington for
Third World malaria control projects. He returned to live
permanently in Cambridge where by day he stares at
spreadsheets and crunches numbers for a living. Sometimes on summer evenings he walks down to Byron's
Pool to throw in twigs. To watch the dragonflies.

Thousand

Gavin Robertson

Jill,
best wishes
Gavin Robertson

HEADLINE
FEATURE

Copyright © 1998 Gavin Robertson

The right of Gavin Robertson to be identified as the Author of
the Work has been asserted by him in accordance with the
Copyright, Designs and Patents Act 1988.

First published in Great Britain in 1998
by HEADLINE BOOK PUBLISHING

First published in paperback in 1999
by HEADLINE BOOK PUBLISHING

A HEADLINE FEATURE paperback

10 9 8 7 6 5 4 3 2 1

All rights reserved. No part of this publication may be
reproduced, stored in a retrieval system, or transmitted,
in any form or by any means without the prior written
permission of the publisher, nor be otherwise circulated
in any form of binding or cover other than that in which
it is published and without a similar condition being
imposed on the subsequent purchaser.

All characters in this publication are fictitious
and any resemblance to real persons, living or dead,
is purely coincidental.

ISBN 0 7472 6021 4

Typeset by
Letterpart Limited, Reigate, Surrey

Printed and bound in Great Britain by
Mackays of Chatham PLC, Chatham, Kent

HEADLINE BOOK PUBLISHING
A division of Hodder Headline PLC
338 Euston Road
London NW1 3BH

for Struan

'It would be far more terrible to mistake a friend than an enemy'

Yevgeny Yevtushenko

Contents

Contents

PART ONE
Washington DC

Chapter One

At the top of the Arlington Cemetery is a row of trees evenly spaced with white stone benches in between. The Englishman, Simon Northcott, was sitting on one of these while Buddy Marlin, the American, walked backwards and forwards in front of him. The late summer sun was catching the first changes in the leaves but today it was still just summer. The grass was being cut and end-of-season tourists were streaming in and out of the distant car park. Neither man had spoken for about five minutes.

Simon looked out over the trees towards the river and at Central Washington on the other side. It looked very neat and ordered. 'Washington's easy,' Buddy had told him once. 'White buildings for politicians and grey for government offices.' Simon smiled as he remembered.

Simon had been new to Washington then. He had come with a background in large-scale agricultural projects. 'Turnkey' had been the buzzword he had adopted. The company he worked for, United Machines, was keen to find development partners for the Third World and Buddy, apparently heading up the newly created Aid, Allocation and Procurement Section of the US State Department had seemed a made-in-heaven partner. The two men had hit it off immediately and their respective masters had been delighted with their early successes. Simon liked the added status of 'Washington' and Buddy revelled in his 'special relationship' partner for his seemingly limitless US Government funds.

If only things could have stayed so straightforward, thought Simon ruefully. Or as innocent.

The two men had been visiting Arlington for about nine years. 'It's something to organise your life around,' Buddy had said at the beginning. The sweeping green slopes were much like war memorial cemeteries the world over. But Kennedy was here as well. The two men no longer believed in him but agreed that he had been important once. Perhaps visiting Arlington was like revisiting themselves when they had believed in things.

People who did not know them well might have asked why, if they spent so much time working together anyway, they should choose a particular place to talk about particular things? Whatever it was there were certainly 'Arlington' topics they rarely spoke of elsewhere. Their secrets seemed safe between the winding black paths and the deaf ears of the dead. They knew from years of experience that nowhere was really 'safe' to talk in Washington. Professional ears were almost everywhere but talking here at least made a gesture that not everything belonged to the

4

world of work. Some things took place out in the rest of their lives and here was as good a place as any to talk about them.

They had been out the night before celebrating Buddy's fifty-second birthday but today Simon thought Buddy looked nearer sixty.

How old do I look? he wondered to himself. People always used to tell him he looked younger than his years but now, at forty-seven, they had stopped saying that. I'll look like Buddy soon unless I watch it, he told himself.

Buddy stopped walking and turned to Simon. He was a tall, untidy looking man. As he looked at Simon he ran one hand over the bald top of his head to the hair which fell down over his collar. He rubbed, almost scratched, his neck before fixing Simon with a stare for a few moments. 'How's Ellen?'

'Fine. Not. Haven't seen her for weeks.' Ex-wife. Non-subject. Small talk.

'And Lewes?'

Son. Sensitive topic.

'He's at Oxford now. I'm afraid I don't get to see him so much now.'

'I didn't ask where he was. How is he?'

'Fine. I don't know that he cares much for me these days. He rather takes his mother's line.'

'I know the feeling,' said Buddy. 'But you still foot the bills don't you?'

'Oh yes,' said Simon looking up. 'His lovely mother sees to that.'

'And it's expensive, right?'

5

Simon sighed. 'Buddy, what do you want here? Yes, he's expensive but I can handle it. And don't ask me about Lewes. For instance, how are your kids? Are they OK?'

Buddy let go of his hair and shrugged. He wore an old leather jacket and put his hands in the side pockets before relaxing his arms. 'Fine too I guess.'

So that was them out of the way.

Buddy looked away over Arlington towards the river before turning back to Simon with another stare. 'Then what are you doing about it?' he asked.

Simon had obviously missed something. 'Sorry?'

'The expensive bit I mean.'

'Well, I worry a lot,' said Simon.

'Me too,' replied Buddy.

'Well, that's what they are isn't it? Worry and expense. Family fun.'

'Sure. But it doesn't leave much for a slice of the sun does it?'

'I suppose not.'

'So?'

'So?' echoed Simon.

'Come on, Simon.'

'Come on what? I don't follow you.'

The American turned away smiling and gave another shrug as if it was time to lighten up. 'Come on, let's go see JF,' he said.

Simon stood up and followed. He was not as tall as Buddy and his slightly out-of-shape suit betrayed his lack of skill at pressing. Any woman looking at the two men would have known they were both in need of a brisk walk around the shops to see about some new clothes.

Simon caught up and walked next to his friend as he set off towards Jackson Circle up by the West Gate as the neat rows of white headstones stretched away from them in all directions.

'How many bank accounts do you have?' asked Buddy.

'Well, about two hundred. You set most of them up so you should know,' replied Simon.

'And how much in each?'

'Again you know. A hundred or so less charges and our trip to Lyons last summer.'

'OK. So far so good.'

'What do you mean?'

'Is it enough? That's what I mean Simon,' said Buddy.

'Come on, Buddy. We set the rules before we did it. We can't take more. I don't have the kit. It doesn't exist. I can't build it.'

'OK. OK. Just think about it though will you?'

'No.'

'Just think. You don't have to actually do anything.'

'The risk is too high. If we went bigger, took more, they would see. You keep telling me that.'

'Not till afterwards. And it was you who said that.'

'But they would still come looking, Buddy. They'd come now if they could.'

'Maybe.'

'Look, Buddy,' Simon went on, 'you've got some debts and I've got some debts. My little game, the scam thing, will see us clear. We're halfway there. If we don't rock the boat we can have enough cash to cover everything by the middle of next year. No one will be any the wiser and we might even have some left over.'

Buddy stopped walking and turned to Simon. 'Debts, huh? I don't remember them being called that at the beginning. At that time your little brochure called them "Investment Opportunities." '

Simon held up his hand. 'OK,' he said, 'it was a mistake. But you were just as keen as I was then. Think back. A couple of new warehouses just outside Cambridge. A new motorway extension practically to the front door planned. If things had worked out we'd have been in on day one. You know we got the places for a song and anyway they might still turn around.'

'No way. No one ever booked any store space from us. And your so-called motorway never materialised and we end up stuck with a ten-year head lease on a couple of storehouses in some goddamn hick town called April twenty miles north of Cambridge that no one, even in England, has ever heard of.'

'March. The place is called March, Buddy. And you forget it was boom time then. Silicon Fen and all that. You know it looked good. It was a chance and we took it.'

Buddy shrugged again. 'Maybe, Si. But the bottom line is that it didn't come home and now we need fifty thou something sterling just to buy out and get back to level. OK, and I admit your latest little scheme can do that for us but it doesn't get us better than level does it? Look, let's hit the button and get some serious money.'

Simon waved his hand in the air but did not answer.

'OK,' continued Buddy, 'try from a different angle. Do this sum for me. Ten thousand accounts. Five thousand in each.'

'Fifty million of course. But that's ridiculous. Madness too. And anyway, I've explained. You can't go that big. The Drifting Table I can build has a much smaller limit.'

'But think about it, Simon. Just for a minute. Assume half each as usual. Gives you twenty-five. And I happen to think that even you could do a lot with twenty-five big ones. And me with my twenty-five? Hell, I could buy a beach in the Caymans, watch the sun go down with a glass in my hand every day of my sweet life.'

'The Caymans?' asked Simon.

'Sure. Cayman Islands. Last piece of heaven left on earth.'

'I don't even know where they are.'

Buddy smiled. 'Don't worry. I'll send you a card. Beaches here to here. Blue sea you wouldn't believe, best scuba reefs in the Caribbean. God's paradise. You know, there's a guy I work with sometimes in the Department has this big poster of the place up on his wall and I asked him about it one day. "Buddy," he says to me, "that place is the dream. One day I'm going and not coming back. I want my kids to grow up with the feel of wet sand between their toes every day." Have you met him? Rolands?'

Simon shook his head. 'Sounds like another dreamer to me.'

'Dreamer? Well it's a damn sight better than dreaming about clearing some lousy debt on some storehouses in the back of beyond.'

'Warehouses,' Simon corrected quietly. 'And I'm not going to go on saying "Sorry" any more. We'll clear it in six months and that's an end to it.'

Buddy took out a cigarette and lit it. Simon took out one of his own and did the same. American cigarettes were all right if you were American.

Buddy blew out a lungful of smoke and watched it drift away before speaking again, 'Anyway,' he said at last, 'about your scam thing. What's so difficult about a bigger Drifting Table? I thought you told me it was just a load of numbers. A page of logs or whatever. Why can't you make it as big as you like?'

Simon tapped the end of his fingers together.

'I'll tell you again,' he said. 'It looks just like a page of numbers; an array to give it its proper name, but the numbers on it aren't fixed. They all move in their rows or columns, in and out like weaving threads. But when they get to the edge they become unstable. And I can only use the middle bit, the stable central part of the table. I get about a hundred crossing points to play with. And I don't know how to build a bigger table. It's as simple as that. Someone else might know but I just don't. It needs a branch of maths called Large Number Theory and I don't know enough about it. They call it LNT for short. It's pretty new.'

Simon hated lying to Buddy.

Away to the right of them, beyond a broken row of trees, a large military funeral was taking place. Six black limousines were lined up on the narrow road. A group of perhaps thirty people were standing around the open grave. To one side a row of marines in dress uniform stood to attention in a line with rifles ready to fire a salute. Behind them was another group of perhaps fifty, some of them with bunches of flowers. Behind them again was a group of Japanese tourists taking photographs.

'Who's that?' asked Simon.

'I don't know. Must be important, the place is pretty full. Used to be any War Dead, now it's only colonels and above.'

'But there isn't a war on.'

'The phrase "active service" comes to mind. They wait till some old retired bird is about to die, cook up some paperwork that pulls him out of retirement to send him on some NATO police operation or whatever. He doesn't actually go of course. He dies instead. But he's on "active service". His family get a free funeral; he gets to lie here; the marines get to fire their guns and the Japanese get their photographs. It's a very fair system.' The two friends laughed.

'See the military in the middle?' Buddy continued. 'The tall one with the flankers? I can't be sure from here but it looks like Warkowski. I didn't know he was in Washington. Ugly enough.'

'You know him? I thought you hated the Military?'

'I do. And mainly because of him. He was my CO in

11

'Nam. Only a colonel then and me a lieutenant. He made it his job to be a bastard. He's probably responsible for more people leaving the Army than any man dead or alive. He's full of shit. If you come across him, steer clear is my advice.'

'Well I think I should be safe from over here don't you?' The two men laughed again.

'But he must have something if he made it to General?' asked Simon.

'Maybe. Only maybe.'

'What did he do after the war?'

'I don't know. I quit the day I got home. I've seen his picture in the papers a few times but I don't know what he does here in Washington. Pushes a desk or something.'

Buddy took out another cigarette and lit it. 'I've got to give this up you know.' He tapped his chest. 'Seriously.'

'We all do,' said Simon, taking out another of his own.

'No. For real,' said Buddy. 'I had my medical last week. The doctor looked me right in the eye and said, "Mr Marlin, you are fifty-two years old and you smoke too much." So I told him I didn't need a doctor to find that out and could have got it from the porter downstairs *and* saved the Department the cost of a medical. I thought that was pretty good but he didn't laugh. I gave up smoking till I was in the elevator down.'

The guard of honour shots suddenly rang out. The two men looked across. The family and senior military were walking back to the limousines. The rest gradually began to disperse. The Japanese changed their films and moved on.

The long black cars drove slowly towards the main gate. Once through, blue lights popped out of covers on the roofs, sirens began and a motorcade of police escorts swung into position. The speed increased from about fifteen to fifty miles an hour.

'Official mourning seems pretty short,' observed Simon.

'Well, no one's going to cry for you either, Argentina.'

Simon stubbed his cigarette out with his foot. 'I know Buddy. I know. So what else cheerful have you got to say?'

'Well actually there is something you might like. It's more of an announcement really.' He lowered his voice. 'You remember JF's speech about asking what you could do for your country?'

'Of course.'

'Well, my period of mourning for him is over. I don't have to do what he said any more. So much crap. And now I'm asking precisely what my country can do for me. And I've decided it can give me a whole load of money as a retirement present.'

'Ah, the emergence of older values. I approve of your announcement,' said Simon.

'Yup. And if my country can do it for me I think it should find it in its heart to do it for you too.'

'But I'm not American.'

'Well, you told me you'd been American for two

days in your life, once when Kennedy was shot and once when Buddy Holly died.'

Simon noticed that a woman away to one side of them was placing a bunch of flowers in front of one of the myriad of white headstones. She knelt, crossed herself and stood up again before moving away. As soon as she reached the main path a man in dark green overalls approached the bunch of flowers from the opposite direction. He picked up the flowers and put them in a plastic rubbish sack and went back between the graves to put the sack on a handcart already piled high with similar sacks. Buddy noticed Simon watching. 'It's a house rule,' he explained. 'No flowers except on Kennedy's grave. It's too messy. Doesn't look good for the visitors. War is the messy bit, dying can be messy too but afterwards Uncle Sam wants you tidy and in line.'

'But it's all right for Kennedy?' asked Simon.

'Sure. Anyway, if you look, his grave isn't in line with the others. Flowers always welcome. It's the military's way of saying "Sorry we shot you. But you were never really one of us." '

'You're not still on about that are you?' asked Simon.

'Of course I am,' replied Buddy. 'It must have been the Military. This Mafia or CIA thing you read about is just smoke. The Italians had no reason to pop him and anyway he was a Catholic.'

Buddy warmed to his theme and held his hands in front of him as if to examine his favourite idea more clearly. 'No,' he continued, 'JF was the first real outsider to get into the White House and the Military didn't like him. It suits them better to have in people they can push about like Carter and Clinton. The people who run America definitely don't want anyone who is a free thinker. You forget that lines of government aren't parallel in America, they converge at the top.'

'So you're saying they just got around some table and decided to take JF out?'

'More or less,' said Buddy, as if surprised that Simon should even ask.

'I don't think people operate like that.'

Buddy was suddenly serious. 'They do. And back there you just saw one of them.'

'That Warkowski man or whatever his name is?'

Buddy did not reply but walked on smoking his cigarette until they had come in sight of Kennedy's Memorial.

They often went there together and as usual stood back about thirty yards in silence while coachloads of tourists poured past them to take close-up pictures. Buddy nodded towards the memorial.

'Look at this place,' he said. 'Just a tourist spot now. Click, click. Walk away. Space Museum next.'

'Come on, Buddy. You can't expect everyone to feel about him the way you do. Half this lot weren't even born then anyway.'

Buddy stubbed out his cigarette with his foot and took out another one.

'You're right. Hell, I know that. Perhaps I don't give a shit about America any more. I look out for me now

15

and there isn't a flag in sight.' He took the unlit cigarette from his mouth and put it back in the packet. 'But if I'm going to do that,' he continued, 'I'm going to need one hell of a sight more money than I have now. For Christ's sake, Simon, get your greedy hat on and make us both rich.'

'I just told you,' said Simon, 'we can't do it. Technical reasons.'

'So you *want* to do it but can't? Is that what you are saying now?'

'No. I *do not* want to do it. But even if I did it's just not that easy. I just don't know how. I understand the *what* but not the *how*,' he said, chopping the air in front of him.

'Then that's not a technical reason. It's an intellectual one. Different problem. Different solution. All you're saying is that you need an intellectual and not a technician,' summed up Buddy, holding his arms wide.

Simon shook his head patiently. 'A bit more than that.'

'How much more?'

Simon spread out his hands.

'OK,' he said, 'so we have a scam going, a simple method to take money from the Dealing Banks without them knowing. We can do it because I know all about their computers. I can hack in and I can hack out. And I have a way of hiding the dealing in the Drifting Table and the Ring Files. So, we go in, make a bit of money, come out and send the money to our accounts.'

'So why not go in and come out with more money?'

'Because of the way it works. The hacking is pretty straightforward. It's not really hacking in the true sense. I get the access codes from you and I go in and use them. The dealing in the middle is the hard bit. I have one way but there are probably others. My way is pretty elegant because it's invisible but a real mathematician could do it better. But it's a mind set I don't have.'

'So we need a mathematician. That's all.'

'Well, that's right. But we haven't got one. There is you and there is me. You with your government access codes and me with my dealing program. No *mathematicians* at home. Besides, we know the rules. I mean it's not exactly legal is it? They'd go completely ape if they even *thought* they knew what we were up to. It doesn't matter at the moment because you're not going to tell anyone and neither am I. But we don't know anyone as well as we know each other. We don't have any risk factor at all at the moment. Bring in an outsider and we'd have to sleep with our eyes open forever. No one. No way.'

'Well,' said Buddy. 'One person. One way.'

'Don't even think about it.'

'She'd be perfect.'

'Perfect nothing. I said don't even think about it.'

'She's the obvious answer. You must have thought about her yourself. She's a propeller-head when it comes to maths. You've seen her fly over a page of numbers like an F-15. We know her. She knows us. And she's even beautiful. And you need someone beautiful in your life.'

'You told me that about her once before, remember?'

'Yes, I do. And I was right. It's not my fault you didn't follow through. She still talks about you, you know.'

'What are you, Buddy? Some sort of lunatic? Am I supposed to go up to her and say, "Sorry things didn't work out, Thousand, but how would you like to try again and by the way how would you like a ten million-dollar homework problem as well?"'

'More or less.'

'Nutcase. Total nutcase.'

'If you know of a better mathematician, tell me.'

'That's not the point.'

'Yes it is.'

'Well,' reasoned Buddy. 'Put aside actually asking her for a moment. Do you think Thousand could do it?'

'The maths? Of course she could,' said Simon.

'Well, that didn't take much thought.'

'No. It didn't. Because I *have* thought about it before. Of course I have. I mean she's not just a bit clever, she's double clever. So she could do the maths but that's not the point. We don't know anything else about her. The person has to come before the maths.'

'Oh, come on. This person did. I've known her for ten years and you've known her for six. That's quite a way back for these days.'

'But that's all at work. The Office. The Department. This has to be something else. We actually hardly know her outside work at all.'

'She likes you.'

'So you said before and look what happened.'

'So, you're both inept. Can I help that?'

A slight edge came into Simon's voice. 'That wasn't it at all. I was in the middle of the divorce thing with Ellen. Terrible state. And Thousand? She could have been in the middle of something too for all I know. Anyway it was a complete disaster. Very embarrassing all round.'

'Like I said, inept.'

'Well, the answer is still the same. We don't know her well enough and that's an end to it.'

'Twenty-five's a lot of money, Simon. If you come up with a better answer, let me know.'

Simon wiped his hand over his face. Of course he had considered Thousand. He knew she would be able to handle all the maths and probably even help with the initial hacking. In fact, for almost anything, he would choose Thousand above other people. What were dreams for if not to choose above others? But that wasn't the point. She was only a dream. He didn't really know her at all and he was equally certain she didn't know him at all either. But Buddy was different. He and Buddy really did know each other. Thick and thin and so on. All he really knew about Thousand to put on paper was that she lived in his life in a special compartment, away and separate from everything else. To be taken out and looked at when things were particularly bad to cheer himself up. That and their Famous Day. Afternoon really. A happy beginning never followed up.

Simon put his hands in his pockets and began

strolling back next to Buddy down the hill to the car park, thinking about Thousand as he went. How many years ago was it now? Four? Maybe five.

He had had to go back to England the next day and then he hadn't written to her because he didn't know what to write and then because he thought it would be the wrong thing to do. Did people who knew each other really write just out of the blue? And then it had seemed too late to write. And besides there really had been disastrous things going on. That was always a good excuse. No one would ever question it. Too personal. But he knew the divorce excuse had been a sham. He hadn't been upset at all really. Not involved even. Just a long series of predictable and mechanical rows. An excuse, should one ever be needed, to drink too much and generally behave badly. So if it wasn't the divorce, why hadn't he followed up their Famous Day? Frightened it might spoil? Find out that the one Good Thing wasn't so good after all? He knew he had never wanted anything as much as Thousand, and if he had eventually found out it wasn't possible it would have been terrible. Better at least to have the Famous Day. But whatever the reason he hadn't asked her out again. They had continued to work in the office as before. The months came and went and she gave every indication she had also put it out of her mind. Certainly that one day was not enough for them to ask her to help with the dealing scam. The scam was real world stuff. Thousand was dream world and of course he knew better than to mix the two. Didn't he?

Simon smiled at Buddy. 'We don't do so badly as it is.'

'No, I suppose not. But you're prepared to take the risks for a few thousand, why not take the same risk for twenty-five million?'

'Simply because they would mind a whole lot more. They'd really come looking instead of being just curious. Anyway, what do you think they would do if they did catch up?'

Buddy did not look at Simon as he answered. 'What they normally do to people they don't like. Shoot them.'

Simon laughed. 'I hardly think so!'

Buddy continued to look ahead. 'They would. Less than *one* million missing and it's all above board: quick trial, early release, no questions. But *above* five they would want it covered up quick sharp. If anyone took *that* much money and they played it by the book there would have to be a Federal trial, an appeal, another trial and so on. Months of it in the papers. Everyone wandering around with egg on their faces. Very embarrassing. So they'd do it the quick way.'

'What, just walk up and shoot someone, that someone being us in this case, in the back of the head?'

Buddy blew into his hands and rubbed them together. 'Not quite,' he said. 'They'd check pretty carefully first. Wheedle the truth out of the guy, get him to admit it first. And only then shoot him! But not in the back of the head, in the mouth.'

'Jesus.'

'It's what the Mafia used to do in the thirties. They

21

never do now but it seems to give the public a nice line. So when you read about a mouth shoot you can know that one of Uncle Sam's own has been taken out.'

'Why are you telling me this?'

'Just so you know. So you know. Because one day you are going to do it.'

'Do what?'

'Take the money.'

'Christ, I've just told you, no.'

'That's today. But *one* day. Sooner or later the temptation will be too much. Maybe not with me. Maybe not even with Thousand. But one day you'll be sitting at your little keyboard and you'll start what iffing.'

'It's not going to happen. But this shooting thing. How come you never told me before?'

'I didn't really know before. Of course I heard rumours. But a couple of weeks ago a Sticky I was talking to told me it actually happens.'

'A Sticky?'

'Woman. Sticky Trap. Washington-speak for one of the women who gets the actual confessions from the bad guys. A Honey Trap I think you Britishers call it. But we call it a Sticky Trap.'

'I don't know. A bit outside my experience. Anyway, I don't think that sort of thing actually goes on. Books and films maybe. But not for real.'

'Yeah, seems incredible. But no more incredible than your game. I mean who would believe someone like you could hack in and out of a Central Bank computer and do a thousand foreign currency deals in less than five seconds?'

'It's not so difficult. Just a sign of the times really.'

'Well, so is Sticky and Shoot. Another sign of the times. Your old friend JFK has been six foot down for a while now. The nice guys don't make the rules any more.'

'Well, if it's all so bloody nasty, that's an even better reason to keep Thousand out of it.'

'Yes, but she's cleverer than us. We just might need someone very bright. We might be doing something silly even now. She could stop us.'

'Leave it Buddy, we're not asking her and that's final.'

'Look,' said Buddy, 'how long have you been coming to see me in Washington?'

'I don't know, must be ten years. Nearly eleven.'

'Ten right. And what was I then?'

'What do you mean?'

'I'll tell you,' said Buddy pointing at Simon. 'New Nations Aid Procurement Officer, Agriculture Infrastructure, State Department. Equivalent to an Army Major. Same pay and all that shit. And you?' he said pointing again. 'What did they call you in those days?'

Simon pushed out his lower lip and thought for a moment. 'Well,' he said, 'the same as now I suppose, Sales Manager, Washington Turnkey Projects.'

'Manager huh? Big department is it?'

'Leave it out Buddy, it's just a title. There's only me and Ginny, you've always known that. United

Machines may be a multinational, but I'm just a small bit of it.'

'And you're *still* a small bit of it ten years on. And have I been promoted? No. Procurement Officer. That's me. We're a bit of a No Win Double, Simon. How do you British put it, passed up?'

'Passed over,' corrected Simon. 'But so what? Plenty of people don't even get as far as us.'

' "So what?" ' Buddy repeated. 'I'll tell you "so what"! In that ten years we must have set up a dozen major projects and maybe fifty small ones. Yes?'

'Sounds about right.'

'And the big ones worth what? Five million, six million each? The others from a half to a million. Still sound about right to you? Take Pakistan five years ago. Biggest rice and cotton irrigation project south of the Himalayas right?' He began to count items off on his fingers. 'Survey. River pumps. Concrete field pipes. Irrigation pumps. Iron pipes. Installation. Drain pipes. Training.' He stopped counting and waved his hand in the air.

'Pipes, pipes, pipes,' he went on. 'You tell me how many goddamn miles of pipes.' He put his hands back in his pockets and blew out his cheeks. 'We must have spent eight months out there one way or another.'

'Nine and a half actually,' said Simon quietly.

'Whatever. And when you got back to Cambridge, did they say, "Hey! Well done Simon, great project, take a raise, take a desk job"? No. I know exactly what they said to you. It was, "By the way Simon, we hear there's a project coming up for bids in Turkey. Why not go to Washington and see if you and your friend Buddy Marlin can't come up with something. Could be big." Hell, Simon, I'd hardly got the top off the Southern Comfort but you were banging at my door.'

'We had to go with it, Buddy, it's what they paid us to do. I found the two Ps, pumps and pipes. You found the two Bs, bucks and backhanders.'

'And that's another thing,' Buddy went on. 'Backhanders. Christ, I've personally watched you push ten grand under a table just to get three pumps through customs without being wrecked. And did *you* take home that much that week? Did I? I don't think so Simon. I really don't think so.'

'Buddy, it's just the business we're in. Part of the costs. "Aid's the name, dollar's the game." You've said so yourself often enough. And anyway, you talk about Pakistan and Turkey. Hell, that was five years ago. In case you've forgotten, we haven't done anything half as big as that for two years at least. You're living in the past.'

'Maybe,' countered Buddy. 'But I've got five years on you and, take it from me, they start to go by awful fast. And in *another* five years I don't want to even *be* here.'

They had reached the car park and when they were in the car Buddy tapped his hands on the steering wheel. 'See this car,' he said. 'Four years old. Half shaft going. Needs new brakes. Leaks like a sieve. Simon, I want better than this and I want it now.'

'Look, we all want it to be better, but we have to

accept things. We had a pretty good run, came close to the money a couple of times but never quite made it. Just shut up and drive me back to the office.'

Buddy did not start the car immediately but lit a cigarette and wound the window down.

' "Close to the money." Oh yeah? OK. So you made good commission on Pakistan but what do you do with it? Put it in your storehouse property deal back in the UK, that's what. Sunk the lot. And not one dime came back did it? Not one. Then when United found out you'd been using their name to set it up, you damn near lost your job. Their blue-eyed boy all of a sudden caught with his pants down in Hicksville Cambridge style. You had to second loan your house and when Ellen found *that* out! Christ, man I could hear her ring hit the floor from here.'

Simon put his head back and looked up at the roof of the car. 'Ellen? I'm afraid it wasn't just that.'

'No?' said Buddy. 'She liked it did she? You losing your shirt like some patsy. Her home going down the tube at the bank. From what I hear, that was her ticket out.'

'Maybe,' said Simon. 'But the rot was already in by then. The rest was . . . oh I don't know, a combination of all sorts of things. She saw the other wives having things we didn't. I kept telling her to hang on. I told her what I was doing with you was worthwhile. Aid. Helping. "Fighting for Strangers", I called it. Just like the song. I told her I was doing the right thing.'

Buddy coughed and threw his cigarette out of the

car and watched it smouldering where it landed. He did not reply.

Simon sat up again. The two men watched as the same group of Japanese tourists who had been at the funeral earlier passed in front of the car on the way to their bus. When they arrived, they lined up against the side while the driver took their picture. Then they changed places and all took a photograph of the driver while he posed with one foot up in the doorway of the bus. Eventually they all climbed aboard and drove away.

Buddy looked back to where his cigarette was still smouldering. 'When she found out about Costa then?' he asked. 'Was that it?'

'Yes, I think so,' said Simon heavily. 'You know I can remember so clearly the first time he approached us that day in Karachi. We'd been having all that hassle with that customs guy. We couldn't get a thing through no matter how hard we tried. Then up comes Costa waving his hands and head from side to side. "Give and take, boys. You have to know how to give and take. Look, I got a cotton shipment due for Netherlands next week. Maybe we swap dock space. What you say?" '

Simon imitated Costa's waving his head and hands from side to side. ' "Leetle bit give. Leetle bit take," ' he said. ' "Not so expenseeve. Just a leetle." '

Buddy laughed out loud. 'Is that your idea of a Colombian accent, Si? Terrible!'

Simon laughed in reply: 'Well, you have to admit he did the trick. And all for a ten thou drop in Zurich.

27

Seemed good value at the time. We both thought so.'

'You're right, Si. But did you guess then what was in with his so-called cotton shipment?'

'Not then. I'm a bit too trusting I suppose.'

'When then?' insisted Buddy. 'When did you see what he was up to?'

'Not till I was on leave in England a month later,' replied Simon. 'When I saw it on television. Biggest shipment of uncut heroin ever seen in Amsterdam, they said. And most of it bad. Kids practically dying on the streets and no one knew who had shipped it.'

'So what made you put two and two together?'

'Well,' Simon went on, locking his fingers on the top of his head. 'The Excise people found one of the empty containers. It was on the TV. Shit, Buddy, it was one of ours.'

'How could you be sure? They all look the same. Millions of them.'

'No,' said Simon resting his head back again. 'After six weeks practically living on the docks in Karachi with it I knew every scratch and dent on that container. It was one of ours. Take it from me.'

'So why did you have to tell Ellen? Bad move Simon.'

'I just sort of blurted it out. We were watching the news. I couldn't believe it. There it was.'

Buddy shook his head to himself.

Another group of tourists began to pass in front of the car towards their waiting bus driver. Cameras at the ready.

'Christ!' cried Buddy angrily as he fired up the

engine. 'I'm not watching this all over again!' He pulled away with a screech of the tyres and nearly knocked one of the tourists over.

When they were out of the car park and driving up the slip road of the bridge Simon turned to Buddy and went on: 'But it was too late to get away from Costa by then, wasn't it? You'd already set up the next container swap in Karachi hadn't you? We were well and truly in bed with him?'

'Yup,' replied the American. 'Face down on the pillow.'

Simon held out his hand in front of him and looked at it. 'So that was it. Shipments going both ways. And not a thing we could do if we wanted to go on with the project. But the real last straw for Ellen was when she found out about that sodding warehouse deal in March. That was quite a night I can tell you.'

'I can imagine,' said Buddy. 'But when your dealing scam began to claw some money back? Couldn't you have changed her mind then?'

'Too little, and way too late. She'd already booked her ticket as you call it. Time was well up for her and me by then. "I've had quite enough of you and your crazy schemes and dreams", she said. "Go and weave them with someone else. Lewes and I are going." Slammed the door and that was it.'

The traffic slowed as they approached Central Washington. Simon looked absently as the faceless government buildings went slowly by.

As they were waiting at a set of lights, Buddy turned to Simon and said. 'You told me last year that there were two years' life at least in your scam. You said by then they would either figure out a way to stop it or change the system so it wouldn't work. Do you still say that?'

Simon sighed. 'Yes, I should think they've seen enough to know someone is up to something. They don't know it all, but yes, the window's closing. Sorry, old friend, but it is. I honestly don't think we can get through it before it shuts.'

'Ask the bloody woman then, give us a chance.'

'No, Buddy, no can do. What part of no don't you understand for God's sake?'

'Sure. But she's not going away. Miss Long Legs and Big Blue Eyes stays centre stage.'

As they drew nearer the State Department, Simon asked himself again about Thousand. Was it really possible to know her well enough to ask her? He didn't think so. Ever polite but oh so cool. Impenetrable blue eyes and so often folded arms. He smiled to himself as he remembered the first time he had met Thousand.

He had gone to make a Washington call on Buddy shortly after a long Far East trip. He had been tired when he had reached Washington the night before but after a heavy night out with Buddy he had been more or less flattened. The fact he was out of clean shirts didn't help and the midsummer heat in the city was all he had been told. Not so much clammy as plain wet. Then he had made a mistake on the underground and finished up walking half a mile and arriving late.

THOUSAND

Buddy had told him a little about Thousand beforehand. 'One cool lady, but you'll like her,' he seemed to remember. But he was quite unprepared for what he saw as he arrived sweating and out of breath at the State Department. Simon was as good as lost forever. She was standing with her back to the window with the light shining through her fair hair. Her arms folded. 'You must be Simon.' She half-smiled and held out her hand. Washington elegance he was expecting but this was something else. 'I'm sorry I'm late,' was all he could manage.

'Don't worry, Buddy's not here yet. He was out last night if you know what I mean.'

'Yes, with me.'

'Ah, well in that case I suppose you'll be needing some coffee. We may have to wait a little time.' Her mouth formed a small smile but it did not reach her eyes.

He often went over that first meeting in his mind. He had stood there frankly amazed. Sometimes he concluded that everything about her was astonishing and the more he got to know her the more astonished he became.

He remembered how he had been staring attentively at her legs while she was on the telephone. He had eventually looked up to meet her expressionless and unblinking stare. He smiled, embarrassed. She had not smiled back.

Then he found himself thinking again about their one time out alone together. It was near Christmas and she, Buddy and Simon had been working on a dreary report all morning. First there had been the figures to go through. Thousand had done her background and so she had sailed them through that part. Then there was the technical section, Simon's part. He went into automatic mode and dictated large chunks to Thousand directly onto the keyboard. Finally Buddy had to summarise and paint on the State Department perspective. He hadn't prepared at all. He hummed and hawed and finally Thousand impatiently made him come up with at least a series of headings she could pad out later.

The report was due in the next day so there hadn't been any time for small talk. At twelve, Buddy had left for another meeting and Simon and Thousand worked on till two. From Buddy's headings they made plausible Introduction and Conclusion sections. Then they put all the sections together and sent the disk down to Secretarial for final polishing. It would be back by five. So that left Simon and Thousand alone in the office. The Devil made work for idle hands.

He said, 'I'm not staying here. Let's go out for some lunch.'

'OK,' she replied. 'We'll go to the Deli on the corner.'

'Deli nothing. We'll go to the Blade's Bar or nothing! You've done a lot this morning. You deserve a drink!'

It was just beginning to snow as they left the main building. The grey light on the white flakes. She shyly took his arm as they crossed the main road at the end of the block and did not let go until they came to the entrance of the wine bar. They went down the narrow steps, shook off the snow from their coats and sat down.

He brought a bottle of wine to their table and sat down opposite her against the wall.

'We've worked together for ages and this is our first drink out,' he said.

'Yes.'

'Funny really.'

'Yes.'

'Do you know this place?' he asked. 'I mean do you come here a lot?'

'No, I haven't been here before.'

'Ah.'

Hard work.

He spent most of that first ten minutes staring at his glass. Whenever he looked up she was looking straight at him. Her amazing eyes seemed to be smiling. Or perhaps they were just being amazing. He remembered to smile himself and then completely forgot what he was going to say. He looked immediately down at his glass again. But when he looked up she was still looking at him. And this time she was definitely smiling.

'I'm sorry. I think I feel a bit awkward,' he said.

'Me too.'

'Don't worry.'

'No.'

'I'm forty-five,' he said, looking down at the table. 'I didn't think you were supposed to feel like this.'

'Nor did I. Don't be. It's only me and you know who I am.'

He looked up at her and she was still smiling.

Later they walked hand in hand down Twenty-first street and came out by Buchan's 'Books 'n' Tapes'.

'Do you like music?' he asked.

'Well, I'm practically a musical dyslexic, but I do really,' she said.

'Come on in then,' he said. 'I've got an idea.'

He walked over to the counter and asked, 'What is the most beautiful music in the shop?'

The girl behind the counter looked surprised.

'You see,' he explained, 'I've a really elegant and beautiful friend and I want to buy her a present. So of course only the best and most beautiful music will do.'

The girl smiled. 'In that case I think I know,' she said and walked over to a rack near the door. 'I think this is it,' she said.

'Yes, but is it really beautiful?'

'Oh yes, heartachingly.'

'Well, it has to be the one then. What is it called?'

'It's the Felix Mendelssohn Violin Concerto in E minor. Opus 64 to be precise.'

'Mendelssohn it is then.'

He took it over to Thousand and gave it to her. 'For you,' he said. 'It has to be for you.'

She looked taken aback. 'Thank you. That was a very nice thing to do.'

'And no. I haven't done this before.'

'I wasn't thinking that.'

'Perhaps, but I want you to know anyway.'

They walked out of the shop and stood looking at each other. It was time to turn the afternoon into an evening. He held her hands and stood in front of her. 'What shall we do now?' he said.

'I don't think it's that simple,' she said. 'I mean, we still have to go to work together in the morning. Everybody there. That sort of thing.'

His heart began to sink. 'What do you mean?'

'Well, you can't go back on some things can you? You can't say they never happened. If you bite an apple it stays bitten. You can't ever go back.'

'I don't want to go back. I want to go forwards,' he said.

'Well, you don't know how things might turn out do you? I mean you can't know.'

'But we don't know what will happen about anything.'

'I'm sorry. It's no. That's just the way it is. Has to be if you like. Sorry.'

'I see.' He let go of her hands. 'I had better be getting back to the hotel. You know.'

'Yes.' The wind blew her hair across her face. Only five minutes ago he might have reached out to brush it away. Now he couldn't.

He turned and walked towards the corner. He tried not to walk slowly so she would have a chance to call out. When he reached the corner he tried not to look back at her but he saw from the corner of his eye that she was already gone.

Simon looked over at Buddy. 'So what's this money thing with you all of a sudden? You look pretty restless all round today.'

35

'Yeah, I guess so, Sime. Sorry I think it's to do with that shipment of yours last month.'

'I thought it was OK. Just a regular batch of water pumps,' said Simon.

'Yes. Those and my US-made pipe work to go with them. About four containers altogether wasn't it?'

'Give or take, yes. I didn't know there was any problem. I thought it was going without a hitch. My pumps arrived Stateside on time and I checked that your pipes were ready for shipment at the same time. Costa was going to take on the crating and ship them out to Manila as usual.'

'Yes,' agreed Buddy. 'That bit went OK. The four crates left the US without a problem but by the time they got to Manila they'd multiplied up to eight.'

'Eight? Where did the other four come from?'

'You might well ask. The ship had four on at Lagos when it docked to drop off some other cargo. But it became eight and went on as if they were an original consignment from here. Costa had them all on the same US paperwork. All the containers had US Custom Seals. God knows how he did it.'

'What was in them? The extra four I mean.'

Buddy took out another cigarette and lit it. He blew out a lung of smoke before answering.

'Costa thought Manila would just take it in as one shipment from here but someone must have tipped them off from Lagos.'

'Buddy, I didn't ask about Lagos. I asked what was *in* them.'

'I don't know exactly.'

'Oh yes you do.'

'You don't want to know anyway.'

'Oh yes I do. If whatever Costa was shipping with my pumps and your pipes was made to look like part of the same shipment then of course I need to know. And you do too. So tell me.'

Buddy wound the car window down and tossed out the barely begun cigarette. 'Well,' he began, 'let's just say the containers started out from Moscow and their first lot of paperwork said Machine Tools.'

'Shit. Arms?'

'Arms.'

'What sort?'

'Light stuff mainly,' began Buddy. 'Hand helds. Shoulder weapons. Maybe mortars as well. Nothing new anyway. Look, you can buy stuff like that by the truckload in Moscow now, you know that. It's the other face of the utopia dividend isn't it?'

'Secondhand military or not,' Simon said, 'he'd have to pay in hard currency. Four containers must be five million US at least. Does Costa have that much clean money in Moscow?'

'No, not that much. Probably not more than a million all in. But he got Moscow to agree to wait full payment till he could ship it to a third party country direct from Manila when he himself got paid after the stuff had landed.'

'Credit from the Moscow Mafia? I don't think so.'

'Why not? Costa may be a crook to you and me but to them he's Triple A-rated. He always pays. Always. It's the way he's gotten to be top of the pile.'

'OK. So now he's lost his shipment. He has to come up with the other half from somewhere. I don't see what it has to do with us.'

'Well,' said Buddy. 'It doesn't directly. But we can help him out. Do him a bit of a favour.'

'I don't see how. If customs in Manila have opened the containers they will have impounded the lot already. Our stuff along with the arms as well I should think.'

'Well, no,' said Buddy. 'That's the only saving grace. Sure, the customs did open up the containers and saw what was in them. But they didn't impound. Only held them up. Officially they are still just delayed in shipment. Costa can get the whole shipment released, our stuff included, if he pays the customs people enough.'

'So? Why doesn't he?'

'The customs people can't risk ever being linked to Costa in Manila and they say they will only accept the money in clean currency in another territory. Washington in this case. Which is a real problem for Costa. He doesn't have enough clean currency at the ready here in Washington. All he can do is borrow from me for seven days, clear the shipment in Manila and pay me off when he can ship enough clean currency into here. Meanwhile the shipment is burning a hole in the docks in Manila and he can't leave it for more than a few more days. A week at most. Hence the hurry.'

'How much does he want? He must have *some* clean money he can use.'

'Not enough. He has to have seventy grand US today. Notes.'

'Seventy? Steep. Even for you. Can you do it?'

'Only maybe.'

'Why for God's sake? The worst that can happen is that Costa loses the shipment and that is his problem. Not yours, you're insured. And certainly not mine. I get paid by Uncle Sam anyway because my sale was to you and not Manila.'

'Well, Sime, think about it. I told you that all the paperwork back up the line has been changed by Costa. It looks as if the whole shipment – pipes, pumps and arms – all originated from here. You and me. He's no bloody fool you know. As far as anyone official is concerned it goes through Costa without touching the sides. He can claim, and back up, that he was only shipping containers already sealed by us here in the States. But Manila now know the real story and hence they are leaning on him and not us. Whatever Manila thinks of us, they know that the arms are not ours. So if I lend Costa the money all the problems go away. The customs get paid off. The shipment is cleared. The pumps and pipes go up country as you planned and the arms vanish off the face of the earth. Look, it's no skin off customs' nose to let the arms in. When the whole country falls to bits in five years or so, which it will, the customs guy just ups sticks and comes over here to start spending his clean sweet dollars he is already piling up. And probably in half a dozen other countries as well I should think.'

'Have you told Jake this? Does he know?'

'No, of course not. He'd go ape-shit.'

'Well, you must have told him something. He's not just going to give you seventy grand to play with for a week is he?'

'No. He thinks the money is for our storehouse deal with Costa in Puerto Rico. Kick start money. Pretty usual. Bigger than before, but still usual.'

'And that's another bloody cock-up. You know it is. It seems to me you are just jumping from one hole into another. You didn't used to do this sort of thing, Buddy. What are you playing at?'

Buddy didn't answer. He shrugged and drove on in silence for a while. Eventually he said, 'It's lots of things Sime. But mainly Costa. Without him we're completely stuffed these days and you know that as well as I do. But more importantly, so does he. I keep telling you the only real way out is for us to buy ourselves out. Once. For all. With enough money we could just pack up and get out. Costa doesn't think we can ever do it and so he thinks he's got us where he wants us.'

'Buddy. Are you mad? Costa's not the only one to think that. So do I. Mr Instant Riches is just not at home today. Sorry.'

'Don't give me that shit Simon. You once said your scam thing was virtually limitless. Well. Is it? OK, so we've creamed a few thousand off so far but I don't see any noughts lining up yet. Do it. Now would be a very good time.'

'For God's sake Buddy! I was just wrong. OK. I

keep telling you I simply can't *go* any bigger with it. I just can't. Not yet.'

'Well, get Thousand in. She could do it. You just said she could. Get her in and that way none of us has to deal with Costa ever again.'

They had arrived at the State Department and Buddy drove the car down to the basement car park.

As they waited for a space, Buddy turned to Simon and said, 'Anyway, what do you make of Costa these days?'

'You know exactly what I think of him,' replied Simon.

'But he's no fool is he?'

'I never said he was a fool. I just said he was a shit.'

They laughed.

'Look,' said Simon. 'That warehouse deal in Puerto Rico. I worked it out. You're going to lose one hell of a slice. How are you going to cover it?'

Buddy did not reply.

Eventually Simon said. 'Oh no! Costa's not going to cover for you is he? That's it isn't it? He's going to do the paperwork on the Rico deal in exchange for the loan.'

"Fraid so.'

'But do you really have to do him such a big favour?'

'Yup.'

'But what's going to happen to the stuff?'

'That's his problem. Storm? Rain? Dockside fire? I don't know.'

Buddy pulled the car into a space and switched off

the engine. He made no move to get out of the car but sat and rested his wrists on top of the steering wheel.

Eventually Simon said, 'You must be out of your fucking mind.'

'Do you think I want to do it?' said Buddy. 'I have sod all choice. And I haven't even told you the worst part.'

'What!'

'He thinks I screwed him on the last deal.'

'No, Buddy. Don't tell me that! Nobody screws on Costa. Not even you.'

'I know. I know. I didn't. I didn't. Well . . .'

'Well what? Nobody goes back on a deal with Costa. Crook he may be but he does not mess on deals. He sticks to his side. If he doesn't like something he just walks away. If he says he'll go with something, then he'll go all the way and expect you to as well.'

'I know, I know.'

'So what happened?'

'You really want to know?'

'Yes. I really want to know.'

'I was drunk.'

'You mean you actually went into a meeting with Costa when you were pissed?'

'No,' replied Buddy. 'I mean I came out of a meeting with Costa pissed.'

'This gets worse. But can you really lay your hands on seventy clean in one day?'

'Sure. I'll get it from the CIA Laundry Bank. There is a sort of panic fund I can use.'

42

'What Laundry fund has got seventy grand cash sitting in it?'

'Just one. It's always there. It's meant to be used for kidnapping and hijacks. It's called the Wall Fund. For when you are up against it. Which, as it turns out, I am.'

'Stall him,' said Simon.

'Tried that,' countered Buddy.

'Try again.'

'Tried that too.'

'Then get something on him.'

'I don't think I can this time.'

'What "this time"? Are there others?'

'Sort of.'

'What sort of?'

'Department. I can't say.'

'The hell you can't. What is it? What on earth have you done?'

'Look, it's nothing. Nothing you and I haven't done before.'

'I don't like this sudden "you and I". Don't put me in the shit too.'

'So what's the difference. A few dollars here and there. We're all at it. Why should Costa be so different? Grow up man. He's a margin man. He has to make more than is on the table too. You know that or he won't play. He wants the same things as us. He's in it for the money too. Just like you and the scam. I don't remember any reluctance on your behalf when you came up with it. A "Golden Guarantee" you said.'

'It was the way of doing it I liked. I just wanted to

know if I could do it. You know that.'

'Well then,' said Buddy, 'that's why we've got to get Thousand in to help. Again. Do all three of us a favour.'

'No. You do me a fucking favour. Forget this Thousand thing. If we involve her the whole thing becomes unmanageable. Dangerous for her as well as us. She's well out of it.'

'Dangerous? Look, we deal with Costa every day. That's dangerous enough isn't it?'

'Yes, but Thousand's never involved.'

'What the hell. You think she can't cope with danger or whatever? She'd be better at it than us. We're just a couple of old fools. Probably make mistakes all the time she wouldn't. She's perfect for it.'

'And even if she was perfect, why should she be interested?'

'Look, Simon, everyone I know would be interested for five million.'

'Anyway, this is way off the subject. We were talking about your cock-up with Costa.' Simon turned to look at his old friend.

They left the car and walked towards the lifts and continued in silence up to Buddy's tenth-floor office.

Thousand was sitting neatly at her desk flicking through a pile of printout. She marked her place with her finger as she looked up and nodded to a file on the edge of her desk.

'Budget allocations, Buddy,' she said. 'I've checked them and they're OK, but you have to sign them before I put them back to Central Data.'

Buddy took the file to another desk and began signing the sheets as Thousand went back to her flicking. Without looking up Buddy said, 'Thousand, I need to talk to Jake Cohen. Tell him I've hit the wall and need that seventy K for tonight. Tell him I'm not pissing about. Remind him I've never used the wall fund before and it's only for six days. Then he can have his precious wall fund back again.'

'Are you sure?' she said.

'Of course I'm bloody sure.'

'Simon?' She looked at him.

'He's right Thou. He has to have it right away.'

'OK.' She marked her place with a pen and went out.

'Quite a girl,' said Simon. 'You ask her to do something like that and she just says "OK." '

'Yes, but she did ask us first.'

'I suppose so.'

'More than that. She asked us both. Not just me. If it was all right with you, she would do it. And you're not even Department.'

Thousand came back into the room. 'Bad news, Buddy,' she said. 'Jake's hopping mad. He got to me before I could call him. Apparently he was watching the monitor screen for you to come in. And he wants you in his office now. He says Costa was on to him an hour ago.'

'Oh, shit,' said Buddy. 'He said he wasn't going to do that again.'

'Needs must, Buddy,' said Thousand.

'Thanks, Thou. Just the sort of Staff Support I needed.'

'Sorry. But don't hang about. Jake sounded pretty urgent.'

Buddy stood up and looked at his desk as if searching for some saving piece of paper to take with him. He shrugged and went out.

Thousand sat down at her desk again and picked up going through the printout where she left off.

'What are you doing?' asked Simon conversationally.

'I'm looking for something,' she said, turning another page.

'I can see that,' he said. 'But aren't you going a bit fast? I should think you'd miss something going at it like that.'

She smiled as she ran her finger down a column of figures. 'Not really. If it's what I think it is, it will pretty much stand out.'

'A mistake? Don't tell me you have actually made a mistake.'

She stopped checking and looked up directly into his eyes. 'Hardly,' she said unsmiling. 'I wrote this allocation system and there are no mistakes in it.'

'So? What then?'

She leaned back in her chair and folded her arms without taking her eyes off him. 'Do you know how these allocations work?' she asked.

'More or less. Not the details of course. Congress or whatever gives you a certain amount to spend on International Aid, the Allocation you call it. Buddy and Co go out and place contracts with people like me who set up the deals. And you keeps tabs on it all.'

She was still staring directly at him.

'And us too I shouldn't wonder,' he added lamely.

She did not answer him directly but asked, 'And do you know how much is involved?'

Simon was not feeling happy under such direct scrutiny. 'Well, I'm not exactly sure,' he began. 'Annually, you mean? In any one year?'

'Annually.'

'Quite a lot. Millions, I should say. Fifteen? As much as twenty?'

'Last year eighty-seven.'

'Really? As much as that?'

She took her eyes off him and looked down again at the printout. 'As much as that. And Congress want to know where every cent goes. Every cent. So my number one task here is to do just that and try to make some sense of the paperwork you two comedians come up with.'

'Good job you're so bloody clever then isn't it,' said Simon slightly irritated. 'And anyway,' he went on, 'we do what we can. You've been in Aid as long as we have and so you should know it's not possible to have everything neat and tidy all the time. Too many people involved. Too many pieces of paper.'

'Oh yes. I know all about your pieces of paper, thank you.'

'Well then,' he said.

'They're not the problem as it turns out.'

'What is then?'

Again she did not reply immediately but tapped the pile of printout. 'This is,' she began. 'Think of the

47

Department as some gigantic trading company. A consortium if you like. Buying. Selling. Marking up. Paying out. And like all big companies we need a lot of actual cash. Day cash. Now I keep that tabbed and hold it in the Federal Bank for whenever we need it. Let's say five or six million. Now I know to the cent how much they are holding for me at any one time.' She pointed to the computer screen on the other side of her desk. 'No problem. But I can't get that' – she pointed at the computer again – 'to square up with this,' she said pointing back at the printout, 'which is the logging transaction list. They should be the same but there's a loose thread somewhere.'

'Loose thread?'

'That's what I call it. Look, a good accounts system is like a huge piece of fabric. Every transaction leads somewhere and the whole thing holds together. If a thread gets broken you have to find it or you can lose the whole thing.'

'Sounds a bit dramatic, Thousand. One broken thread and you lose the whole thing? Surely not.'

'Well. Not on its own. But if someone has started some serious unpicking I have to know where.'

'What counts as serious unpicking? How much are you talking about?'

'I'm not sure yet,' she said, beginning to run her fingers down the columns again.

'Well, I'd better shut up and let you get on with it then hadn't I? Can't have you dropping a stitch can we?'

'Don't make light of it, Simon,' she said without

looking up. 'Congress is pretty tight with its loose change.'

'Good. I can sleep at night then.'

She looked back up at him. 'I like to think so Simon.'

Their eyes met again. Did the woman never blink?

'By the way,' she said at last. 'What has Buddy got up to with Costa that he needs seventy K for?'

'Don't ask me. I'm not even "Department".' He held up his hands and put inverted commas around the word 'Department'.

'I asked you because you know and not because you are Department, Simon.'

'Sorry. Well the Laundry Bank, the CIA legit bit, apparently keep some sort of panic fund in readies for emergencies like today.'

'But Costa's not an emergency is he?'

'He is for Buddy today. Look, it's OK. I'll wait for him. You can get away.'

'No. I'll wait. If he actually gets the money, someone from here will have to go with him to Costa later on. I don't know what time Buddy has in mind, so I'll wait to see what happens.'

'It doesn't have to be you. Someone from one of the other departments could go. Bradley, someone like that.'

Thousand laughed. 'Bradley? He's the last one Buddy would take. They hate each other and Buddy would never admit to Bradley that there had been a screw-up.'

Simon said, 'Who said anything about a screw-up?

It's just an emergency, not a screw-up.'

Thousand folded her arms and looked at Simon with her head on one side. 'Maybe,' she said. 'Anyway, while you are here there is something quite different I wanted to ask you. Buddy tells me you are quite a computer chess buff?'

'I play, quite a lot actually. But this is a funny time to ask.'

' "Quite a lot actually." Very English! Buddy says you play on the top Internet league. And you have to be pretty good for that. But what I was going to ask you was why you chose chess instead of Go?'

'Go? Isn't that the Japanese game with black and white counters? Pick and place and that sort of thing. I didn't think there was much to it. Intricate, perhaps. But hardly strategic. Not my sort of game at all. No fun for me.'

'Don't let the Japanese hear you! It's their national game. At least as complicated as chess and probably more so. They have levels of Go Masters a bit like Karate belts. Seven actually. The top ones are practically national heroes.'

'I didn't know that. Clever old Japanese.'

'Well, I know you are pretty good at programming and Go is a natural for machine solving. Much more than chess really. I mean chess is what they call an infinite game because the pieces move which means you can get the same configuration at two different stages of the same game.'

'Yes, but that never happens,' interrupted Simon.

'No, I know, but it remains a theoretical possibility

and so the game remains open-ended in the mathematical sense. You can never know all the possible moves. But Go is different. A finite number of moves and no moving of pieces once played. It's theoretically possible to calculate every possible game play.'

'I should have thought that made it a bit simple.'

She smiled. 'It only sounds that way. But the Go board is bigger than the chess board, nineteen by nineteen rather than eight by eight and so the actual number of possible configurations is immense. Only a really big computer could ever hope to come close. Perhaps one of the big Cray 900s or something.'

'I'm not sure I understand why you are telling me all this. You tell me Buddy is halfway through the biggest cock-up of all time and you want to discuss board games?'

She ignored him. 'You see I was on an Internet conference last night and it seems that some guys at Cambridge in England think there is a better way of doing the maths using that latest LNT.'

'LNT? What's that?'

'Sorry, Large Number Theory, Drifting Tables and that sort of thing.'

'Really? I haven't heard of that before. Sounds fascinating. What do you call them? Drift Nets? Sounds like fishing to me.'

'Drifting Tables, Simon, Drifting Tables.'

'No. Never heard of them. Not my style at all really. I must be a chess man at heart after all.'

'Oh, really. I thought it would be right up your street from what Buddy said.'

Shit. What had Buddy said? 'No, as I said, fishing. Sounds like fishing to me.'

She smiled. 'You're good Simon. Very good.'

He looked at her as briefly and blankly as he could. What the hell did she know?

The telephone on the desk rang. She picked it up. 'Oh, OK, Buddy. I'm sorry. Yes, of course I'll wait. Simon says he will too. No? OK. Well I'll tell him you'll call him at the Watergate later shall I? Yes. Yes. Good luck.' She put the phone down. 'That was Buddy. Apparently Jake is stalling for some reason. He wants to take it to the Long Table. Buddy has to wait till Jake calls him. Could be an hour or so. He says not to wait and he'll call you later to let you know what happens.'

Simon looked at his watch. 'Yes, I've several calls to make from the hotel. Good luck and I'll see you both in the morning.'

'Yes of course. I guess we'll have to finish our Go and chess chat another time.'

'It's a promise. Bye.'

Close. A bit too close.

Chapter Two

Jake Cohen came back into his office where Buddy Marlin was waiting for him. He was the same age and height as Buddy but looked younger and fitter. Close cropped grey hair and a smart city suit further marked him apart from Simon's friend.

He sat down at his desk and squared up some loose papers in front of him in a crisp, businesslike manner. 'They'll be ready in about five minutes,' he began. 'Chief says he wants the Long Room bug swept before we go in. And that's code for he's really fed up. You watch your step is my advice.'

'Look, it's no big deal Jake,' returned Buddy. 'We don't need the Chief. You can give the go-ahead. It's only Costa. We both know him. Why draw all the others in?'

'Because I say so, Buddy. I'm the one has to make up the returns and I'm fed up with yours. You're becoming a liability around here.'

'What's that supposed to mean?'

'It means you make too many mistakes.'

'I do not.'

'Well, your request for seventy in old notes at two hours' notice hardly smacks of success to me.'

'Oh come on Jake. It's just for a deal. You know Costa.'

'It's a screw-up, Buddy. I've been doing this long enough to know one. Seventy. Old notes. Who rides a high deal on those terms?'

'You have to roll with men like Costa, you know that.'

'With maybe. Over I don't think so.'

'OK, so it's a tough deal,' replied Buddy. 'But it's coming back. Costa is the only one who can shift that stuff. Even the Chief would go along with that. And don't forget you were in on the idea too. You signed the invoice.'

'Spare the violin, Marlin. Let's not piss about. Now, if I can squeeze you the money, you make damn sure Costa takes it out on the first flight or I'll have you. If so much as one of those bills hits the streets, you are out for good and I'll do the kicking.'

'Look, don't worry, Jake. It'll go out tonight. I'm taking him to the airport myself right after the drop. At least I got that.'

The intercom on the desk flashed. 'They are ready for you now in the Long Room, sir.'

The two men walked in silence out of the office, along the corridor and into the lift at the end. Jake Cohen took out a key from his pocket, unlocked a small flap next to the lift buttons and punched a sequence into a key-pad. The lights on the floor indicator went out and the lift car went straight down to ten floors below street level.

An armed marine was waiting for them. 'Please come this way, sirs.' They followed him along a brightly lit corridor to a red steel door. 'May I see your identity card Brigadier? Yours too Colonel Marlin.' The marine took them and scrutinised them. 'Thank you. Now please key in this day's access code on the pad here.'

Both men silently obeyed. A light above the door flashed green. 'Thank you again, sirs. The Chief will see you right away.'

'Thank you, Disley. Remember me to your father,' said Jake as they went past into the Long Room.

General Warkowski was sitting alone and unsmiling at the opposite side of a long, polished wooden table. He was still in full dress uniform from the funeral earlier in the day. In front of him was a black briefcase. Next to the case was his cap with its row of polished stars across the brim.

He nodded at the two men in recognition rather than greeting. These were his subordinate officers and he wanted to press on with the matter in hand. 'Sit down gentlemen. I don't want to be here so let's make it short.'

Jake and Buddy sat down next to each other.

Warkowski spread out his hands flat on the table. 'Now,' he began, 'Brigadier Cohen here says you need seventy for this man Costa. Is that right, Colonel?'

'Yes, sir,' said Buddy. 'It's exceptional I know, but I've dealt with him before. It's an ordinary commodity drop but he has to pay the customs and local officials or it won't go through. He's made some sort of mistake on timing or something and I said I could help him out. I know I should have checked with you and the Brigadier first but there wasn't time. It's only for six days and all the original money will go out of the States. None of it will stay. I can guarantee that, sir.'

'Do I look like a virgin to you Colonel?' said Warkowski.

'Sir?'

'Someone to mess with, Marlin. Someone to play with.'

'No sir, of course not sir.'

'Then don't try to put your hand up my jumper. I know exactly what's going on.'

'Sir?'

'Shut up Colonel. I had to bury a good soldier this afternoon. Better than you ever will be. I come back here to a red light flashing on my desk simply because some jerk wants seventy K to cover a screw-up.'

'Sir. It is exceptional.'

'I'll come to that. But do you know what makes it worse?'

'No sir.'

'I said shut up. What makes it worse is that you are a Military. And if Costa screws you, he screws me too. And I can really do without that. And I mean really.'

Warkowski pushed the briefcase across the table and said, 'Now you take this Goddamn money out of here and follow it all the way to the airport. And in six days I want it back on this table in different notes or you are out for good. Is that A1 clear colonel?'

'Yes sir. Thank you sir.'

'And another thing. Is that idiot Englishman involved?'

'You mean Dr Northcott sir? No, he is not involved at all. And with respect sir, he's not an idiot at all. He's very clever sir, very good at what he does.'

'Well if he's so bloody clever, how come he's working with a joker like you?'

'Aid, sir. He thinks of it as International Aid.'

'Huh. But he's a hacker too isn't he?'

'I don't think so sir. That's not him at all. He hardly uses a computer at all.'

'Not what I heard. The Feds tell me someone has been going into his Amex Account to change hotel codes. You have to be a hacker for that, and no one is going into an account except the owner of that account are they?'

'Quite extraordinary sir. I'll take it up with him myself.'

'The hell you will. I want to see what he's up to. There's more hacking going on in Washington than at a lumberjack's wedding. And I want to know what he's into. You've got a computer expert in house. Hundred or whatever her name is. Get her to look into it.'

'Yes sir. That would be Major Nocta. They call her Thousand, sir.'

'Whatever. Tell her she's got three days. Then get rid of him if she finds anything. I don't need God-damn meddlers in this place.'

'But he's the best we have sir. He has gotten us the best contacts we have ever had. Africa, South America. Far East. If it wasn't for him we would not be in half the places we are sir. He's perfect sir.'

'Perfect nothing. I can't take a chance. So I say let Major Nocta key-stroke follow him for a week.'

'And then sir?'

'I just told you Colonel. But it depends on what we get. If he is just hacking his own credit cards we drop him. If he's into anything else then that is something else. Something else altogether.'

Buddy gripped the case so hard his hands hurt. 'Yes sir,' he said quietly.

'Right. Out. Both of you. And you Brigadier,' Warkowski pointed at Jake Cohen. 'You bring her report to me in person. Understand?'

'Yes sir,' said Jake. 'Thank you sir.'

Jake and Buddy went out. In the lift, and away from the armed marine, Buddy said, 'Shit, Jake. I've never seen the Chief like that. What the hell has happened?'

Jake shrugged.

'And Simon,' Buddy went on: 'Warkowski's flipped. He's our best man. You know that.'

Jake shrugged again.

'And anyway there is nothing to find. OK, so he fiddles his hotel bills. Half bloody Washington does that. It's just a game for him. But he's not a serious hacker. Not the type. And as for sending Thousand after him, that's plain ridiculous. Simon would see. Warkowski's completely wrong. Simon's not an idiot.'

Jake said, 'Warkowski didn't get to be head of Ops

by being wrong. How can you be so sure Simon's clean?'

'Because I know him. Ten years. Probably more.'

The lift opened at their floor. They walked through to Jake's office and shut the door.

Buddy sat down with the case on his knees and flipped the catches. He opened the lid.

'Jake. What the fuck's going on? These are new notes. Costa has to have old. You know that.'

'Sorry. That's all you get.'

'Old notes, Jake. He can't use new ones, even from the Laundry.'

'Sure he can. You said yourself he was taking them out of the country. So no difference to him. He can rewash them anywhere.'

'Don't do this to me Jake. You know me too well.'

'Do what? You asked me for two quite separate favours. First the money and then the old notes. Well, take the money first. Seventy. It's too much. Nobody needs seventy cash. Even if this was for the warehouse deal, which it isn't. Thirty would do. So we're asking for something a bit different aren't we? You're off the main line. Outside your jurisdiction. Either you have miscalculated or he's got you over a barrel. And knowing you, I strongly suspect the latter. But you are a field operator. I have to listen to you. I've always backed you up to now. But old notes? No. That's something else.'

'Jake, I simply cannot take him new notes. I struck the deal with old.'

'Yes, and that's the second favour you asked. A

straight deal never needs old notes. We both know that. Now if it's a bent deal I should have been told a long time ago. So what do we have? A bent deal and over the limit. And you sit there pretending to be a nun. I won't be made a fool of. Now you take this money and do what you can with it. I've gone out on a limb far enough for you on this one. Now what's it going to be, take it or walk away?'

'I can try him. That's all.'

'Good. Same language time.'

'He's not going to like it. How is he going to trust me next time?'

'Your problem, Colonel.'

'Well, you certainly know how to make a girl feel special.'

'Look, Buddy, this is the last time. I know what he wants that money for as well as you do and it's not on. Now you find a way to take this money to him and tell him to piss off. He thinks he's dealing with you and he's got you stuffed. OK, but you're Government property. My property. That you've screwed up is completely down to you but until I throw you out you are still all mine. He messes with you and he messes with me. All of us. Warkowski too. You heard the man. I won't have it. So you can tell him it's our rules or nothing. And my rules are old notes for small deals, new notes for big deals. Big deals and old notes means Costa's up to something I don't like. And if I don't like it I don't play. And you can quote me on that.'

'But I agreed,' protested Buddy.

'And I didn't,' rounded Jake. 'It is not your money. You should not have agreed. If you didn't like it you should have walked away. Rule one of negotiation. Now, if you couldn't walk away because of something I don't even want to think about, then Costa's got something over you. You are in way too deep Buddy. At the very least you should have called. But my phone stayed cold. So you went out too far, too deep. And now you have to swim back alone. And I've not changed any of the rules. You just forgot them. I should have refused outright but this is the first time you've called The Wall and so I have to go along. But I won't go to old notes. You should have known that.'

They both sat staring at the case open on the desk between them.

Jake looked up at Buddy. 'Who is going to Costa with you?'

'Thousand,' replied Buddy. 'She's good. You know that.'

'What does she carry?'

'Walther P37. Issue.'

'And you?'

'The same, Jake.'

'Great. Peashooters. What a fuck-up.'

'Look this is just a handover, Jake. Not the OK Corral. It's at a hotel for God's sake.'

'Still a bit thin. And who's in the back-up car?'

'There isn't one. Not for the handover. I've got to use one car from my house. They'll follow all the way. If they see another car they won't play. You know that, Jake.'

'I know fuck all apparently. New notes. Heavy case. Peashooters. No back-up. Now what kind of set-up is this Buddy?'

Buddy spread out his hands on the desk between them. 'Costa thinks the money is coming from somewhere else. If he thought it was direct State Department cash he would back out. We'd lose the shipment pay-out. All of it. I keep telling you, only Costa can shift it. And that is the total extent of his hold on me. No more. There is no secret agenda. It's just a big one-off. If we behave differently he'll know and he'll back out, and we'd lose him for good. And no one will thank you Jake if we lose Costa. Not even the Chief. We both know the CIA use him too. So you actually need him far more than I do. This is bloody play-acting.'

Jake scratched his neck. 'So where is this "somewhere else" you skated over? Why isn't State Department money good enough for him. Always was in my day.'

'Maybe. But not any more. Costa knows our regulations as well as we do. Better probably. He knows perfectly well that fifty thousand is my limit. And even for that he gets three people turning up and a back-up car as well. This way he won't suspect anything. It puts me more on his side. And because of that he thinks he's pulled one over on me. So I get a better deal. It's all worked out. I'm a pro. I know what I am doing.'

'So, Mr Pro. Tell me the nitty then.'

'Right. I go from here with the money alone. Drive home. At seven, Thousand comes to my place in her car. Then we go in my car straight to Costa. Hand it over. Phone in. He goes to the airport within the hour. Flies out. Does his deal in Puerto Rico. Comes back with the seed money in three days, washed, pressed and wrapped. Hassle over.'

'Your bit is OK. His bit doesn't sound so good.'

'Why?' asked Buddy.

'Well. Why should he fly out with it at all? Even Costa can use 70K in the States.'

'But he can make it grow faster in Puerto Rico. He can kick start the whole storehouse deal from there. And believe me, he stands to make a great deal more than a simple doubling. Don't worry. He'll take it. I know him.'

'OK. But you still haven't told me where he thinks the money is coming from.'

'Well. Not State Department.'

'So where, wise guy?'

'Are you sure you want to know?'

'Not really. So spoil my day.'

Buddy looked straight at Jake and took a deep breath. 'Well, actually he thinks I stole it from the Department. He thinks it's hot.'

'What! Are you completely mad, Buddy?'

'Not at all. I told him I have a scam to cream money out of the system. A good one. Computer hacking. That sort of thing.'

'Shit, Buddy. This is one hell of a mess.'

'No it isn't. It's all worked out to the finest detail. No screw-up is possible.' But I could do with a drink, he added to himself.

Jake leant back in his chair. 'Buddy, I just don't want to hear any more. But you listen to me and listen good. Official Time, Colonel. You screw up on this one and you are finished. You've gone way out of your depth here and I'm on tippy toes too. I want you back on dry land real soon. Me too. No more silly set-ups. Ever.'

'Thanks Jake.'

'Thank me when it's over.'

'I will.'

Buddy took the case and left the room. Twenty minutes to his house. Twenty-one to a decent drink.

Warkowski was at the head of the long wooden table again. Three men were seated to either side of him. Two of them had also been at the funeral and were, like the general, still in dress uniform. The remaining four wore dark suits, white shirts and anonymous-looking ties. 'So gentlemen,' began Warkowski, 'welcome back. What do we have? South America first. What is your line on da Costa, Williams?'

The man in a suit on the left began: 'He is a difficult man to get near, General. He knows he is followed everywhere in the States so he takes care never to slip up or even to try to lose his tail. We try to bug his hotel of course but it's only a gesture. He finds us all the time. A man with his resources has all the best equipment. Most of it at least as good as ours, but we keep trying. But I'm afraid we haven't gotten lucky yet.'

'And out of the States?' asked Warkowski.

'Better sir. Puerto Rico say he's not expected there for five days but apparently this money really is going there tomorrow. All of the 70K. But I don't think it will be the same money. My bet is that he will use street money in Puerto Rico and keep the fresh money for use in Washington in the usual way. That way he is covered both ends.'

'And this warehouse shit of Marlin's in Miami? Is Costa really going to ship to Puerto Rico?'

'I believe so yes, sir. For him it's a form of cover. Profitable enough for him to have legitimate accounts with large sums going in and out. Most of it goes to Zurich and back but he keeps enough here in the States to run the straight side of his businesses. We can't get anything on him that way sir, but if he uses those new notes you gave Cohen and Marlin we can nail him. We have all the numbers circulated and we will know the hour and place they enter the banking system. My guess would be about midday tomorrow.'

'And if he refuses the new notes?'

'I really don't think he will sir. He will know of course that Marlin's got them from somewhere odd but he won't think they are batched if he thinks they are a straight lift from the normal banking system. My bet is that he will go with them because he's already committed to using money at both ends.'

Warkowski turned to the man on his right. 'What is the Pentagon line on all this, Joe?'

'Williams's right sir. We know Costa has a deal going down tonight here in Washington. It's a shipment out of Belfast bound for Madrid – AK47s mainly, some grenades. Old stuff. It's not 70K. But I think he will use about half of the Washington money for it.'

'But why would the Irish take new notes any more than Costa?' asked Warkowski.

'They won't want to at all, but our man in the Falls Road says the nationals are pretty strapped for cash now. That's why they are selling the stuff in the first place. They won't want the new notes and may even haggle at the edges but they will take them.'

'And the timing?' asked Warkowski. 'Is Williams right when he says the money will come into the banks tomorrow?'

'I'm sure of it. Definitely if the Irish are involved. They don't know how to behave. They always spend at least some straight away. Girls mainly but always some drugs. Crack is so much cheaper here, they can't resist a bit of dealing on the side. They look on it like duty-free shopping. I'd say midday sir. One o'clock at the latest.'

Warkowski looked at the man sitting next down the table. 'What does Dublin say, Sean?'

'Williams and Joe are both right. Dublin expect about 30K to land in two days.'

'So that's 30K accounted for. What about the other 40?'

'Well, that's not so good, sir. I'd say the bulk of it will be going up and down the drug chain here some time over the next twelve to twenty-four hours. We have to wait for him to cut down his latest shipment. I want to give him eighteen hours outside. That should make enough separate deals going down for there to be at least some of the notes in the crack houses. I say we do a heavy swoop on the five we have been watching most. And if we find so much as one of our notes there we've got his balls in a drawer.'

'You may not,' replied Warkowski. 'As soon as he sees the new notes he will know it's too much of a risk to stay Stateside. He'll fly out as planned.'

'Well, that's possible, General, but with evidence as hard as numbered notes we can shut down his operation. At least for six months. He'll be back of course but it gives us time to put more deep cover agents in like now. I know it's a roundabout, but it's better than nothing.'

'Too many "ifs" but I have to go with you. That will be all, gentlemen. Thank you.'

The civilians at the table stood up and left just the two men in uniform sitting on either side of the general.

'I guess that just leaves the home team,' said Warkowski. 'You first, Rolands. Does the Fed Bank agree with what you've heard so far?'

Colonel Rolands was a large man with a round face. He wore horn-rimmed glasses which he pushed up onto the bridge of his nose with one finger as he began to speak. 'Yes General. But only as far as it goes. We are pretty confident from our end. Now, I don't know all the details of what we've heard this afternoon yet but my people are confident that Colonel Marlin is doing another set of deals with Costa or at least is setting up to do so. Of course he's moving money in and out of his own and the official accounts all the time and we do monitor that. There is nothing so unusual about his personal spending pattern but he is dealing far more with Costa than would be usual. Several transfers a week now instead of the one or two a month we had a year or so back.'

'How much each time?'

'Only within Department limits. Never more than five thousand and all authorised by Cohen at least five days in advance. He's within his bounds of authority but definitely near the top end. I'd say it shows too close an association with Costa. I told Cohen to raise it with him but apparently Marlin's explanation was that it was a "tricky period". His words, sir.'

'And is it?'

'Well, I'm afraid I'd have to agree with him there, sir. Commodity trading is pretty low just now with the Russians off the scene and trading legit chemicals and equipment is undoubtedly difficult.'

'So what's your problem?'

'Well, sir.' Rolands shifted uneasily in his chair. 'In order to work with Costa direct, Colonel Marlin has to have access to Federal Bank codes to activate certain accounts there and also here and at the Laundry. But there is other money going in and out of the Laundry we cannot account for. The amounts debited and credited always match but the money is certainly outside the system for a finite time and its whereabouts then is unknown to us at this time.'

'Speak English, Rolands. What you're telling me is

that you don't have a fucking clue where it goes. Is that right?'

'Yes, sir.'

'Thank you. That's better. Now if you don't know where it goes I presume you know how much is always missing and for how long?'

'Oh, yes, sir. But it's really weird. The amounts are never more than a few thousand – eight or ten perhaps. And the time is never more than fifteen seconds.'

'Fifteen seconds?' barked Warkowski angrily. 'Look, are you wasting my time or what?'

'Well, in banking terms that is quite a significant period. There could be many thousands of transactions over that time. The official accounting period is still a whole minute and so technically the account does not actually move at all and is never out of balance. But we do believe the money is being used within that minute even if we don't know what for.'

Rolands pushed his glasses up to the bridge of his nose again.

Warkowski drummed his fingers on the table in front of him. 'Looks as though we are back to not a fucking clue.'

'Well, not quite sir. The obvious place for short-term money is the Foreign Exchanges. The amount of money moving there is very large. Often billions in any one minute and even a big currency like the Mark or Yen can alter measurably from one minute to the next. And because the normal amounts are so large, it makes only a few thousand impossible to trace. But our man Marlin, if it is him, always takes out and puts back the money in the last minute of Forex trading.'

'May I come in here sir?' The speaker was the other, much younger man, with a thin face.

'Yes, Bradley, what is it?' said the general.

'Sir, Colonel Rolands here told me about this phantom dealing yesterday and I've done some checking on the times. When it's happened, and it's only been five times so far, Colonel Marlin has been on a scrambler telephone to the same person.'

'Who?'

'The Englishman, sir, Simon Northcott.'

'So that bastard's involved is he?'

'There is no direct evidence, sir, but I believe yes, he is involved.'

Warkowski rubbed the side of his face. 'What are they saying? Bring me a transcription.'

'Well, that's a problem at this time sir.' And now it was Bradley's turn to move uneasily in his chair. 'I don't have the de-encryption authority. It's within Brigadier Cohen's jurisdiction and he was unwilling to share that with me.'

'Was he now? Well, he's never asked me about it. Tell Cohen to check with me and then by Christ he'll give it to you. No, better still, I'll give the authority myself. Come to me after this meeting and I'll get Disley to fix a meeting for you direct with the telephone people. What the hell is Cohen pissing about for?'

'Thank you sir.' Bradley was comfortable again.

Warkowski rubbed the side of his face again and

then asked, 'Anything else on this Englishman?'

'Yes sir.' Bradley was coming to the part he had been looking forward to. 'I checked with Major Nocta, Colonel Marlin's number two. She confirms he's not just the salesman he makes himself out to be. She says he's big on computer programming. Quite a computer freak actually, uses PCs the way most people use telephones. He plays top level computer chess and can hack into most non-government mainframes. It may be nothing sir but it could well be that Marlin is using him to play the banks.'

'Shit. Is she sure about this?'

'Yes sir. She has been watching him now for four years under the guise of working with him. I'd say she knows him pretty well.'

'Any chance she knows him a bit too well?'

'Absolutely not sir. Nocta is one of our very best people. Best in her year at West Point. Laude cum Laude at Yale. Faultless deep cover ever since. She is behind a lot of the success Cohen has been having in Iran and New Vietnam. She says Northcott tried it on with her some time ago. She immediately rejected his advances and reported the whole thing in the usual way to her head of section, Jake Cohen. I think she could be very useful to us.'

Bradley allowed himself a self-satisfied smile.

'OK, Bradley,' said Warkowski, 'but get her to check out Marlin's activities first.'

'Sir?' asked Bradley, his smile vanishing.

'Yes, her first call is to me and not him or Cohen. I need to know what he's up to with Costa or whoever.

It's nothing she shouldn't be expected to do with the way he's carrying on. Tell her it's priority and fully confidential. Tell her there might be promotion in it for her if she does a good job.'

'Promotion sir?'

'I didn't say there would be. Just tell her there might be.'

'Yes sir.'

'And give her three days.'

'And after that sir?'

'Depends what we turn up. Use your initiative. Does that present you with a problem, Bradley? Look, Marlin's been good. Very good. But he isn't now is he? I don't think he has anything to contribute apart from the information he has. When I have that he's no use to me any more. He's a liability as it is. Do you understand?'

'Yes sir.'

'Good. That just leaves the Englishman. And the trouble is we don't know exactly what he is into and how deep. I want that information. I guess we'll have to Sticky him. Is that on? Who is available?'

Bradley was really enjoying himself again. 'I've already looked into it sir. Because I came to the same conclusion as you. From our eight operatives, I came up with a short list of two. Dodsey and Booker. Dodsey may be too young at twenty-five to be credible but Booker would be perfect because of her special situation.'

'Which is?'

'She is Colonel Marlin's sister. She may even have

72

met the subject socially but he would have no idea what she does. No one in the Department knows. Not even Cohen. She always runs the same deep cover so that would not be a problem. She is also the best we have by a long way and three days would easily be enough for her to get everything we need. And that would give us the same three days Nocta could use for Marlin himself.'

'But what if Marlin contacts Northcott while the operation is running? He'll know immediately what's going on.'

'I don't think so sir. Booker says that even Marlin does not know what she does. He knows she's Agency of course but he thinks she is more mainstream. Data Ops, setting up stations and that sort of thing.' Bradley leant back in his chair and smiled again.

'Northcott will be in Cambridge, England all next week,' he went on, 'and I can have Booker there on some conference or other. And if we make it completely clear to her that Colonel Marlin himself is not involved at all there should be no problem. In fact I suggest we tell her Marlin and Nocta have been acting to entrap Northcott for several months.'

'OK. But I want Marlin out of Washington and off the phone for the three days. We can't run any risk of the two idiots getting together at all.'

'Yes, sir. Very good idea.'

'And don't take any action on Northcott until I have seen Booker's report. That has to be clear.'

'Yes, sir.'

'But Colonel Marlin is a different matter.'

'Yes, sir.'

General Warkowski flicked his teeth with his thumbnail and thought for a moment before looking at Bradley and saying, 'OK, what's Booker's current assignment?'

'The Washington sleepers, sir.'

'That should be nearly finished by now,' said Warkowski. 'How many left?'

'That's right sir,' replied Bradley. 'They are on the last one today. In fact,' he went on after checking his watch, 'it should all be done in about fifteen minutes.'

Warkowski turned to Rolands. 'See that?' he said, indicating Bradley. 'He keeps in touch. I like that.'

'It's admirable sir,' replied Rolands pushing his glasses back to the bridge of his nose. 'But the Washington sleepers? Do I know that project sir?'

'No you don't.' Warkowski turned without elaborating further back to Bradley. 'Who's she working with?'

'Sergeant Buller, sir. He hasn't been with us long but he's very good.'

'One of your protégés is he Major?' asked Warkowski. 'I think I remember the name: some sort of pistol marksman isn't he? How is he under pressure? What experience has he got?'

'He served in Grenada sir,' said Bradley hopefully.

Warkowski gave Bradley an irritated look. 'I asked about experience, not summer camp.'

Bradley looked down at the table. 'Yes sir,' he said quietly.

An uncomfortable pause fell across the three men.

Eventually Rolands, after checking his glasses again, said, 'General, if I might ask, Major Booker, sir. Does she know much about computing? This Foreign Exchange thing is pretty complicated. I mean how much briefing will she need?'

'Hardly any Rolands; no more than you're going to put on one side of a piece of paper for her. Her job is people. And I think you'll find she knows all about them.'

'Of course General,' agreed Rolands, 'but I was just wondering . . .'

Warkowski cut him short. 'Well don't wonder then. Hell, she didn't know about Washington sleepers before she began the current assignment but I'd say she's made a pretty good job. Tell him Bradley.'

'The Sleepers?'

'That's what I said.'

Major Bradley clasped his hands and began. 'These Sleepers are the KGB deep cover agents here in Washington. They are outside the intelligence community but can be called up for specific works.'

'KGB?' asked Rolands. 'I thought they weren't a problem any more, no USSR and all that.'

'That's right,' agreed Bradley. 'The KGB in its old form is largely disbanded. But it all went wrong for them so fast they had no time to call the sleepers back home. They all are, or rather were, still in place.'

'Doing what?' asked Rolands, puzzled.

'You name it,' gestured Bradley. 'Cleaners, waiters, hospital porters, bank clerks. Normal immigrant jobs.'

'But how do we know who they are?' went on

Rolands. 'Now they don't even have a chain of command.'

'Well, that's down to the General,' said Bradley and smiled hopefully at his boss.

But the general did not respond. 'Cut the crap Bradley. I said to tell Rolands about the project, not give him a history lesson.' He turned away from Bradley to Rolands. 'Let's just say that Kalashnikovs and counterfeit Levis are not all you can buy in Moscow these days.'

'Files sir?' asked Rolands incredulously. 'KGB files?'

'Sure, why not?'

'But how do we know the information is good? That the names we get really are sleepers?'

'Two ways,' said Warkowski, tapping his fingers and thumb. 'One, I never buy bad files and two, Booker. She checks them out. I presume you know the meaning of the words "Sticky" and "Close Surveillance"?'

'Of course sir.'

'So, she checks them out. Gets to know them, gets friendly, sees what they know and when she's sure they are who we think they are, she sees if they know anything else. Then she introduces them to Sergeant Bullock or whatever his name is.'

' "Introduces"?' queried Rolands open-mouthed.

Warkowski raised his eyes to the ceiling in mock despair. 'Christ, do I have to spell it out for you?'

'No, no sir,' said Rolands apologetically. 'I understand.' He looked down at his hands with his mouth still open.

But Warkowski had already turned back to Bradley. 'OK, that wraps it up. Get me Marlin's file and the Englishman's. Have stuff ready for Booker and tell her I want her here for briefing as soon as she calls in. I want her to start right away. That's it then. Get on with it.'

'Yes, sir. I'm very confident.'

'Good, Bradley. I don't want to be disappointed. I don't *do* disappointment.'

Warkowski sat in thought for some time after Bradley and Rolands had left. He picked up his cap and looked at the row of hard-won stars. God, he thought. I'm tired. I never used to feel like this. Mustn't let this Marlin business get to me. He used to be twenty-four carat, and I thought he still was. Maybe he has been deep cover for too long. And if he has, what about the others? Nocta? Cohen? No way of telling. Perhaps time to call them all in and lay out a new board with new players. But who? Bradley would never be good enough. Too squirmy. No guts. Not like Buddy Marlin at all. Not in the old days anyway. But that seemed a long time ago. Probably was. His own fault for not keeping in touch more. It still seemed barely credible that things had gone so wrong without him hearing anything about it.

He leaned forward and pressed the intercom. 'Any transcript from that tape yet?'

'I'm afraid not sir. We've enhanced it all we can but there is too much background. The voices we have are definitely Marlin and Northcott but the boys don't think they will ever be able to sort out more than a few words. They can go on trying if you like, sir.'

'No. Call it off then. We'll flush them out some other way.' But if a bloody cemetery wasn't quiet enough to overhear a conversation, wherever would be?

Back in Arlington Cemetery, Major Madeline Booker, dressed in civilian clothes, was preparing to 'introduce' her sleeper, Mikael Lomakin, to Sergeant Buller.

She was sitting hand in hand with her man on one of the stone benches at the very top of the cemetery. The ground to the left of them dipped away from the main part, to where the maintenance sheds were. Three men in gardeners' overalls were standing next to one of the large handcarts used for the rubbish sacks. Out of sight of everyone they could have been three friends enjoying a quiet smoke before going home.

Madeline was wearing a plain black raincoat over an equally plain blue dress. On her feet she wore sensible brown shoes with low heels, suitable for the city librarian she was being. Most of her long blonde hair was tucked into a green headscarf. 'Blue and green should never be seen,' she had told herself as she had put it on earlier. 'Without something in between.' In this case duty. The scarf had been a present from the Russian and he was disappointed if she did not wear it the entire time.

She looked at him sitting next to her; his shapeless grey flannel suit was shiny at the elbows and knees. She squeezed his hand gently and smiled.

'I'm so glad we came here,' she said. 'I wanted to

show you Washington as the sun goes down. It's beautiful now, but in a week all the leaves will be red or bright yellow for the Fall. I just love the colours of autumn.'

The man smiled at her from his broad face and pale blue eyes. 'I think it sad place, Madeline, but you make anywhere special. I happy to be here with you.'

She smiled back at him. 'You are so sweet Mishca.'

'Ah, Mishca, I like it when you call me that. I have been Mikael all my time in America. I think you make me feel at home.'

'I read about the name during the Moscow Olympics,' she said. 'That little bear thing on all the badges, he was called Mischca. They said then it was short for Mikael. The children's name for it.'

'Yes,' he said. 'Is right. And what children say for Mikael in America?'

She thought for a moment, 'Well, our Mikael is called Michael, and we say "Mickey" for that.'

'Mickey? Like Mickey Mouse? I think I like that. You call me Mickey. I will be a real American soon.'

She laughed gently and linked her hands around his arm. The material feeling rough and grubby to her carefully kept hands.

That's right, she thought to herself. You are a bloody Mickey Mouse.

She was glad the assignment was nearly over. His accent and poor vocabulary were beginning to irritate her intensely. His smell, the way he was always touching her face. But she smiled at him as brightly as ever. 'I'm not sure,' she said playfully. 'That would mean I

79

would have to be *Minnie* Mouse and I don't know about that!'

'OK. Is good. I to wait.' He reached over and tapped the end of her nose gently with one finger.

She smiled eagerly and pressed herself against his arm. 'Do you think you would have liked to have children of your own?' she asked.

'Oh yes. But son. I would have liked son,' he said. Then, after thinking for a moment, he added, 'I would have call him Yuri.'

'Yuri?'

'From Gagarin. When I was young man I admire Gagarin. First cosmonaut. He was very brave Soviet man. Hero man for me.'

Mikael nodded at himself and went on looking out over the river towards Washington. A stillness had come over the afternoon and neither of them spoke for a short while.

'I'm so looking forward to this weekend,' she said eventually.

'Yes, Chicago. I want to meet your mother. She sound very kind. Will we stay in hotel or at apartment?'

'At the apartment. But there's only two bedrooms so you'll have to bed down in the living room.'

'Why for? You not tell her we sleeping?' he said slightly surprised. 'She not like?'

'No. She definitely "not like". She is very old-fashioned. She thinks people have to be married before that sort of thing.'

'I see,' he said patiently. 'America is different place.

But is good.' He smiled approvingly and leant back comfortably.

The sun began to dip behind the buildings in the distance and a cooler breeze sprung up. He didn't seem to notice but continued to smile contentedly. She did not interrupt his thoughts but, under the pretence of brushing a hair from her face, she stole a sideways glance at where the three men were waiting by the handcart. She gave a very slight shake of her head. They could wait until she was good and ready.

'You know,' Mikael suddenly said brightly, 'is very funny. Ten years I sleep for Soviet Union and is secret. Now I sleep with you and is still secret! Joke, no?'

She laughed despite herself. Then she sat up and tugged playfully at his arm. 'You are *such* a funny person.' Then more seriously she said, 'But you shouldn't talk about any of that. You said you would try to forget it. It's all done now. They aren't going to contact you. You said yourself that they have forgotten about you. All the people who knew you here have been replaced and none of the old people are left.'

He sighed. 'I know Madeline. But is difficult for me. I train as soldier, learn English to come here and start hidden life in Washington. I work as a hospital man. I am always ready for embassy people if they need safe place. I keep the Canada passports for them. Dollars. Many things. But now is five years and they not sign me.'

'Signal,' she corrected him absently. 'Signal.'

'Yes. Signal. Each once a year before I have signal. Now not.'

'I told you, Mishca, don't worry. It is all done. You can forget it. Start again.' She looked up into his troubled blue eyes. She leaned up and kissed him gently on the lips. 'Start again. With me.'

'But if communists come back?' he went on. 'Maybe they need sleepings here again. Maybe they can find me again.'

Maddie glanced down and smiled. Well, she said to herself, I think I can make sure there is no possibility of that.

She looked away from him towards the three gardeners. One was standing apart looking openly at her and Mikael and then his watch.

She gave a small sigh. Perhaps it was time enough after all. No point putting it off any more. She checked to see that Mikael was looking away from her and then nodded almost imperceptibly at the gardener before standing up.

'Come on Mickey Man,' she said. 'Cheer up. If we go to the car and drive into town, we'll have time for a hot dog or something before our movie.'

The Russian brightened and stood up next to her. 'You are right, Madeline. I promise not to talk it out any more.'

She turned towards the sheds. 'We can go this way,' she said. 'There is a short cut to the side road of the car park I know. It'll be quicker.'

'Are you sure Madeline, it looks like no road to me.'

'Trust me,' she said, linking her arm in his and giving him an affectionate squeeze. 'Trust me.'

In a few moments the dip in the path had taken them

completely out of sight of the rest of the cemetery.

As they reached the man dressed as a gardener who had been standing apart, he stepped back as if to let the couple pass more easily. But as they drew level he stepped forward again and suddenly kicked Mikael hard to one side of the knee and almost with the same movement shoved the Russian backwards so he fell to the ground. The gardener then stamped on the neck of the fallen man and kept his foot pushed hard down whilst he pulled a pistol with a long-nosed silencer on it out from his overalls. The gun was pressed hard against Mikael's chest. There were two rapid 'thwacks' and the Russian's body went suddenly and completely limp.

No sooner was this done than the other two men came quickly from around the back of the cart with a large sack. They reached down, folded the body roughly in half and pushed it inside the sack. One of them tied the neck before both men picked up the bundle and heaved it on the top of the barrow and then began wheeling it away towards the sheds.

Fifteen seconds. Perhaps less. Maddie Booker and Sergeant Buller were left standing alone by the path.

'Christ,' she said. 'Do you have to be quite so bloody brutal?'

Buller was tall and broad, he had very dark skin and his hair looked as though it had been straightened.

'I'm not brutal,' he said. 'I'm just efficient. What did you want me to do. Ask him if he wanted a smoke first? Anyway,' he went on, 'it was your idea to do him here. I don't see why we couldn't have done him, and all the others, at their apartments.'

'Because, dear Sergeant,' she said with an edge to her voice, 'you and your goons would look a bit odd going up and down stairs with your fucking trolley.'

'OK, OK,' he said putting up his hands. 'Only a suggestion Maddie. Maybe for next time.'

'There isn't a next time,' she said. 'He's the last one. And another thing, it's Major Booker to you, not Maddie.'

Buller shrugged as if it didn't matter to him what he called her. He took out a cigarette and lit it without offering one to her.

'You're too uptight,' he said. 'You should relax about it. We should get to know each other better. Have a drink. You know.'

She took out one of her own cigarettes and lit it without replying.

'Well?' he said. 'How about it?'

Maddie fixed him with as direct a stare as she could manage. 'Sorry, Sergeant, the next two million years are busy.'

Buller shrugged again, 'Suit yourself. But tell me, after one of these jobs, do you go home and have a bath, a shower maybe?'

'What! What did you ask?'

'I don't. Not me. Not for twenty-four hours. I like to keep it on me. The moment.'

She tossed her cigarette aside and stubbed it out with her toe. 'You're an animal, Buller, a frigging animal.'

He suddenly pointed his finger angrily at her. 'No,' he said. 'No. I'm not an animal. I'm as good at my job as you think you are at yours. Look at this path! Go on, look where I did it.'

She shook her head in disbelief before looking down to where he was pointing.

'So what – it's a path,' she said dryly.

'Yeah,' he went on. 'But is there a mark on it? Do you see any blood? No. And is it all kicked up where he struggled? No. It's tidy. And why? Because I use split nose, low velocity rounds. I set them up myself, special like. They don't go through, but you can take it from me that he's cat food inside. Dead in less than two seconds. One soft mush from neck to guts. And that's one hell of a pro job.'

She shook her head again. 'Well I'm sure the Chief will be impressed. I'll make a note to put it in my report. Now, if you don't mind I'm going now. Bath to take, you know how it is.'

'See,' he said smiling. 'You do take a bath after one of these, I thought you did.'

She turned to walk away and over her shoulder said to him, 'Not because of the job, Buller. I don't give two cents for it. No, I'm going to have a bath because I've been talking to you. Two hours' soaking should do it.'

Chapter Three

Simon stopped off at Buchan's 'Books 'n' Tapes' on his way back to the Watergate Hotel.

'Do you have anything on the game Go?' he asked the young man at the counter.

'Oh, yes, sir. We've a whole new section over there. Computer play or traditional?'

'I don't know yet. A friend was telling me about the game. I usually play computer chess.'

'Well, you'll like Go I'm sure. It's more logical than chess. I play a lot myself. If you're on the net I'd be happy to show you. There are quite a few club sites. The best players are still all Japanese but you can enter at lots of levels.'

'Thank you,' said Simon. 'I just might take you up. But I want to sort out the basics first. What's the best book?'

'Well, that has to be Korschelt's *Theory and Practice*. It's an absolute classic. Pretty old now and pre-computer of course. But I think it's still the best introduction. Some of the Go Web Sites are set up to play the teaching games from the book.'

'Sounds good. Do you have the addresses? I'm hopeless at searching for Web sites.'

'Sure. I'll put them inside the cover. Better still, I'll give you my home bulletin board number and leave a file for you there with all you need. But it won't be till later. I don't get off until eight.'

Simon laughed. 'I think I can wait that long! Thank you.'

He paid for the book and went out to find a taxi. He smiled again thinking of the young man in the shop. Couldn't be more than twenty. Great to be that enthusiastic. And that young. It seemed a long time since he was that enthusiastic about anything. Or that young come to that. Maybe Buddy was right about getting on with things. Perhaps he really should do something before he forgot what wanting something felt like. Well, actually, there was one thing he still wanted. A person. Always had. But best not to think about her. Wiser to stick to what he was good at. Keyboards, numbers, dreams. He could get by with them. At least most of the time.

At the same time that Simon was leaving the shop, Buddy was opening the front door of his house at Great Falls and kicking the mail aside. Probably all junk or bills. He dropped his coat on the floor in the hall and walked into the large sitting room. Picture windows gave out onto an overgrown lawn and beyond to the woods. The last of the afternoon light showed the first of the leaves turning to red. The view was one of the main reasons for choosing the house when Buddy and Susan had found it. He did not look out.

He took a bottle from a side table and poured himself a starter which he drank immediately and then a larger, main drink, which he took to the big chair which faced the white ashes of a dead fire in the grate. Just before he sat down he returned to the side table to collect the bottle. Just in case.

He stretched out his legs towards the fireplace and waited for Thousand to arrive.

The meeting with Costa was not one he was looking forward to. But there did not seem any way to avoid it. Well, almost no way. He poured himself another drink. Slightly larger this time.

By then Simon was at his hotel. He collected his key and messages and went up to his room. He stayed at the Watergate Hotel because it was Washington's most expensive hotel. 'Look,' he had explained at the office, 'I'm meant to be putting big deals together. I can hardly ask people to meet me at a Howard Johnson, can I? Besides, all Buddy Marlin's other people stay at the Watergate. Even the Colombians. And anyway it would look odd if I switched now.' And so his director had reluctantly agreed. Simon was happy and regarded it as a victory of sorts. But, in reality, Buddy didn't mind where he stayed and Simon had never met any of 'Buddy's people,' whoever they were.

In his room he poured himself a beer from the fridge and went over to sit in a large armchair by the window. The hotel looked over the quiet waters of the Potomac river. The evening was just beginning to turn dark and lights were coming on in the buildings on the other side of the river. Simon blew out his cheeks and stared down into his glass. Buddy was right of course. One day he would do it. The scam. The hit. The Dream. Call it whatever. It wouldn't be just for the money. Simon knew it wasn't about that. He wanted someone to do it with. He was waiting for that. Buddy was fun and seemed more than willing to go ahead but Simon didn't really want to do it with Buddy. So how long should he wait? Actually until that afternoon it had never occurred to him that Buddy might just want to do it for the money either. Regardless of any associated fun or risk. Want it enough in fact to involve Thousand. Which complicated things. Because she was the real reason Simon was waiting. Yes, he was waiting for Thousand, he admitted to himself. He smiled ruefully at his reflection in the window as he sat there in the darkening room. Ridiculous. It was never going to come to anything at all. Never had done. Never would. That really would be going too far. He rested his head back against the chair and began to drift off to sleep.

He seemed to be standing by the white benches again in Arlington. Buddy was standing down near Kennedy's memorial and waving up at him. Behind him, and further away, stood Thousand. She had her arms folded and was shaking her head. She did not seem to be smiling.

An hour later he awoke with a start at the sound of the telephone. It was Thousand.

'I'm glad you're in. Look. It's Buddy. He can't go to Costa tonight.'

'But I thought it was all fixed. Has the time been changed?'

'No. Buddy has changed the rules.'

'How?'

'By becoming totally out of it. He just called me. He's not going to be able to hand the money over without falling down. Let alone being able to drive to the hotel.'

'I thought you were only going with him riding shotgun. Can't you do it alone?'

'No way, Simon. Not to Costa. There has to be two people. It's seventy K of Uncle Sam's. It needs two people at a handover. Even one like this.'

'So why ring me? I can't go. I'm not Department. I'm not even an American.'

'That doesn't matter. We can fudge that. But I won't tell anyone in the Department that Buddy can't go because that would mean telling them why he can't go and I won't do that. They think he's pretty much of a lush as it is.'

'Well, just take a guard. Someone from security, the Laundry.'

'I can't do that for the same reason,' she went on. 'I want someone I know when I go in front of Costa. Someone I can trust. Please.'

'OK, I'll do it. But on one condition.'

'What?'

'I'll think of one. Do you want me to come over now?'

'Yes, we are going to be an hour late as it is. I had to come all the way back to the office to call you.'

'Why didn't you ring from Buddy's or the car?'

'I wanted a quiet phone.'

'You went all the way back to the Department just to get a scrambler phone? It's only a cash drop Thousand, not some sort of State secret, you know.'

'Simon there are all sorts of complications. We haven't time to talk about them now. Just hurry on over.'

'On my way.'

'Go to the back entrance of the block. I'll wait for you in the lobby. We'll go out to Buddy in my car. I want them to think you are at my place already. It will look more natural that way.'

'Who? Who is "they"?'

'Costa's lot. We'll be followed till we get to him. They'll be outside my place already.'

'Why? What's going on Thousand? Is there something I don't know?'

'Oh yes, Simon. I should say that's probably true. But please go now. It's going to be bad enough without Buddy and we're going to be late as it is. Please hurry. Bye.' Click.

Buddy lived about ten miles west of Washington in a small house in Great Falls. Long before his wife had left him he often told her they would buy a retirement home near the river. Simon thought Buddy had bought the house as they were splitting up in a last-ditch attempt to make her stay.

Simon took the wheel of Thousand's car and, as he

drove out along Leesburg with the river away and down to their right, he remembered how he and Ellen had come there that last summer on her one and only visit to Washington with him to meet up with Buddy and Susan to see the new house. All four of them had known that it would be no dual retirement home for Buddy and Susan but each of them kept up the pretence for the others. Things would work out. Difficulties could be smoothed over. Only five years ago and yet it seemed so much more. Time went by slowly when the heart of it was dead.

Simon looked in the rearview mirror. Thousand was right. A large black car was tailing them about a hundred yards behind. It made him feel distinctly uneasy.

Thousand broke into his thoughts. 'I grew up near here,' she said. 'Just over the river there at Cabin John Park. My father was a cop at Glen Echo.'

'Fairfax County, eh? I had you down as more of a West Coast type. You know, California Girl and all that.'

'No. Not at all. All that came later when I went to Cal Tech. I nearly didn't come back actually. I think part of me still wishes I had stayed in LA. But things happen. My mother died and I came back to be near Dad. Then he died and I just sort of lost momentum and stayed. But I think it's time to go again now.'

'What do you mean?'

'Oh, I don't know, perhaps it's just me,' she said quietly looking away to where the ground fell away to the dark river. 'But I think there is a sort of greyness about Washington and the Department now. A few years ago, working for you and Buddy it all seemed so – oh I don't know, so possible I think. All that sending you two to new places, new schemes coming on almost every month. You coming back with new ideas. It was fun. Frankly I loved it.'

'And now?'

'Sort of went a bit wrong didn't it? I mean when you two were married it was different somehow. Not only the work to look forward to but I loved hearing about the children when they were little. Probably because you both talked about them with such enthusiasm. It was catching. There always seemed to be a new photograph to see or a new story. You must have thought it a bit odd. Me liking to hear about the children so much but never doing anything about having my own.'

'I don't think so. Parents never think it odd when people ask about their children. I noticed more what you thought later of course. Famous Day and all that.

'I got a bit carried away didn't I?' he continued. 'I think you were right to turn me down before I did anything really silly.'

'I didn't actually turn you down, Simon. You know it wasn't really like that.'

'Well, it came to the same thing didn't it?' he said looking again into the rearview mirror.

'Look, I said I'm sorry.'

'Yes. But you don't have to be.'

She turned her head completely away from him and looked out the side window. 'Why do you call it our

Famous Day? What do you mean?'

'Just that. A One Day. Things seemed to me right as never before. You know that.'

'And you didn't want to spoil it? Is that why you never asked me out again?'

'Something like that. Only more complicated.'

She smiled to herself. 'And you think it was all a long time ago anyway don't you?'

'Well? Isn't it?'

'Not really,' she said. 'I remember it as though it was yesterday.'

They had arrived at Buddy's house. Thousand asked Simon to drive right into the open garage under the house. They walked up the dark stairs into the main part of the house without talking.

Buddy was lying sprawled out asleep on the floor by the easy chair when they went into the sitting room. A glass was lolling out of his hand and the bottle was lying on its side next to him. The briefcase with its neat rows of notes was open next to his head.

Thousand hardly looked at him as she kneeled down, clicked the case shut and stood up again. 'Shall we go then?' she said quickly.

'What about Buddy? We can't leave him like this. I mean do you think he'll be all right?'

'Of course he will. People get good at what they spend a lot of time doing. He'll be fine. He's doing his Special Subject isn't he? Let's go.'

'You're embarrassed aren't you? That's it. You're embarrassed for him.'

'Of course I'm bloody embarrassed. I know him.

He's not some wino. He's my boss. Please let's go now,' she said quickly, walking towards the door.

'But he's not my boss. He's my friend. I can't leave him like this.'

She stopped and turned to face him. 'You can and you will. He's fine. He'll *be* fine. We have to go now.'

'All heart, the Ice Queen.'

'Don't call me that. I hate it,' she snapped.

'Well, at least you know your name.'

'Of course I know what people call me. Look, we have no time to stand here bickering. We have got what we came for and we have to go to Costa.' And with that she walked out of the room. Simon followed.

They hardly spoke as they drove away from the house until they passed Spring Hill and were on the long straight Leesburg Road, just west of Langley Forest. Simon checked the mirror and, sure enough, the same black car was following them as they drove back to Washington.

'Did he tell you about his medical?' asked Thousand.

'A bit.'

'There is rather more to it than "a bit" I'm afraid.'

'What do you mean?'

'Well, let's just say it's not good. Not at all.'

'How do you know? Are you going to tell me you hacked into his medical record?'

'No. Not that. Jake told me.'

'And?'

'Not long. A year at the outside.'

'Jesus. His liver?'

'Yes, but not in the way he thinks.'

'Jesus again,' said Simon.

'It's not simple apparently,' she added. 'And they can't be sure yet. But all this drinking isn't helping him. Nor the smoking. He's not giving himself a chance.'

'So? Are you going to stop him?'

'If I could. And you would too. But sometimes I don't think he wants to be stopped.'

'Of course he does,' said Simon. 'All alcoholics want someone to put their arms around them and stop them. That's why they drink. To be stopped. But they never *do* stop till they see they have to do it themselves.'

'He's not an alcoholic. He just drinks all the time. There is a difference you know.'

'Well, yes. I do know actually.'

'Because you used to drink a lot?'

'Yes. And with Buddy. You know we used to drink a hell of a lot. But only ever to get drunk. Never just for drinking's sake.'

'Well. You stopped and he didn't.'

'Yes. A year or so back. But at least he doesn't drink as much as he used to.'

'I'm afraid he does,' she said thoughtfully. 'He makes an effort when you are here. But when you're not it can be pretty terrible. He's made a lot of enemies in the Department. And it's not as though he can point at what he is doing and tell them to back off. They all want his job. Particularly Bradley. And it's more than just snapping at his heels. And this trick,' she indicated the briefcase on her knees, 'isn't going to help. Jake can't go on carrying him.'

'So what can Jake do? Retire him or something?'

'Or something.'

'What's that supposed to mean?'

They reached the old chain bridge and turned right along Palisades Park. All the time Simon was checking the mirror. They were still there.

'Perhaps I'm not really sure,' she said at last. 'I don't know much about these things. No proper experience. But there is a bad feeling. I've seen Bradley looking at Buddy. Really fed up. A sort of "one more time old man" look.'

'It's not up to Bradley. Jake's the man.'

'You don't know that.'

'Well, Jake's head of department isn't he? Bradley's just a Field Organiser. Same as you.'

'Thanks for the "just".'

'Oh, I didn't mean it in that way.'

'I know. Forget it,' she replied. 'But the point is that Bradley is, well, in such a good position. He sits on all sorts of committees. He knows the right people. He's Kappa Alpha from Harvard, that sort of thing.'

'Kappa what?'

'Kappa Alpha. It's a Fraternity. A Frat House. In England you have the Masons I guess and over here we have the Frat Houses. Most of the top people in State are Kappa Alphas. The same way that most of your Overseas Development People are Masons. It goes with the job.'

'Am I too late to join?'

'Kappas yes. The Masons I don't know.'

'I meant the Kappas. And I could be a Mason for all you know.'

'You're not. I do know.'

'Don't.'

'Do.'

'How?'

She laughed.

'You know far too much,' he said.

'Maybe.'

San Antonio da Costa had taken a top-floor suite at the Ritz Carlton on 23rd Street. He was a small and fastidiously dressed man and this evening wore his customary expensive Italian blazer and perfectly pressed trousers. All that set him off from the Washington businessman he would like to be were a rather too heavy gold watch, just too many rings and a pair of grey crocodile skin shoes. Simon had once told Buddy that Costa did not know what it felt like to wear a shirt that had been ironed more than four hours ago.

But what had always impressed Buddy and Simon more was the fact that Costa never met them alone. The tall and unsmiling Raôl was never more than six feet away and two further 'associates' were always in the room. 'Don't make a sudden move or one of them will shoot your hand off.' Buddy had once joked.

Tonight was no exception, and the two associates sat at the far side of the large room watching quietly as ever.

Costa himself was sitting in a sofa in front of a small glass-topped table when Simon and Thousand arrived. He waved them to sit down opposite.

'Miss Nocta,' Costa began, 'I was expecting Mr Marlin. Why has he not come?'

'I'm sorry Mr da Costa, he has to leave for a special conference in Chicago first thing in the morning and he has to attend a briefing session before that so he asked Dr Northcott to come with me instead.'

' "Briefing Session", "Special Conference", "urgent visits to Chicago". What an exciting world Mr Marlin must live in. So far removed from my life as a simple businessman.' Then he turned to one side and spoke briskly to the man behind him. 'Raõl, check the morning flights to Chicago.'

Simon looked at his shoes. Oh shit.

Thousand handed the case to Costa and he placed it carefully on the small table in front of him and clicked open the lid. He immediately pursed his lips and looked up angrily. 'What is this? This was not my agreement. I see now why he did not come. This is not acceptable. No.'

'Mr da Costa,' said Thousand evenly, 'I am very aware of what you and Buddy negotiated. I know he said he would do his very best to get you old notes but he did explain it might not be possible at such short notice.'

'He emphatically said he would do it. I will not accept this at all.'

'There is really no problem,' she continued. 'These notes are anonymously sourced. Old notes would have meant obtaining them from elsewhere or changing them for you in advance and we did not want to attract that sort of attention.'

Costa waved his hand extravagantly. 'That is your matter. What I am aware of as much as you or Mr Marlin is that new notes are of no use to me at all. They are worth twenty cents on the dollar at best. This is completely inadequate. I will not accept.'

Thousand went on in her quiet voice, 'Mr da Costa, I think we are all aware that this is an exceptional transaction in many ways. But I have authorisation from Mr Marlin to give these notes to you in the complete confidence that they will be very suitable for you. Dr Northcott here will tell you the same. You have conducted business with him and Mr Marlin on many occasions in the past and today is no different.'

Costa turned to Simon and put up his palms in a theatrical shrug. 'So, Simoon, what do you say to this ridiculous situation? Do I look like the fool this woman takes me for?'

'Not at all, Santo. It's fine. I was as alarmed as Buddy when I saw the notes. Of course I was. You know we were expecting the old notes you requested. But he tells me these are properly sourced and I have used new notes from the same source for this type of work on several occasions. Yes, they are new notes but they are not batched in any way. You have my word on it and you have Buddy's word too. He asked me to come particularly to set your mind at rest. Miss Nocta here is perfectly correct. There is no problem.'

'Your word, Simoon; Buddy's word. Interesting

commodities in uncertain times.'

'Possibly, Santo. But you know my word is good. And so is Buddy's. We have dealt together too often for this to come between us.'

Costa leant back and moved his eyes from Simon to Thousand and back again.

Raōl came back over from the telephone and leaned over to whisper in Costa's ear.

Costa nodded. 'Very well. It seems Mr Marlin really is due in Chicago tomorrow. If what you tell me about the money is also correct I will reluctantly accept. But reluctantly. The days of new notes are over. I will not take them again. I only take them this time because you are here Simoon. I sometimes think that the only people I can trust in Washington are you and me. But then of course, we are not American.' He smiled thinly at his little joke.

'Santo, there is no problem. I'll tell Buddy you don't like it but honestly he had no choice at this short notice.'

'Very well.' Costa stood up. 'But one more thing, Simoon. I am sorry to have to say it but I think you have to be careful of our friend Buddy Marlin. He is careless now.'

'Careless?' asked Simon.

'Yes. I think that is the word. You and me, we are different perhaps. We deal in many places in many ways. Buddy deals only from Washington. The world is changing. The famous mighty dollar is now not so famous. We will use dollars yes, but what you and I sell is no longer American. Soon we will not even use dollars. Old or new. I think you know what I mean. And it is in this new world that our old friend is careless. He does not know how careful he has to be. Tell him I am sorry but I cannot take the old risks any more. Now, please, I have much to do if I am to rescue this business.' He picked up the telephone in front of him. The meeting was over.

When the door had closed, Costa put down the phone and picked up the case without closing it and turned to the man who had checked the Chicago flight. 'Raõl, take these on the midnight flight to Grand Cayman. Be at the George Town London and Provincial Bank Office when it opens in the morning. It is on the top floor of the Pan Bank building. Ask for Lockton. He will give you ninety cents on the dollar in old notes. Return on the ten o'clock flight. You will not of course be checked on the way out. If you are stopped on the way back ask for Chief Customs Officer O'Mara. It will be five hundred dollars which you may take from the case. I can tell you my old friend, I spit on these pathetic Americans. I spit.'

In the lift down, Thousand turned to Simon and asked what Costa had meant about the new ways and Buddy being careless.

'It's something he was on about last time we met,' replied Simon. 'It seems he has got it into his head that we can work with him through his bank for deals like tonight. We used to call this sort of thing "suitcase money" because it couldn't be traced but he now thinks electronic transfer can be made untraceable. He wants to be modern I suppose, that's all.'

'But that's not possible, Si. Even Costa should know that. And anyway the Department would never sanction it. You might be able to make the money disappear once it was in the system but it would have to have a start point. It could be back-audited.'

'I'm not saying it could be done. Just that Costa wants to try it. Or rather he would if Buddy was more adept. Or not "careless" as Costa puts it.'

'Meaning?'

'Meaning that Costa knows as well as I do that Buddy doesn't have the computer skills to make the money disappear before it reaches him.'

'And you do? Is that what he was saying?'

'Well, he thinks I do. That's all.'

'And do you?' asked Thousand.

'No. Of course not.'

'Oh, Simon, what the hell are you up to? If Costa thinks you can do it he must have some idea you can. That you have the skills. Exactly what have you told him?'

'Nothing. Practically nothing.'

'Tell me the "practically" bit.'

'No.'

'Yes.'

'No. Well. The three of us, Costa, Buddy and I, were having dinner a couple of days ago. Top floor of the Marriott. Big dinner. Oysters, all that sort of thing. Anyway when the bill finally came it was about three times what Buddy and I expected. I guess I was a bit pissed so I adjusted the total on my Amex card for a joke.'

'What? At the table. Then and there?'

'Yes, sorry. Costa thought it was a huge joke.'

'I'll bet he did. How the hell did you do it?'

'Not so difficult really. Went into the account and changed a few numbers, that's all.'

'Tell me how.'

'You just get access to the Amex mainframe in New York and make the changes. College stuff.'

'Accessing a bank mainframe in New York from a restaurant in DC. Doesn't sound like college stuff to me. What did you do? Just whip out your lap-top and modem it up or what?'

'More or less.'

'How the hell did you get into the mainframe? It's an International Corporation for God's sake!'

'I think that was the bit Costa liked. But actually you just have to have a few identity codes.'

'Where the hell did you get those?'

'Hey? What is all this? I have to have some secrets you know.'

'Oh, Simon. I don't think you have any idea what you have done.'

'It wasn't serious. Just a party trick. I told you I was a bit pissed. I probably wouldn't have done it otherwise.'

'And did Buddy see what you did?'

'He may have done. But he wasn't exactly connecting. He was a bit far gone if you know what I mean. I don't think he really saw.'

'Well, I think he did.'

'Why?'

'Because. That's all.'

The lift arrived at the car park level and the doors hissed quietly open. They walked out into the dark car park towards the car.

Thousand paused before getting in and looked over the car at Simon. 'Oh, hell. You might as well know. You'll find out soon enough anyway. Jake Cohen thinks Buddy's got his fingers in the jar.'

'Oh, don't be ridiculous. I told you it was just a dinner table thing. Just fiddling expenses. Half Washington's at it in one way or another.'

'Maybe. But not using mainframes.'

'Well. All right. It's not *that* easy. Buddy couldn't do it even if you showed him. You know that.'

'Well, he must have remembered enough to try it or something. Jake is really serious. They all are. Hopping mad in fact. Apparently someone went and borrowed some central funds from somewhere. I don't know the details. And they think it might be Buddy. They're not sure.'

Simon thought for a moment before replying. 'Well, if they're not sure, it's all right isn't it?'

'Like hell. Jake's having it checked out really properly by all staff.'

'By "all staff" eh? What do you think *that* means?'

'I think you know what it means. Sorry.'

'Hell, Thousand. You? He's your own boss. They can't be serious. You can't do that. They can't ask you.'

'Well. Who would you rather did it? Bradley? Central Data? Look, Simon, you've got to tell me what he did. Or, or, or something.'

'Or? Or?'

'Look. It's a mess. I'm sorry.'

'A mess? Is that what you call it?' started Simon. ' "I shopped my boss and friend but I was only following orders." Is that what you'll say?'

They climbed into the car and Simon took the wheel. As the car pulled out from the ramp down onto the street he turned to her and said, 'It gets you down doesn't it?'

'Costa? Well of course it does.'

'Don't let it get to you. Think of it as not real. Just a game.'

'But it's not a game. It's our work. It's what we're supposed to do. I mean if people were to ask what I did I would have to say "I deal with Costa. And when I'm not dealing with Costa, I'm dealing with someone who is." So it's not a game. Real life. It's what I'd say I do.'

'So who asks?'

'Well. If they did.'

'They don't though, do they?'

'No, they don't. People just don't know.' She folded her arms tightly as if she was cold and then relaxed before continuing, 'Perhaps it doesn't really matter. But it all seems so shabby, such a sham. I mean did you honestly think when you first came to Washington that you'd finish up taking a briefcase of drugs money from one man who's lost his nerve to another who never had any?'

They drove in silence. Simon checked the mirror. No car.

'No,' he said eventually. 'I didn't think it would come to this. None of us did. Especially not Buddy. I suppose him not coming tonight is his way of admitting Costa and his lot have finally beaten him. But he still has to go on. Maybe hoping that one day something good will come from it all. But I don't think he believes it will any more than we do. But he goes on. We just have to help him a bit more than we used to.'

'Because of the drink you mean?'

'Of course. But we don't help him because of the drink. We help him because we knew him before.'

Thousand unfolded her arms and pressed her hands up to the side of her neck. 'He always drank.'

'But you say not like now.'

'No. Not like now.'

'His friends will help him because they know him. Not because they have to,' said Simon.

'Possibly,' she replied. 'But tonight we did have to do it. Would I have done this with that loathsome man if I had had a choice?'

'Well, in a way you did have a choice. You chose to be Buddy's friend. And then you chose to call me. You could have walked away. Telephoned Security. I don't know.'

'It doesn't make it a good choice though does it?'

'Good and right aren't the same thing, Thousand.'

'Since when?'

'Since Costa.'

'That makes him sound important. Central. I don't like that.'

'He is important. And don't put it all down to

Costa. He's in the same system as we are. Blame the system if you have to blame anything.'

'That's too simple. Glib. Don't come the glib with me, Simon.'

'Why is it easier to blame the system than Costa? I'd say it's about the same. Part of the same thing. "System" only means "people".'

'I suppose so,' she said. 'It's our fault too. We let Costa move in. He targeted Buddy a long time ago. Went for the weakest part.'

'And so you think us going along with it makes us weak too?'

'Yes I do. And I feel so guilty too. I mean that was real money. Going to real drugs. In the place I live. But what can I do?'

'Like I said. Shrug it off. Don't let it get to you. And anyway, I didn't think that money was going to drugs. Isn't he going to take it to Puerto Rico for this chemical thing.'

Thousand shut her eyes. 'Maybe eventually. But he's going to multiply it up several times by dealing here in Washington first. You do know that don't you?'

'Perhaps. Look, Thousand, I don't have any magic answers on this. I hate it as much as you do. I'm not older. Not wiser. I just don't have the answer. It's just shitty. We just have to shut up and do it.'

They drove in silence again for a while. The traffic was building up. People coming into the city for the theatres, restaurants. Nights out with friends.

She sighed. 'Perhaps you're right. But I still wish I

knew where it all went wrong.'

'Yes, that would be nice. But I don't think there was any one moment you could point to. We just got gradually overtaken. That's all. You have to turn away from it. Find something outside the system to concentrate on. It's what people do. What families are for I suppose.'

'And children too?' she said.

'Not necessarily.'

'But I think it's true. Children are the greatest escape of all. Perhaps when they are little people love them only for what they are. But as they grow up I think they have to carry their parents' dreams too as often as not. Dreams look more possible carried by children.'

'That's pretty perceptive. From someone who never had any children.'

'Not really,' she said. 'Of course I don't know about particular children. But children in general. Of course I know. If you know about dreams, you know about children.'

'Why didn't you have any then?'

'Complicated. Well, perhaps not really. I did want them. Still do. Any woman who says she doesn't want children is fooling no one in my opinion. It really is that simple.'

'Too sweeping, Thou.'

'No. I think women who decide not to have children get a bit of a shock when the old clock thing starts to tick a bit louder.'

'And does that include you?'

'Partly. But I'm not too old you know. I've still got time to panic.'

He laughed. 'Yes. Plenty of time for that. But somehow you don't look the panicky type. But what about all those people who can't have children? Or who really have left it too late? It does happen you know.'

The car waited at a set of lights. Thousand stared absently as people crossed in front of them. 'Well, they can still have their dreams,' she said. 'It's not people without children who are sad, it's people without dreams.'

'That's a nice way of putting it.'

'Thanks,' she said. 'I used to have lots of dreams you know. I think that's why children didn't seem so important. But now with this Costa thing the dream front has taken a bit of a knock. A hell of a knock actually. That's probably why I'm rattling on about children. Sorry.'

'Don't be. So no dreams left?'

'Oh, yes. Some. And you?'

'Oh, yes.'

They were out of the main traffic now. The roads were almost deserted as they approached the block where Thousand lived in Columbia Heights.

'And Buddy's dreams?' she asked.

'I don't know. My guess is that he's about plumb out of dreams right now. Plumb out.'

Simon pulled over just short of the main entrance to the apartments. He switched off the ignition. 'What was this Chicago thing? I thought Costa had us there. Buddy didn't mention it at all earlier today.'

'It wasn't on until after you'd left. It's just a conference thing Jake wants him to go to. There is always
some meeting or other he is meant to be going to. But
he doesn't actually go unless Jake makes him.'

'Sounds like Jake wanting Buddy out of Washington for a bit to me.'

'Something like that.'

'Still, it gives you a chance to grub about in his desk
doesn't it?'

'Shut up, Simon. I don't want to do it at all. You
know that.'

'Anyway he won't be able to go. Not in the morning. You saw the state he was in.'

'Then he'll just have to go later on the shuttle. I can
change the flight,' she said with irritation.

'But won't he think this sudden Chicago thing is a
bit too much of a coincidence? Just after this money
thing?'

'Not really. He'll expect a bit of a pistol whipping
from Jake. Buddy hates going to meetings. It's a start.'

'Too petty. Not Jake's way. Even Buddy will see that.'

'Look, I don't know. Jake just wants him out of
Washington. Period. Anyway it's nothing to do with
you. Department.'

' "Department." Thanks. So it's all right for me to
carry cash about for him when he can't stand up but
not all right for me to ask what's going on the next
day. Thanks, Thousand. But then you're his special
side-kick aren't you? Allowed to know everything.
Allowed to dole out the shitty bits to me when you
feel like it.'

'You know it's not like that, Simon. And it really is Department stuff. Internal. You're well out of it. And it would be easier for me and for you too if you stayed out.'

'Hey, hang on there. One minute, we're talking about the Department and the next thing it's you and me. Sorry, but I missed the connection.'

She didn't reply immediately. 'I'm sorry. I didn't mean to snap at you. But there is a lot going on all of a sudden. I don't know all of it but I do know that in Washington nothing is ever what it seems. It's all hidden agendas and sub-plots. You know that. And even something straightforward as Buddy's Chicago trip. It may not be as simple as it looks.'

'Do you mean there is something catastrophic you haven't told me?'

'Sort of. It's a bit like this.' She drew two overlapping circles on the windscreen in front of her. 'This is you and me. And this bit,' she said, indicating the overlapping part, 'we know about. But the rest is unseen. We don't know all sorts of things about each other at all.'

Simon was sure he had seen the same diagram somewhere before. A magazine perhaps.

'What? Bad things you mean?' he said.

'Could be. Yes.'

'Look, I don't need disclaimers. Not from you of all people.'

'What do you mean, "disclaimers"?'

'Sort of advance warnings about things. So you can say afterwards, "Well, I did warn you." '

'I am sort of warning you.'

'Who are you trying to protect? Me or you?'

'Both of us,' she answered quickly. Too quickly, he thought. She hadn't had time to think about it. Too pat.

'There are all sorts of reasons running against us, Simon. I'm sorry, but you just have to accept it.'

'Ah, "reasons against",' he said. 'You know, sometimes I used to actually count the reasons against us getting together. Overwhelming. But then I would remember how I felt when I saw you. I'd lose my place and have to start counting all over again.'

She did not reply. The two of them just sat looking out of the car onto the road in front of them.

Eventually he reached out and took her hand gently. She did not resist. First fingers entwined, then fingers flat out against each other and then entwined again. The lights at the intersection a hundred yards away changed from red to green and back to red.

'Come up for coffee,' she said. 'There is something I want to show you.'

'I don't think that is such a good idea.'

'I've got proper coffee. The stuff Costa brings for Buddy. Costa may be awful but his coffee is brilliant. And yesterday I bought a special jug for making it in. With a plunger.'

'It's called a Cafetière.'

'Yes. That's it.'

He smiled at her. 'OK. But first we have to let go hands.'

Thousand's apartment was on the top floor of the

block. It was much larger and more luxurious than Simon expected. Thickly carpeted and very quiet. It was on the corner of the building and floor-to-ceiling windows looked out south and east over the city. To the south all the floodlit memorials of central Washington were clearly visible. To the east the eye was drawn to follow the curve of the Michigan Highway around McMillan Lake and out to the parkland beyond.

'This is some view Thousand. It's fantastic. The whole place. Simply amazing. I had no idea you lived in a place like this,' he said walking over to the east side windows.

'I know, I was very lucky. I have one of the best views in Washington. Frankly the view from these two windows was the reason I took the place.'

'But inside too. It's huge. It must cost a fortune.'

'You're wondering how I can afford it.'

'I didn't say so.'

'First not to.'

'First of who?' he asked.

'Ah,' she smiled. 'That might be telling.'

She went over to the open-plan kitchen area and began to make the coffee. 'It's simple really,' she said. 'It depends what you want to spend your money on. Most people have expensive families and holidays. I have the windows.'

'Perhaps,' said Simon as he turned and walked over to the windows that faced south. 'I don't think people really choose families and holidays. They tend to come along with the people you share with.'

'Thanks.'

'Sorry, I didn't mean it unkindly. It's just that expensive things sort of happen regardless. You don't realise they are going to happen when you start out.'

'Then people had better think more before they go in for things.'

'But who does?'

'I did.'

'Did you get it right?'

'I've still got the windows. You got the divorce,' she said.

'My turn to say "Thanks".'

'And my turn to say "Sorry".'

'Two "sorry"s in two minutes. Some start, Thousand.'

'We're not starting out Simon. We've known each other six years altogether.'

She walked over and stood next to him as he looked out over the lights of the city.

'It looks beautiful from here,' she said. 'You can't tell from way up here what a complicated place it really is.'

'It's just Washington being its usual self,' he said. 'Washington Games. That's all.' He took her hand gently and asked, 'Tell me, what do you really want from the place?'

From the kitchen side of the room came a loud click as the kettle switched itself off.

'It's boiling,' he said. 'Coffee time.'

'I don't want coffee, Simon.'

'What do you want then?'

'I want Out.'

'And?'

'And.'

She turned and went over to a small table to pick up a hollow copper ball about the size of an orange. The top was open and small star shapes were cut into the sides. She came back and held it out to him. 'This is what I wanted to show you. It's the first thing I bought for this place. The day I moved in. Actually I want to give it to you. Think of it as a sort of talisman.'

'Talisman?'

'Yes. Something to look over you.'

He took it from her and examined it. Inside was a small night light candle.

'You haven't used it,' he said.

'No. You can think of it as a symbol.'

'What do you mean?'

'Well, look at it. It's unlit. Never used. Not got going properly.'

'Like us, you mean? Famous Day?'

'A bit.'

'Thank you,' he said. 'But why do you think I'm going to need a talisman?'

'I just do. And it's something just in case. But it's a happy thing too. I bought it back when everything still seemed possible. Think of it as a candle ball of happy beginnings. Nothing dreadful has happened to it. Look after it. You never know.'

'Don't worry. I will look after it.' He lifted her hands and gently kissed her fingers. 'Thank you.'

PART TWO
Cambridge, England

Chapter Four

By ten o'clock the next morning, Simon was in a taxi going to the airport. He took out his lap-top and hooked in a modem link to the local phone system. From there he accessed the international lines and dialled London to open a link to the United Machines account at Heathrow. He cancelled his noon British Airways flight on economy class via Dublin and changed it for a first class seat on a slightly earlier direct flight by Virgin Airways. He thought after all his years with the company it was no more than he deserved. Or them come to that. Next he opened a line to the company dollar account in New York and made the necessary currency adjustments so the transactions would not show on the monthly log. What were a few dollars here or there?

Just over one hour later he was sitting comfortably on the top deck of a 747 with a large gin in his hand. The ice in it clinked quietly as the aeroplane levelled out at its cruising height. Out of the window he could see bright sunlight on the white cloud cover. In the distance the horizon was a deep blue. This was the best part of any journey. He finished his drink and held his empty glass out into the aisle for the cabin staff to see. Why not? he thought. Nothing much else to do today.

During lunch he asked for a telephone and called Buddy at home. The line rang for a full five minutes before it was answered.

'Why aren't you in Chicago yet?' asked Simon.

'Piss off. I'm going at six. But thanks for last night.'

'Don't thank me. Thank Lady Long Legs.'

'Both of you. Did it go all right?'

Simon knew it was an open line. 'Ears. Buddy. Ears. But yes, the old man seemed pleased. But he was surprised at the pristine state of the goods. He had expected something secondhand.'

'I know. But was the amount right? I didn't check.'

'Definitely. More than enough. In fact the lady and I felt we should take a little for our troubles.'

'Christ! You didn't lift any did you?'

'No. But serve you right if we did. She was really hacked off.'

'Yes. But she's a good woman. I keep telling you that. Anyway, are you still in town?'

'No. On my way home. I should be back with you in about a week as planned. Meanwhile have fun in the Windy City.'

'No chance. I feel terrible.'

'Bye.'

Simon pressed the off button on the handset. He stared down at it. 'And look after yourself big man. Look after yourself.'

Next he called Thousand. She picked up at the first ring.

'Hi, Si. You made your flight then?' she asked.

'Yes. All well on the ground?'

'Sort of. I can't raise our friend at home.'

'Don't worry. I've just spoken to him. He thinks he can go at six.'

'OK,' she said. 'But it seems our other friend didn't leave Washington this morning either.'

'Don't worry. He's just sent the goods on ahead. That's all that matters. He never carries that much luggage himself. He gets that animal to do it.'

'Seems a lot to trust an animal with.'

'He doesn't have to trust him. He owns him. And his mother.'

'If you say so. And by the way, I had an e-mail from Harvey at the bookshop. He says you really do want to learn about Go.'

'How the hell did he know I knew you?'

'It's on the net, Simon.'

'What is? You and me?'

'Not quite. Apparently you asked him for some stuff. So he looked you up in the directory from your credit card and sent it to you in case you couldn't find him. And while he was in your box he saw some mail from me. And he knows who I am because we play the same Go league table. Two and two.'

'How the hell can he look at my e-mail? It's a secure box.'

'Of course it is. But people who want to can look anywhere. It's one of those things you would say half

Washington is up to. You of all people should know that. Just because he works in a shop doesn't mean he's a simpleton.'

'Oh, well. I suppose it doesn't matter. Anyway, what is the mail from you? You only saw me yesterday. A true confession perhaps?'

'No such luck,' she went on. 'Just a routine request for last month's United Machines transactions. You haven't sent them to me yet.'

'OK. I'll do it when I get in to the office in the morning. I'd do it from here but I don't think Aeroflot run to digital lines.'

'I thought you'd switched to Virgin?'

'Nosey Parker!'

He heard her laugh. 'Well, you take care of yourself Mr Experienced Traveller. I'll call you at the office tomorrow. Bye.'

He handed the telephone to the hostess and called for another large gin. He leant his head back. Buddy was right. She was a good woman.

At the same time that Simon was settling back into his seat, Maddie Booker was sitting reading a file opposite General Warkowski at the Long Table.

Her blonde hair was pulled back from her face and she wore little make-up. Perhaps just enough to cover the fine lines at the sides of her eyes and mouth. Her small and carefully manicured hands smoothed down the pages as she read. When she had finished she looked up at the general with a slightly puzzled expression. 'Simon Northcott? Are you sure, sir?'

'Of course I'm not sure. That's why I want him stickied. You have to check.'

'But he works with my brother. Can't he tell you if Northcott's up to anything?'

Warkowski leaned back in his chair and put his hands behind his head. 'About your brother then. How much do you see of him?'

'Very little these days. We're not very close.'

'And why is that then?'

'Well, sir, I would say he disapproves of me.'

'Does he know what you do?'

'Not really. He knows I sometimes work with Colonel Rolands but that is as far as it goes. I suppose he knows Rolands does Covert Data Surveillance. Perhaps he doesn't think that is work for a woman. My brother has always been rather old-fashioned in his view of women.'

'And what do you think, Major? Are you old fashioned too?'

'Sir. I've been doing Close Surveillance for ten years now. I know it doesn't suit everyone but I like it.'

'You're good too.'

'I hope so. I take a pride in it.'

'I like that. A soldier should take pride in what he does.'

'Yes, sir.'

Warkowski stood up and walked backwards and forwards the length of the Long Table.

After about a minute he stopped pacing and turned towards Maddie. 'Do you remember what I told you when you first started this work? About involvement?'

'Yes, sir. You said that if ever I felt I was getting personally involved with a target in any way, then I should tell you and you would pull me out.' She leaned forwards and put her elbows on the table. 'But that has never happened, sir.'

'And this time? Will the fact that this Northcott man is a friend of your brother make it difficult?'

Without hesitation she replied, 'No, sir. I will remain detached. It's just that I thought my brother could tell you right away what I might take some days to find out.'

'And if I told you I thought your brother was involved too? What then?'

Maddie relaxed back in her chair and smiled. 'Well, I'd have to say your information was suspect, sir. Colonel Marlin and I may not be all that close but I know him well enough to say that this stuff is way out of his league.' She waved at the file in front of her.

Warkowski sat down again. 'Good. I wanted to hear you say it. It's my reading of Marlin too.' But there was a slight hesitancy in his voice.

She leaned slightly forward. 'I am sure I can handle it sir. I want the case.'

'Good again. But what about the other man, Northcott's friend, Lessing. The university one?'

She turned over the pages in front of her and looked up again. 'I can't tell from this. I need more. Is this really all we have?'

'We should have more. Lessing is a British academic so he should have his own file. I've told Bradley to look into it and give you the update.'

'Can't I do that sir? I might find something Bradley would miss.'

'No. I want you over in England now. Look, you may not like Bradley much but I think you will find he's pretty thorough. He's made a good job of the Northcott update and he can do the same for Lessing.'

'Possibly, sir, but what is the urgency? It would only take me a day.'

'Because I don't have a day, Major. My decision, not yours.'

Maddie looked down at the file again.

Warkowski stood up and began his pacing again. 'Your part in this,' he began, 'is to get close to Northcott and see if he's involved in the Data Access. Rolands thinks he is but you have to check for us. I'll take it from there. As far as Lessing goes, my guess is that if Northcott isn't our man, then it has to be Lessing. Maybe both. Could be two ends of the same pole for all I know. But you let me decide what to do in any event. You've got what you have to do. And the reason it's urgent is because Rolands says it is. Good enough for me, good enough for you. I've got the best team there is and I trust them.

'Your brother, Colonel Marlin,' continued the general, 'has reported he suspects files in Washington are being interfered with from Cambridge, England. He told his section head. But we have reason to believe from other sources that the problem may be a great deal more serious than either Colonel Marlin or Brigadier Cohen imagine. We need to identify the source as soon as possible before significant file compromise takes place.

When she asked what 'other sources' meant, Warkowski had simply said 'Federal', and 'You don't need to know which department. But it is significantly important for us to act immediately.' Then Warkowski had fixed her with that icy stare of his. 'This is priority, Major. I don't see your end of it as being complicated. But if it goes well, they will notice it all the way to the top. There could even be promotion in it for you.'

Promotion? Well, that would be nice. Overdue of course, but still nice.

'Yes, sir.'

Warkowski pointed at her. 'This isn't some crackpot operation, Major. Someone's into Uncle Sam for one hell of a lot of money. My job is to stop them and your job is to do what I say. Rolands tells me that person or persons unknown are using this department's computer as some sort of conduit. Now I don't give a shit if Fed Bank can't look after its own money but I'll be in hell before they use my machine to get at it. Playing games with money is one thing, playing games with America is quite another.' He gave her a tight little smile and waved her towards the door. 'Dismissed.'

Five minutes later she was sitting down in Bradley's office as he passed her the Lessing file. It was a bare and featureless room decorated only by a framed commendation on one wall and a photograph of a rather mousy-looking woman on the desk. Could there actually be a Mrs Bradley? speculated Maddie. She smiled to herself as she leaned forward over the file. If there really was a Mrs Bradley then the commendation should be on her wall. She began to read.

Bradley stood up and came around to her side of the desk and stood over her.

She did not like him standing so close. 'I'll take it with me and read it on the plane,' she said.

'No. You'll read it here and leave it with me. I think you know the rules.'

'Then go and sit down. You're blocking my light.'

He went back to his side of the desk and sat down again with a forced smile.

The file on Bellman Lessing was only three pages long and it did not take her long to finish it. The first two sheets were standard stuff and largely repeated the section she had seen in Simon Northcott's file. Details of his lectureship at Cambridge, where he lived, his family, his friends. What university committees he sat on, his salary and spending patterns. All standard stuff and obviously not updated recently. But the last page was different. It was a detailed surveillance report containing a list of all his contacts with American citizens over the last two years and she was surprised to see her brother's name mentioned twice and then further references to transcripts of telephone conversations.

Maddie looked up at Bradley who was still holding his smile. 'These meetings with my brother,' she said. 'Why didn't the Chief mention them? Does he know?'

Bradley shrugged. 'Maybe. But the Chief has a lot of files to deal with. He can't read them all.'

'Well, I'm glad he's got you then,' she said sharply. 'You look as though you read a lot of files. But just maybe this last page wasn't *in* the file that you gave the Chief.'

'I'm glad I didn't hear that, Major,' smiled Bradley. 'But *you* had better read that page pretty good. And remember it too. Use it to start your "conversations" with Lessing and Northcott. That is if you need a lead in, which I doubt from what I hear.'

She looked up angrily. 'You watch it, Bradley. What I do and how I do it is up to me. You can sit here pushing files up Warkowski all day as far as I care but someone has actually to go out there and round these people up. I'm Field and you're Paper. And next time the chief asks you for a file don't you hold back everything newer than two years or he'll get to hear about it from me personally. Is that clear?'

Bradley smiled again. 'Oh dear, Major. I seem to have touched a nerve. So sorry. Now you hurry along or you'll miss your nice shiny plane. The one in the field.'

She stood up and walked out without another word. Bradley picked up the file and locked it in the top drawer of his desk.

Simon woke up in his cottage at about ten the following morning. He telephoned his office to say he was sick and would not be in until about four that afternoon.

He showered and read the paper for half an hour

before walking into town for a haircut at Remi's and a coffee at Clowns. Both Italian and each the best anywhere at what they did. He asked himself, and not for the first time, why, if the best shops were Italian, he didn't just go to Rome and have done with it? He walked over the Backs to the University Library and browsed at random for two hours. There wouldn't be a library like this in Rome. Perhaps there was a reason to stay after all. Oh, yes. And work. He looked at his watch. Sighed and set off towards the United Machines office above the off-licence in King's Parade.

His secretary, Ginny, looked up as he walked in. 'Miracle Cure, I suppose,' she said.

'Something like that. Any messages?'

'Only two. One from Bell Lessing and one from Thousand.'

'Thousand first.'

'She wants your transaction file again.'

'I know. I talked to her from the plane yesterday. I said I would send it to her today but tomorrow will do.'

'Well, she said she couldn't wait for you to get in so she asked me to e-mail it for you.'

'But it's not ready yet. It'll take me about an hour.'

'I know that. But she said she had to have it right away. Some panic or other. So she asked me to send her your entire key-stroke back-up for the US work for the month and she said she would take it from that.'

'Did you send it? All of it?'

'Yes. I hope that was all right?'

'I suppose so. But there is a lot of other garbage in there as well. You know how hopeless I am with directories. It could take her ages to go through it all to find the transactions. I'd better call her.'

'Well, actually she said it wouldn't take her all that long because she said she knew what to look for. And I didn't know if you would be in or not. What with you being so ill and all.'

'Irony taken Ginny. And what did Bell want?'

'Better news. He wants you to join him at high table at his college tonight.'

'That is most definitely better news. Did you accept for me.'

'Yes. I thought you might just recover enough in time.'

'Good. I'd better go home and get ready then hadn't I?'

'Simon! You have only just got here.'

'So? KK isn't here today is he?'

'No. But there is something you still have to do.'

'Like what?'

'Like those.' She pointed to a large pile of green printout.

'Are those the six months' figures?'

'Yes. And they're awful. At least your bits are.'

'Well, I'd better not look at them had I? I'm very easily upset you know.'

'It's the third disastrous six months in a row. It's not funny at all, Simon. And I think it really matters this time.'

'Why? What does that mean? Have you heard something? Come on.'

'Well, sort of,' began Ginny. 'It's only a rumour, but the holding company is taking a bit of an interest. More than a bit of an interest in fact.'

'And what is that supposed to mean?'

'You know what it means.'

'Only threats. Nothing to worry about.'

'If you say so.'

'I do. Anything else?'

'No, but you had better be here the day after tomorrow at ten. KK's called a meeting to discuss the figures.'

'OK. I'll come in at half eight tomorrow and read them.'

Simon left the office and walked down King's Parade past the Chapel towards his home in Trumpington. It was a warm afternoon. Still summer, really, he thought. All the trees were still green and there was the smell of freshly cut grass as he passed the playing fields. There was little traffic and the gentle sounds of a cricket match drifted over from the Leys School. A cricket ball being struck. A ripple of polite applause. Dear England, he thought, I love you very much.

He arrived at Lacrima Christi College at six. He knew Bell Lessing would not be in his room but it was never locked and so he let himself in and sat down in a faded leather armchair by the open hearth. When Bell had become a fellow of Lacrima about twenty years ago, they both remarked that an open fire seemed an antiquated luxury. But they had come to see it as more of a practicality when they had investigated the thickness of the walls one drunken evening the following winter. They were some two feet of solid sandstone. Putting in central heating would have deterred even the most enthusiastic plumber. Simon smiled at how long ago that seemed.

He rested his head back and stared up to admire the ornate plasterwork of the ceiling. The open fire meant that the ceiling was always slightly sooty, but the college in its wisdom had never cleaned it but only repainted it periodically. The result was that the elaborate central rose and the botanic effect cornice were gradually filling in and becoming obscured. Bell never seemed to notice and Simon had never felt it his place to mention it. He just took it as a further example of how people with beautiful things rarely looked after them. Simon thought it probably applied to Bell's job as well. After all, the life of a Cambridge don looked pretty idyllic: little work, safe for life and an excuse to read and write more or less what one wanted. Bell never appreciated that fully, Simon thought, didn't know how lucky he was. It once occurred to Simon that perhaps he too had been free to make what he could of his own life. But it was probably too late to make fundamental changes now. Besides, he didn't really want to strike out in any new directions any more. Bell had waved him off into new lives quite often enough but had also been there when Simon returned home a little wiser and secretly a little sadder each time. 'No joy, Si?' he could hear Bell saying. 'Don't worry. You'll think of something. You always do.'

Up until now. Now he was fresh out of new ideas. He wasn't sure if he was tired or just bored. Getting old even. Whatever it was he seemed to be in his 'wilderness years' as he put it to Bell. His present job was going badly but not disastrously so. He had a house. Some friends. Sometimes that seemed enough. But it was the other times that worried him.

Times such as those he spent sitting at his computer keyboard at home watching the exchange tables of the international banks from around the world. Huge sums of money flowing backwards and forwards. Billions. It was like leaning over the back of a boat watching the wake. If you watched long enough you lost track of individual waves and it became one continuous flow pattern that rolled away into the distance. The market's screens were like that if you looked at them long enough.

During one late-night drinking bout, Simon had been telling Bell about this. He had turned on Bell's own computer and accessed the bank files from there. Bell was sitting next to him at the desk but was not really concentrating. His head tending to loll forward onto his chest. 'I don't see what you mean, Si. It's just numbers. Tables of numbers. Not like a ship at all.'

'Wake, Bell. Ship's wake.'

'Of course. But why do you look at them? You don't understand them. You're not a banker.'

'No,' agreed Simon. 'But we're looking at a lot of money swilling about and I'm not part of it. It's disturbing.'

'Ridiculous. You don't feel like that if you see a famous painting or car or something do you? You're not part of that world either. It's called the Planet Rich.' He found this vastly amusing.

'No,' Simon went on. 'But I don't know about paintings or cars. But I do know all about computers. I should be able to make some money from them.'

'Well. Write a proper program then. A game or something. Lots of money in that.'

'But that would mean knowing about business too. And we both know I'm no good at that. I need to find a way of making money from computers without being in business. That's why I look at these screens. There must be a way. This screen here is a window on the most money changing hands anywhere in history. If I could just see a pattern, or something to latch on to, there might be a way. But I can't. That's what is so frustrating. And yet all the people behind these numbers are making thousands as we watch them. Patterns of numbers. Like the wake. Very nice but not exactly a money spinner.'

But Bell's head had nodded again and Simon was left watching the numbers move and change on his own.

In the Court outside Bell Lessing's window some undergraduates passed by shouting and laughing at each other. Bell woke with a start. 'Afraid you lost me there for a moment, Si. Look, why don't I go and get a bottle of port before the manciple locks the cellar for the night.'

Bell went out and Simon leaned back in his chair

with his eyes still fixed on the screen. Then quite suddenly the numbers on the screen stopped changing. First individually and then in clusters. Soon the whole screen was locked for about five seconds. Then as quickly as they had stopped the numbers began to change again. Outside in the college Simon heard the chapel clock strike midnight. The hairs on the back of his neck stood up and he stared open-mouthed at the flickering screen. 'Yes!' he shouted. 'That is it. That is it! I am home!' Somewhere in the back of his life a huge hourglass was picked up and turned over. Nothing would ever be the same again.

Just then Bell returned with the port. 'Lucky actually,' he said. 'That bastard was trying to lock up early. But I told him. Oh yes, I told him. Anyway here we are. Taylor's sixty-eight.'

'But I've done it!' cried Simon. 'I've cracked it. Midnight. I must have been mad not to see it before.'

Bell was searching for the ever-elusive corkscrew. 'What are you on about old man? Have you seen the bloody thingamajig?'

'Bell, while you were out the whole screen locked. All the numbers froze. Then started again. I thought it was a line fault because I've seen it before but never realised what time it was. But the clock did it. Midnight. The end of the dealing day on the London exchange. All deals have to be cleared by then. They start again immediately but there *is* a moment at exactly midnight when all the currencies are still.'

'Yes, very interesting Si. Ah! here we are.' He had found the corkscrew.

'I was looking for a pattern wasn't I Bell? I haven't found one but I've seen something better, a discontinuity. An actual data discontinuity.'

'Lost me again. Here. Hold this for me will you?' Bell passed him the errant corkscrew and set off to the other side of the room looking for the glasses.

'I just know I can do it now, Bell. I just know it.'

That had been five years ago. He smiled at himself when he remembered how easy he thought it was going to be. And also how easy some other things had looked. He had been happily married then. Lewes was only about fourteen. 'Look, darling,' he had told Ellen, 'we won't have to worry about money ever again.' The dreams didn't have a limit. Not then.

But reality with its sticky tentacles had slowly engulfed him. The money thing was not going to be at all easy and anyway Ellen was not going to be satisfied with just the promise of money. She had grown tired of his dreaming and scheming. She had wanted a happiness he increasingly could not provide. Looking forward to things when you were young was easy, but with each succeeding year it became more difficult when the dreams were as far away as ever.

That warehouse business had certainly been the last straw. Enough was enough and she had moved on, taking Lewes with her. He had gone through his divorce like a sleepwalker. Not being able to do anything about it and not being sure if he wanted to. He felt like one of her endless garden landscape plans. Delayed, postponed and then eventually abandoned altogether. But in the background of his life he had continued to work away at his system.

He had tried patiently to describe it to Bell on a number of occasions in the months following the initial discovery.

'The discontinuity was the key. I found out that it was caused by a very slight rise in the major currencies at the end of the dealing day. Midnight London. And I think it's midnight on all other markets too. It looks as though the whole thing takes thirty seconds but that is down to transmission delay and satellite bounce. The actual event only takes about fifteen seconds.

'I couldn't see why it happened at first,' he went on. 'Then I realised it didn't really matter just so long as it was predictable. Later I found it has something to do with how the computers close their books. As the deals close down at the end of trading, they move all loose cash and incomplete transactions into the main currencies which causes a slight rise in them. The effect is small but it *is* there and it's there every single time. Maybe as little as a thousandth of a per cent, but it always happens.'

'A thousandth of a per cent, Si? Doesn't look much of a margin to me.'

'It isn't. But it is always there and always in the same direction. If I can ride enough on that few seconds, I can write my own ticket.'

'Well, if it's so bloody easy, why don't the banks do it themselves?'

'They don't see it. Their machines do it for them.

Anyway, remember it's a very small rise in their terms.'

Bell was still looking doubtful.

'Look, it'll work like this,' began Simon. 'I'll find a way to hack into the banks' mainframes.' He pushed his hand out in front of him, cutting the air. 'Then I'll take a file up to the communication satellites that link the big financial centres: New York, London, Tokyo, whatever.' He reached his hand above his head and spread out his fingers. 'Then I bounce the file from satellite to satellite right around the globe.' With this he flicked his hand at points around an imaginary circle above him. 'Bounce, bounce, bounce, without coming down at all. And that's the file that will do the dealing but they can't see it because it's only on the satellites and not in the ground computers. So then I literally fill the file with money and store the amounts in a big net of numbers, a Drifting Table. Then, when I'm ready, I drop the money down from the satellites into whatever accounts I choose.' He banged his hand down on his knee. 'Christ, Bell, they won't know what's going on! They won't be able to see it!'

Bell put his head on one side and pursed his lips forward with an expression between not believing and not understanding.

'Show me then,' he said.

But of course Simon couldn't.

Because he had soon discovered that it was not simply a matter of understanding the discontinuity and how much it represented. To ride enough money on the margin he soon found he had to tackle whole areas of mathematics and computing that were new to him.

His first set of problems had been with coming to grips with the Large Number Theory. LNT he had needed to store and manipulate his data. There were plenty of books on the subject but he made slow progress.

Then he had to learn how to use the international communication satellite system because that was where he would have to tap into the dealing streams. He was daunted at first but soon found it was not too different from land line telephone hacking. Only the scale and speed were different and they were things he could manage.

Next came the problem of how to ride his files up to the communication satellites without being noticed and to hide the files once they got there. He rejected viruses as being too clumsy and had gone for Side Files, packages of data that could ride alongside other signals by using the same frequency. Once the data was 'up' as he called it, he used ring files that bounced completely around the globe from satellite to satellite without coming down. He found that by doing this he could be 'in' the dealing system without being detected from the ground stations of the banks. He could 'borrow' money from any account he chose, use it for any amount of dealing within the magic eight seconds, pocket the profits and return the original money to its account before it was officially missing.

Finally he had started developing his own version of Mathematical Drifting Tables to store the files in while he called them down into the banking system. This had taken him the longest. The lie he had told Buddy at Arlington would have actually been the truth a year ago. But now it was all in place. The codes he found he could get from Buddy at the CIA Laundry bank had sealed his success. They cut down the time on normal telephone lines from five minutes to less than the magic thirty seconds needed to complete the sequence. Two seconds to get in. Ten to get the files up. Ten more to establish the ring files and build the Drifting Tables. That left just eight to complete the deals and drop the money back down to terrestrial bank accounts and come out of the system. Not long. But enough.

But the longer he spent at it the more dangerous he had seen it was. Straight theft really, no matter how he dressed it up. He couldn't see the banks thinking it was just the harmless game it had seemed that first evening in college with Bell. It had been a turning point for so much.

He never thought there could be anything even as remotely important. Then came Thousand. That had been more important hadn't it? But he had never told anyone. It had to remain locked up inside him.

He wished he hadn't started thinking about her. It always disturbed him and reminded him what a mess his life really was. How far he was from anything he really wanted. From home. And here he was supposed to be having a pleasant dinner with an old friend. Normal life. Boring. But no more turning points, thank you.

He dozed off and slept until Bell blustered into the room half an hour later.

'Wake up, Si. Have you been drinking already? And if not, why not? There's loads of sherry in the cupboard you know.'

Two large glasses later and they were walking over the lawn towards the Senior Common Room.

'I appreciate your invitation to dine, Bell, but it's not guest night or anything is it?'

'No, my boy, it is not. I am under instructions from the Master to bring you. Apparently he's been landed with some American computer woman and he wants someone to talk to her at table. And you, erudite Dr Northcott, are that man.'

'Well, I'm flattered. But perhaps you should have asked someone from the Maths Department, someone who actually knows what they are talking about rather than some hobbyist like me.'

'No, no. The Master was insistent. Don't ask me why. Anyway, the fewer people we have from the Maths Department in Lacrima the happier I will be. And by the way, the old man says this woman is quite a looker.'

'I should have thought he was a bit past that sort of thing. How is his heart by the way?'

'Too bloody good.'

The two of them smiled. It was an open secret that Bell Lessing was next in line for Master of Lacrima Christi.

Bell flicked out the wings of his gown. 'Talking of

Maths, how is that dealing program of yours coming along?'

'Not very well. I haven't had much time lately. One thing and another.'

'Pity. The college could do with a decent endowment just now. You would become a fellow you know. A hundred grand would see it.'

Simon slapped his friend on the shoulder. 'Bell, if I had a hundred grand, I don't think I would put it in your wine cellar. Fellowship or not.'

'I know. Just thought I would remind you what a corrupt lot we all are. But seriously, you should finish the program and see it through. No one else can write it you know.'

'Maybe I'll get more time this winter. How is your one going?'

' "Lessing's Stock Exchange Trader" I've decided to call it. Fine actually. I have a beta version testing with two of the telephone brokers.'

'Brilliant. I had no idea it was finished. How far ahead of the market can it keep?' teased Simon. He already knew the answer.

'Well. It doesn't actually run *ahead* at this stage. It sort of *tracks* the process and charts the trends.'

'So? When *will* it run ahead?'

'Frankly, old man, I may need a smidgen of help from you on that one. I am not really in your league when it comes to raw programming am I?'

Simon smiled at the grass. 'OK. I'll show you again. But it might cost you another dinner or two.'

'You're on. But what I really need is for you to

actually write chunks of it for me. I really am frightfully busy. Commission basis of course.'

'Bell, don't get me wrong, but what you are actually saying is that you haven't a clue and you want me to do it. Is that it?'

'No. No. It's just that I don't get much machine time these days and you never left me much in the way of notes to go on or anything. And you are so much faster than me.'

'Flattery. Flattery. I'll put something together and e-mail it to your disk stack on the mainframe.'

'Good. But be circumspect. It's still more than my life is worth for anyone to know you have access there.'

Bell pushed the tall door to the Senior Common Room open. 'Here we are then,' he whispered loudly. 'Chin out, stomach in, and let's see this woman the Master has for us.'

As they entered the Senior Common Room, they looked around for likely candidates. It wasn't very difficult.

She was standing in the middle of an admiring crowd next to the Master. Her long blonde hair fell down over the bare shoulders of a low cut scarlet dress that would do the Master's heart no good at all. She was laughing and talking animatedly to him. One hand on his arm and the other waving a cigarette around. The Master looked confused on both counts.

'Ah, Master, good evening,' said Bell, striding across the room with his black gown flowing behind him. 'This must be Dr Booker.'

Without waiting for an answer he turned to the woman and extended his hand. 'Welcome to Lacrima Christi, my dear. How do you do. I'm Bell Lessing and the Master has told me all about you.'

She gave Bell a very full smile. 'Hello. Yes, I'm Maddie Booker. How did you know it was me?'

'My dear, the Master described you perfectly. But where are my manners? May I introduce another guest this evening, Dr Simon Northcott.'

Simon shook her hand. 'How do you do. I'm sorry, but you look horribly familiar to me. Haven't we met somewhere before?'

Bell stepped in immediately. 'Simon! What a ridiculous line!'

The woman threw back her hair and laughed. 'You are both right I think. I'm Buddy Marlin's sister. Hello Simon.' She squeezed his hand and gave him a very direct smile.

'Good Lord, so you are,' said Simon. 'I must have seen your photo a hundred times at Buddy's house. I'm sorry I didn't recognise you. We were all going to meet up at the Ohio Conference last year but I think you were called away or something.'

'I know. I was really cross. Sometimes I think I spend half my life being called away from things I want to do.' She beamed.

'Let's hope it won't happen here. You must be here for the Data Protocol conference this week.'

'Only as proxy. My professor has gone ill and so I have to deputise for him at some of the meetings. I have to take notes for him of some of the papers. But

I expect they will go straight over the top of my head.'

Bell was not to be put off. 'Don't confine yourself to the conference. You must let me show you around the colleges as well. Quite fascinating.'

'That's very kind. But I don't know that I shall have much time.'

'We'll see,' said Simon. Then he leaned forward. 'You must have made quite an impression on the Master. He doesn't normally let people smoke in here.'

'Oh no! I never thought. I should have realised there were no ashtrays. What shall I do with it?'

'No problem. Give it to me,' said Simon.

He walked with the cigarette in his hand over to the side door leading to the kitchens. And while I'm at it I'll get the manciple to change the seating at table, he thought.

However he was pleasantly surprised to see from the seating plan that he was already due to sit next to Maddie Booker and only two down from the Master at that. By normal protocol he would be much further down the table. As far as the end if it had been left to the Master, he thought, as the old boy never tired of pointing out to Bell that Simon was 'not college' at all. Perhaps this woman was more senior than Simon and Bell thought.

Bell was deep in conversation with her when Simon returned.

'Oh, yes,' he was saying. 'So much of it is done by computers these days. We're not quite as old-fashioned as everyone thinks.'

She turned to Simon and gave him another smile. 'Professor Lessing here was telling me about his work. I knew he was an economist from his books but he tells me he teaches programming as well.'

That's news to me, thought Simon. 'He has many talents.' Give the man enough rope.

'Buddy says you are a bit of a computer whizz as well. Is that right?' she questioned.

'Not really. Interested in a lay sort of way but not a whizz by any means. Actually I think you are the real whizz around here if I remember Buddy correctly. Don't you teach Large Number Theory at Ohio?'

'Large Number Theory,' Bell sprung in. 'I've always been fascinated by that.'

Maddie put her hand on Bell's arm. 'Work, work, work. Tell me about yourself instead, Professor.'

'Oh, I'm far too dull. And call me Bell, everyone does.'

It's doctor not professor anyway, thought Simon. But you had to admire the old fool's pace if nothing else.

Just then a large gong sounded and the fellows and their assorted guests began filing into the huge, vaulted dining hall.

Simon hardly had a chance to talk to her during the first part of the meal. Bell monopolised her and left Simon talking to a rather dull historian opposite who specialised in seventeenth-century Fen village life. Simon could just about manage a series of 'oh really's' and 'who would have thought that's'.

But towards the end of the meal, Bell's drinking

was slowing him up. During a lull, Maddie turned to Simon. 'Actually, now I'm in Cambridge, and have found you, there is something I want to ask you about Buddy.'

'His illness you mean?'

'Yes. You don't mind do you? You see, Buddy doesn't know it all yet. I think it is down to me to sort of rally his friends round or something. He's going to need a lot of support and I guess you know him as well as anyone.'

'Yes, I suppose so. But I don't think it's anything dramatic. Not yet at least.'

'Let's hope not. But I've got to start somewhere. Would tomorrow be all right?'

'Yes, of course. I'll give you a call. Are you staying here in college?'

'No. A hotel. I'm afraid I've forgotten its name. It's by the river.'

'The Wallingford. You must be pretty important.'

'Oh, no. Don't forget I'm standing in for my professor.'

'Of course. But I don't need to ring you. Why don't I come and pick you up about one. That way you get lunch as well.'

'Yes, I'll be free. Are you sure you don't mind?'

Bell leant heavily across. 'Is my friend Simon leading you astray young lady?' he breathed.

'Not yet, Professor. No such luck.'

'Bell, my dear, call me Bell.'

'All right, I'll call you Bell if you will call me Maddie instead of young lady.'

She smiled at Simon and gave a tiny shrug.

By the time the port was coming round Bell had finally decided his bread would be better buttered by the Master than Maddie and so he turned to his right, leaving Maddie free to concentrate on Simon.

'What do you think of our famous economist?' he asked.

'Bell? Well, he's not quite the dry academic you'd think from his books or articles. He looks as though he has spent a fair time pursuing the pleasures of the flesh as well.'

Simon laughed. 'Yes. But I'm afraid one or two of them are a bit of a memory for him now.'

She gave another of her little shrugs. 'But he's obviously clever. He was telling me all about some Stock Exchange program he has written. Apparently he can go in and out of the dealing system in less than a minute to strike a deal. Is that really possible?'

'I shouldn't have thought so,' he said cautiously. 'But, even if he could, he wouldn't come out ahead any more than anyone else who knew the market. Prices have to be going your way no matter how fast you trade.'

'Well, he says he can do that too. He can see at certain times what is going to happen. Does that sound right or have I got it all wrong? I'm afraid I wasn't concentrating all that hard.'

'He could be right for all I know. He's a man of many talents.'

'Yes, he told me that too.' The big smile again. 'But does he do all his own programming? He doesn't really look the type.'

'Oh, yes. I'm sure that bit is true. It's when he tells you that his wife, Lizzie, doesn't understand him that you have to be a bit careful.'

Another smile. 'I thought you were supposed to be his friend.'

'I am. But I also double up as his cardiologist. I mean you do look a bit young for him.'

'Thanks for the compliment. But actually I'm the same age as both of you.'

'Eh? How do you know that?'

'Well,' she said brightly, 'he told me you were both the same age at some point during dinner and I already know from Buddy how old you are. Voila. Two and two.'

'Why should Buddy tell you how old I am?'

'I don't remember how it came up. We must have been talking about family birthdays or something. Anyway, don't let's talk about our age. It's so depressing.'

'Quite right,' Simon said. Going reasonably he thought.

Any further conversation was halted by a loud scrape on the stone floor as the Master's chair went back and he stood up to say grace. He had obviously finished his meal. The fact that other people were eating was really neither here nor there.

Simon was outmanoeuvred at coffee by Bell and several others so he spent another half hour with the Fen historian before he made his excuses and left. As he went he gave Maddie a little nod and received an encouraging smile in return.

He walked the two miles home and, as he turned up the lane to his cottage, he could hear his telephone ringing. He thought whoever it was would have given up by the time he had walked the rest of the way, unlocked the door and gone in. But it was still ringing.

'Hello. Simon here.'

'Oh, I thought I would have got your answering machine.' It was Thousand. 'Sorry to ring you. But I'm checking the phone list and I thought you might have moved. I'm doing everyone. You should leave it switched on. Anyone might need to be in touch.'

'Thousand. It's half past bloody midnight. What on earth are you on about?'

'Oh, God. So it is for you. I didn't think about the time. I'm really sorry. But don't hang up. I actually have a message for you. Well, for Maddie Booker really. I think you were going to meet her tonight?'

'Maddie? How did you know she was in Cambridge?'

'I didn't. Buddy called me. Apparently he tried to ring her where he thought she was staying. Couldn't get through or something.'

'Odd. She's staying at a hotel.'

'I think he thought she would be staying in some college or other. Anyway could you ask her to ring him tomorrow your time?'

'All right. But have you got his Chicago number?'

'No. He didn't give it to me. Perhaps she knows it.'

'Sounds a bit odd to me.'

'Don't blame me. I'm just passing it on. What do you think of her by the way?'

'Maddie? Yes. Fine. Do you know her?'

'Sort of. Apparently she's got a bit of a reputation. One of the girls was telling me.'

'What?'

'Oh, I don't really know. Canteen gossip. Just you be careful, Simon.'

'Well, thank you, Thousand. But I think I can look after myself.'

'I doubt it. But there is one other thing.'

'Oh, yes?'

'That data Ginny e-mailed for me. I didn't find what I was looking for. Do you want me to wipe the file?'

'I told Ginny you wouldn't be able to make head nor tail of it. You'll have to wait until I can sort it out for you.'

'That's OK. No rush,' she said.

'But she said you couldn't wait. That's why she sent you the whole key-stroke back-up.'

'Oh yes. Well. I did want it but that particular panic is over. There wasn't anything in the file I wanted in the end. It can wait until next week now. Bring a copy. I can wipe this one.'

'Thank you. I don't like to have copies of things on other people's machines,' he said. 'You never know who is going to look do you?'

'Quite. Well I think that's it. And don't go mad. Remember what I told you.'

'Told me? You haven't told me anything.'

'About Maddie.'

'Oh, for Christ's sake. I've only just met the bloody woman and you're warning me off already. Look, she's a perfectly ordinary woman. Buddy's sister. That's all.'

'Just you be careful, that's all.'

'Yes, mother. Thank you mother. Mind your own bloody business, mother.'

'This is ridiculous.'

'Yes it is. It's late and I'm pissed. I'm going to bed. Good night Thousand. Sweet dreams.'

Simon replaced the receiver. Odd. Thousand had never telephoned him at home before. He didn't know she even had his number. He took out one of his business cards from his wallet to double check. No. Just his work number. Funny girl, Thousand. Well, woman really. Funny woman. Anyway she must be pretty bored if all she could think of to do was check the Department phone lists. Couldn't be very interesting.

He decided that he really was too tired to think about it and so he went up to bed. But as he was almost asleep another odd thing occurred to him. How come Maddie knew about Bell's work before meeting him? Why should she bother to have read his books if she was a mathematician? Curious. Perhaps there was something he didn't know.

Chapter Five

Maddie lay back on her bed and lit a cigarette and looked at her watch. One a.m. London time. She reached for the phone and dialled Washington. Six rings.

'Department of Building and Works. Linda Hart speaking. How may I help you?'

Five words. Three words. Five words.

'Oh, I'm sorry,' said Maddie. 'I must have the wrong number.'

'No problem. You have a nice day now,' replied the voice but left the connection open.

Two. Six.

Maddie keyed the numbers onto the telephone. The line went dead for ten seconds. Then a hiss as the scrambler cut in.

'General Warkowski, please. This is Major Booker.'

'One moment please.' Another ten seconds. The hiss changed in pitch.

'Warkowski.'

'General. I think we are clear. This Northcott is a complete naive. He can't possibly be our man.

He is a complete innocent.'

'One of the innocents, eh? Well we all know what happened to them. How much does he know about hacking? Remember he can work his Amex Account. Have you asked him about that yet?'

'Not yet sir.'

'Then why are you ringing me with half a report?'

'I thought you would like to hear sir. A progress report.'

'Look, don't ring me up with half a report. I'm busy. Find out how he did it. Get the name of the person who taught him. I want a full breakdown. Give it another two days and then call me again. I may need to keep him on the field even if he is our man.'

'May I ask why, sir?'

'I've got Major Nocta checking him out from this end but Cohen says she hasn't come up with anything at all yet. Now we know all about this card thing, and if he can hide it from Nocta and Cohen he must be pretty damn good. I want all of him.'

'There may be nothing to find, sir.'

'I don't make mistakes. I don't *do* mistakes. Now get to it.'

'Yes sir.' But the line had already gone dead.

Maddie was not waiting for Simon in the foyer of the hotel when he arrived to collect her promptly at one the next day. He sat and waited for ten minutes and then went to the desk to ask for her.

'Are you Dr Northcott?' the concierge asked.

'Yes. I was due to meet her here at one.'

'I'm sorry sir. I didn't realise it was you. She asked me to tell you to go up. Room 412, the river side.'

Maddie had thought she would start the day from her room so that he would feel more comfortable if they came back later. It was only a small thing but she prided herself on her professionalism. When he knocked she was sitting on the bed pretending to read a magazine.

'Thanks for coming up, Simon. I was expecting a call so didn't come down but I guess it doesn't matter. They can always take a message for me at the desk.'

'From Buddy?'

'Buddy?' she said, puzzled.

'Apparently he has been trying to reach you. I had a message from my office to tell you to ring him.'

'Oh. OK. Thanks. But no. This was just those people in London I've got to see before some meeting in DC next week. Not frightfully interesting. Let's go. I'll ring Buddy when I get back. It's way too early for him just now.'

'I suppose so. He's in Chicago. Do you know where he stays there?'

'Yes. Hilton.' She picked up her coat from the end of the bed. 'So, where are we going?'

'Well, you won't need that for a start. It will be really warm today. We're having an Indian Summer.'

'Indian what?'

'English for a hot September. Don't ask me why. All you need know is that it will be a beautiful day. Cambridge at its best for a new visitor.'

'If you say so. But don't tramp me round looking at

the sites for hours. Just give me the Senior Citizens' tour. The one with sitting down.'

'OK. In that case for madam we will skip the colleges and go straight to a rather good wine bar I know.'

'You are a tour guide after my own heart.' She smiled.

Well, he thought. I might just be that. 'Shades it is then.'

'Shades?'

'I don't expect it's called that any more. These places are always changing names. It's right in the middle of town so I suppose it counts as being on the tour.'

They found a quiet corner in the wine bar. It had indeed changed its name but the brick vaults of the converted wine cellar were unchanged and the wine was still reasonably priced.

Simon set a bottle of Chardonnay down between them in a bucket of ice.

'What did you want to ask about Buddy?' Simon asked. 'Are you worried about what is going to happen?'

'I guess so. When you hear that someone close to you is probably terminally ill you see a grisly sequence beginning to unfold. You wonder what you can do to help. I know that the two of you have been friends for a long time so I'm sort of sounding you out.'

Simon poured them both a glass of wine and pushed one across the wooden table towards Maddie.

The sun was coming through the skylight above them onto the table and made a pattern of gold bars on the old oak.

'You mean if he has to go into hospital for treatment or something?' he said.

'Yes.'

'Wow. I never really thought of it like that. You don't. I suppose I've never worked with anyone this has happened to before.'

'Perhaps I shouldn't have asked you. I don't really know how well you know him outside work at all. I've made all sorts of assumptions.'

'Pretty well. We travelled together a lot. And whenever I was in Washington we spent a lot of time together. Families knew each other. That sort of thing. But it was really work we had in common. We needed each other. I had to sell him my project ideas, equipment and so on, and he had to find recipients for US Aid. He could have used one of a dozen manufacturers but he chose us because he thought I knew so many people.'

'And did you?'

'A few. I've been selling one thing or another to those places for quite a few years. But if you tell people you can get them United States Aid, they always see you. I think I looked better than I was. I expect you think that is dishonest.'

'No. No. I don't. But why didn't he go to them directly?'

'He could have done that in an ideal world but in reality he needed a sort of intermediary. An agent both sides he could strike deals with and someone who could legitimately hand over a commission. When governments do business there always has to be someone in between to pass money over.'

'I don't understand.'

'Oil the wheels if you like.'

'Bribes. You mean bribes don't you?'

'Not really. It's not like that. It's the way business is done. A few per cent here. A few per cent there. Introduction fees. Setting-up costs. It's not so different from your famous American free lunch.'

' "There is no such thing as free lunch." '

'Exactly. But anyway, you must know all this. You know what Buddy does and you don't look the naive type to me. Besides, he isn't involved personally.'

'And you are I suppose?'

'As much as anyone. But I don't think of it as dishonest. It's just a cultural thing. They have different words for it in different places. Pishkesh in Iran. Dash in Nigeria. Bucksheesh. That sort of thing.'

'It's still bribes though isn't it?'

'No. And anyway, why all this third degree?' he asked.

He lifted his glass up and looked critically at the colour.

'Sorry,' she said, 'I didn't mean to grill you. It's just that I'm interested in what you do.'

'It doesn't matter. Most people aren't, I think. So I don't think about it much. I think of it as work and kind of switch off when I come home to Cambridge.' He sniffed the wine and took a sip.

'And what *is* at home?' she asked playfully. 'Some fearfully clever and beautiful academic or other?'

'No such luck. I think I am still sort of coming to land after my divorce really. I haven't thought about things much. I must seem rather dull to you. Work I don't care for a great deal and home I haven't thought about.'

'Not at all. You sell yourself short. I certainly haven't come out to lunch because I think you are dull. You were really interesting last night talking about Bell and that dealing thing. You're really into that sort of thing aren't you?'

'But it's all a bit abstract don't you think?' he said and pointed to her glass. 'Come on, drink up.'

'It seems to be about money,' she replied. 'I don't think that's very abstract.'

'No. It's not really about money. It's about whether it can be done or not.'

'What? Work the system?' she said taking a small sip.

'Yes. That's a good way of putting it. Beating the system. You see, with ordinary gambling, there really isn't a way of winning. Take casino roulette, it's weighted in favour of the house because of the two greens between the red and black. The mathematics are always weighted against you. You can't win in the long run. Or horses. You can't ever know as much as the insiders. That's why they put horses up for betting in the first place for God's sake. But the financial markets are different. No one group is in control and the maths don't look too bad. If you could find out something about how markets moved the insiders didn't know, you could make a killing.'

'And is that what Bell Lessing does?' she said as she put her glass down.

'He would like to. But it's a bit of a Holy Grail. It keeps everyone busy looking but there isn't anything to find in the end.'

'But Bell said during dinner that you'd cracked it. Found a discontinuation or something.'

'Discontinuity. That's what I found. But what he didn't tell you is that the next bit threw us. Writing the machine code to take advantage of it was something else. We never came close.'

'Machine code? Not an ordinary program?'

'No such luck.'

'Why not?'

'Tecky reasons. All about how the big computers work. Proper machine code is much faster. But anyway, once I saw clear that it could be done in theory, I cooled off. Besides, making serious money at it would mean taking it away from someone else. Stealing.'

'At market dealing? I should have thought it was every man for himself. And I wouldn't have thought you would have any scruples in that department. Not after what you do anyway.'

'Maybe,' he said, pouring himself another glass. 'But what if they came and asked for their ball back? They might not be very nice people, you know.'

'I see what you mean. So what happened to it?'

'Well, Bell went on with his bit and I more or less dropped out.'

'So it's down to him now is it, the writing bit?'

'Meant to be. He boasts about it but I don't know how much he has actually done. He boasts about so many things you can't tell what's real and what isn't.'

'Wait a minute,' she said holding her hand up. 'I think I've missed something. If this dealing thing isn't properly finished, then how come he is ready to sell it to brokers?'

'Ah,' smiled Simon knowingly. 'For one thing he's only got a beta version, and for another he wants a Stock Exchange version. No one will mind that.'

'And yours?'

'I was looking at the foreign exchange markets. Forex. Where the really big money is and where the real trouble would have been. You see, Stock Exchanges are open access but the Forex is pretty much a closed shop and the rules are complicated.'

'And so you never did anything more about your one?'

'No. I just didn't know enough about Forex. It looked like a dream. But I woke up eventually.'

'Sounds quite a dream to me. The money and all that.'

'Like I said. I woke up. Real world.'

She left it there for a while and moved onto other things. She finished her glass and encouraged him to do the same with his second one.

But he went on anyway. 'Besides,' he said reflectively, 'I think at some point Bell's and my dreams got a bit out of step. He found he was getting what he wanted out of life and so we weren't after the same things any more.'

'Is that your defensive way of saying he has more money these days than you? I can't believe he has a fraction of the money your little game would net.'

Simon swilled the wine around in his glass before replying. 'It is a bit like that. But not in the way you think. You see, ten years ago we both had everything still in front of us. Things we wanted. Not just for ourselves but for our families as well. They were realistic goals rather than dreams. The polite word would be ambition I expect. And I think he more or less got what he wanted and I didn't. In the old days all that seemed to be between us and what we wanted was money. But as time went by we saw it wasn't that at all. So we lost what we had in common and now keep up with each other out of politeness as much as anything. That and to talk about the times when we did have things in common. Old men's talk.'

She smiled at him encouragingly. 'That sounds a bit introspective and not very convincing. I'm sure old Bell doesn't see it like that. And anyway, the main reason you just told me that you didn't go ahead with the thing was because you couldn't do it.'

'Perhaps.'

'And when you found you couldn't do it you gave up and Bell had to give it up too because you were the brains behind the whole thing: is that right?'

'I didn't say I was the brains.'

'You didn't have to. It's pretty obvious that you are more intelligent than Bell. So I'm putting two and two together and coming up with him doing the pushing and you doing the head work.'

Simon smiled down at his glass. 'Me the clever one? I don't think so. He's the Cambridge don and I'm the travelling salesman. Unfortunately it is the world making judgments about intelligence and not you.'

She reached out and put her hand on his. 'Look, Simon, I told you. Don't sell yourself short. People's lives rise and fall. So he is up now and you are down. Everything could change.' As she spoke she leaned slightly towards him.

He looked at her, smiled again. 'Who is being the dreamer now?'

'I've got it from you,' she said almost in a whisper. 'You are a "Weaver of Dreams and Teller of Stories." '

'That's a funny expression.'

'Well, it's true. I think you can get people to believe in things.'

'Like Bell you mean?'

'Yes. He seriously believes in the dealing thing or whatever you call it.'

He sat back. 'Scam. It's just called a scam.'

'But not just Bell. Look at Buddy. He was really fed up with this Aid thing before you came along. And then with you he sort of kicked into gear again. Started going to places again and getting on with things. He used to talk about you so much in the early days. Still does as a matter of fact.'

'Well, Maddie, it's nice to hear you say that. But my little dream didn't really get Buddy very far at the end of the day did it? I bet he drinks as much now as he ever did before I met him.'

'Possibly. But without you I think he would have given up ages ago. And that is why you are going to be so important to him now.'

'The illness you mean?'

'Yes.'

'Look,' shrugged Simon. 'If there were any way on earth I could actually *do* something, I would. You know that. But I honestly don't see how I can do anything at all on a strictly practical level. And you know that as well.'

'Well, what about your money thing? And I won't call it a scam because that's a horrid word. Anyway, the Forex thing. Couldn't you do it with Buddy? That'd be something for him wouldn't it?'

'Look, I don't know why you keep on about it,' he said leaning right back. 'It's almost as if you are questioning me. I'll say it again. It was a nice idea, a weaver's dream if you like. But it's not on for all sorts of reasons. And if Bell and I can't do the maths, then Buddy certainly can't. End of story. Time for another glass.'

But she was not to be deterred and moved her other hand over and put it on Simon's wrist.

'I'm sorry. I didn't mean to upset you.'

'I didn't say I was upset.'

She very gently squeezed his hand. 'You didn't have to. You've gone all sort of defensive.'

'Look, what is all this?' he said, taking his hand away. 'One minute we are having a nice quiet lunch and the next you're telling me about my feelings. Back off will you, Maddie.'

I haven't time to do that she thought. But she withdrew her hands to her side of the table and put them around her glass. 'Sorry,' she said. 'I'm always getting ahead of myself. It's the Buddy thing. Sort of unbalanced me I expect.'

'Probably just that. No need to apologise.' He continued to stare down at the table, not sure what to do next.

He poured them each another glass. She decided to press on.

'Is United Machines a big company?'

'Huge. We used to be even bigger but have been rather overtaken recently. Still quite well known though. The stuff's pretty good. Irrigation pumps for the Third World, all that sort of thing. Rugged and reliable and very British. But they are also rather simple which has been our downfall in a way.'

'How's that?'

'Well, an irrigation pump doesn't have to be very sophisticated. You just have to be able to turn it on and it pumps up water ten or fifteen feet. The simpler the better really because then it can be mended locally. But nowadays there are all sorts of refinements. Electronic controls, remote sensing, radio operation and so on. Third World governments all want to be modern and so they are easily dazzled by flashy things. And that of course means Japanese or Korean. We still only make the old "one man and his dog" pumps, and that's why we've had to go into project management.'

'But can't the aid givers like Buddy tell them what to buy? It's donated money after all?'

'To some extent. And that's how we scrape by. That and Buddy being able to set up service depot agreements with some US staff actually based in the local country. That is expensive and that's why Buddy stays on top. He's got quite a lot of clout in Washington. He works under Jake but Jake doesn't seem to do very much.'

'Jake?'

'Jake Cohen. He's semi-retired. Just seems to sign things.'

Maddie tried not to smile. She could imagine Jake Cohen's face at being described as 'semi-retired'.

'Sounds a good job to have,' she said encouragingly. 'How long has he been doing it?'

'Since the section was set up by Carter back in the seventies. I think he has always been a State Department administrator. He leaves all the field operations to me and Buddy. I like him but he's not terribly effective if you know what I mean.'

'I think so. And isn't there some terribly clever woman there as well?'

'Thousand. That would be her. Did Buddy say she was clever?'

'Yes. He said she was called Thousand because when she was at university she was so clever everyone thought she had an IQ of a thousand.'

Simon laughed. 'Not quite. Her real name is Kay. So Thousand is a sort of pun because of "K" being about a thousand in computer-speak.'

'Oh dear. How prosaic. So isn't she clever after all?'

'Oh, yes. She has brains all right. Sometimes I

wonder what she is wasting her time for in Aid Procurement. She could get a better job. Much better.'

'What is she like?'

'Quite good looking really. Tall. Fair. Blue eyes.'

Maddie squeezed his arm. 'I didn't mean that, silly. I mean what is she like as a person?'

'Oh. I don't really know. We work together a lot but she never comes out with me and Buddy. I think she is rather quiet actually.'

'She sounds a bit dull to me.'

'I wouldn't say that. Just quiet.'

'Well, anyway. Is that it? Just the three of them? Not much of a department.'

'No. It's only small. It just handles the procurement and the setting up of the project. The main Overseas Aid thing is based somewhere else. Part of Agriculture I think. Jake's lot comes under the State Department for financial reasons.'

'Financial?'

'Yes. It's only small but it handles a lot of money so it's in the State Department so it can use the internal bank.'

'A bank? I didn't know there was one there.'

'Some of the money can be as much as tens of thousands in cash so the politicians want to keep it separate from the mainstream.'

'Cash? Large amounts? Sounds a bit dodgy to me.'

'That's why they want it separate. The cash sort of oils the wheels of procurement you might say.'

'Ah. That must be where the famous Mr Costa comes in.'

'Costa? Did Buddy tell you about Costa?'

Maddie backtracked. 'Once or twice in passing. But he sounds really dreadful. I think Buddy used the words "fucking parasite".'

Simon put his head back and laughed. 'Yes. That would about sum him up. If you wanted to be polite that is.' And then Maddie laughed too. Good. Opening made.

'What is this Mr Costa really like then,' she asked. 'Do you work with him too?'

'Oh, yes. All the time. Costa's not his full name. He is San Antonio Fabian Jesus da Costa. He says he is Colombian but I think he's half-Lebanese. Too clever to be anything else. Not a nice person at all.'

'What does he do that is so terrible?'

'He's a wheeler-dealer on a major scale. Arms, drugs, prostitution, that sort of thing.'

'What! Why do you have anything to do with him?'

'No choice really. And if it wasn't him then it would be someone else. He helps us get deals we couldn't hope for otherwise. He knows all about shipping things in and out of Third World ports. And that is important to us. Any pumps or something left at a dock would be stolen within a week. He can get things through customs and shifted up country within forty-eight hours or so. Spares. Whatever.'

'More bribes.'

'Yes. I suppose so. More bribes. But at least the pumps end up where Buddy and I want them to go. Without him we would be nowhere.'

'I can see why you need him, but what does he get

out of it? Silly question. Money I suppose.'

'Yes, mainly,' he said. 'There are people like Costa everywhere you look in Third World trade and you can't operate without them. It's an open secret and everyone goes along with it. But my lot, United Bloody Machines, being very British and all that, would rather swim on alone. I keep telling them they can forget about reliable shipments without an "agent" to help.'

'Couldn't you use someone else though? Someone a bit less awful?'

'Not really. American Aid is pretty big business. While any number of people will *tell* you they would make a good agent, we have to have someone as big as Costa. One of our shipments might be a million dollars or more and we have to have someone we know can actually deliver.'

'It's just the money then? A slice off the top every time you move goods.'

'Not just that. But he does make a lot. No. The real reason he likes us, needs us, is that we give him access to the bank thing I was telling you about.'

'How does that help him?'

'Well. When I tell you we call the bank "The Laundry" you will begin to see. We wash his money. Change it into dollars from whatever it happens to be in: cruzeiros, pesos, whatever. And no questions asked. Even the Swiss won't do that since Lockheed. And because it's a bank he can borrow too. He might want to borrow twenty thousand for a week or so to kick start some deal or something.'

'And then pay it back just like a proper bank. Interest and all?'

Simon laughed again. 'No way. One for one. Costa plays hardball.'

'I can definitely see why it has to be so separate now. I had no idea this sort of thing went on. But why on earth would the US government want to be involved at all? If it ever got out!'

'Well, if Costa didn't use Washington he would have to go to Tokyo or Seoul even. At least this way they can keep tabs on him.'

'It all sounds so awful.'

Simon shrugged and looked down at his glass. 'I suppose it is really. But I try not to think about it. I keep my bit clean. Keep the pumps selling. It's all I know. I have to do it.'

She finished her glass. 'Perhaps we should get out of here. What are you going to show me next in famous Cambridge after the famous wine bar?'

He relaxed and sat back. 'It depends how much time you have. The best things are the inside of the University Library and the Real Tennis Courts. Take your pick. Oh, yes. And Byron's Pool. All guaranteed top attractions and not a tourist at any of them.'

'Can we walk to them?'

'Yes. The library and tennis courts are about ten minutes away but we'll need to go by car to Byron's Pool as it's near Grantchester.'

'What is Byron's Pool?'

'It's just a widening in the river really. It's as far upstream from Cambridge as you can go in a punt.

It's where Cambridge begins if you like. We could go around a dozen colleges and you would never remember any of them. But a perfect pool on a perfect afternoon? That will stay with you. And there is no point being a tourist if you are going to forget everything is there? Besides, I know it is Buddy's favourite place in Cambridge. Perhaps if we go there we might think of something for him too.'

Maddie looked at him and smiled. You're not what I expected at all, she thought. I thought you were going to be like Buddy. A shadow man. Living in the past. Or at least some sort of computer freak. But you are neither. And I didn't expect to like you. But I do.

Be careful, Maddie, she told herself. Remember what you are here for. And that there is not long to get it.

She waited a moment longer and decided that was enough eye contact for now. 'You've gone quiet again. Are you thinking about Buddy?'

'No, actually. I was thinking it has been rather a long time since I did this. You know. Asking someone new out for lunch.'

She smiled at him. 'I think you are doing pretty well. For an old man anyway.'

She reached over and brushed an imaginary hair from his forehead. 'That's better. And anyway I'm not exactly "new". We've known about each other for quite a few years even if we haven't actually met.'

'I suppose so. Buddy's told me quite a lot about you over the years.'

She stiffened ever so slightly and then forced herself to relax.

'Really? What terrible things has he told you?' He hadn't noticed. Good.

'I'm trying to remember. Just about when you were children and I think you were married at some point?'

'I was. But that was more than ten years ago. He ran off with someone else. One of his students. It was practically an occupational hazard in those days if you were a university teacher like him. People used to sort of accept it. But that didn't make it easier for me. I was pretty cut up really. It must have taken me a good two years to come to terms with it and pull myself together again. I couldn't talk about it for ages.'

'I'm sorry. I don't mean to pry.'

'Oh it doesn't matter now. It's just like talking about someone else. Buddy thought I should have stuck it out till Henry came back. Buddy probably told you that.'

'No.'

'Well, anyway I couldn't have. There weren't any children and there didn't seem any point going on. And when he *did* eventually want to come back I just didn't like him enough any more. As a man. I probably shouldn't have married him in the first place. I was very young. I just drifted into it without thinking. And then when I did think about it, I found it was too late and I saw I didn't really care at all. That must make me sound a bit of a bitch really.'

'No. Not at all. You might have stayed if he hadn't had his little fling.'

'Yes. I think I would have. Out of inertia. Henry wasn't really a bad person. But once things were broken between us I knew it was over. He couldn't accept it. He still thinks I'll go back to him one day. I think what he did wasn't really so unforgivable. But it's just that I personally didn't want to forgive him.' She shrugged. 'And you and Ellie?'

'Ellie. Why do you call her that?'

'I thought that was her name. Your wife. Ex-wife.'

'Ellen. Not Ellie. Ellie was her pet name before we got married.' He smiled as he remembered. 'Then after the wedding she told me she didn't care for it at all. So it was Ellen ever after. Funny you should use that name. It really takes me back.'

'Ellen. Ellie. Whatever. But what did happen?' And why the hell weren't the files up to date?

'It was just a sort of "project abandoned",' he was saying. 'There wasn't one particular thing. Neither of us ran off with someone else or anything exciting like that. No. One day we just started dividing things up ready for me to move out.'

'What about the children?'

'Just one. Lewes. I suppose it must have affected him but maybe it was better than watching Ellen and me endlessly bitching at each other. I don't know at all. Actually it is that part that goes on being wrong. Even now.'

'No closure you mean?'

'Closure? That's an American expression. I'm not sure I know what it means.'

'Finishing. Rounding off.'

'Well, it's wrong then. There is no tidy finishing off or rounding out a marriage. Even when it is supposed to be completely done. If you go on thinking about the children, and everyone does, then that part of the marriage stays too. You can't just say "Closure" and walk away.'

'I think you can. Or have to try. Maybe you should try.'

'No. You can't just open and shut relationships like boxes. You get enmeshed. Part of you stays tangled up. If I made "closure", as you put it, I'd be denying the good things that came from those years. And there were some. And must have been for her too.'

Wise up, Simon, she thought. Opening and shutting relationships? I do it for a living. Anyone can walk away from anything if they want to. But I don't want philosophy from him she told herself. I want answers.

She rested her head on her chin. 'But I bet Ellen would have liked the money thing. Didn't she keep on pushing you?'

'Not really. She never believed I could do it. As a matter of fact I don't remember her believing I could do anything at all. In a row once I told her I'd cracked it and she just threw up her hands and told me to get real.'

'But you hadn't really cracked it, had you? You must admit she was right.'

He sighed. 'That's true. I'd done all the difficult bits but hadn't started the long slog that came next. It was only the details that took time. Once I'd seen the discontinuity I knew it could be made to work one day.'

'You sound pretty certain.'

'I am. But you keep coming back to it. We are going round in circles. These glasses are empty. Let's go to Byron's.'

'Hey! Don't rush me. I can only drink slowly. So tell me more about Lewes. What made you choose such a funny-sounding name.'

'It's not funny-sounding,' he said. 'I used it because it's the name of a town on the South Coast where my mother's people came from. I'm afraid it was a compromise name really. I should have liked to give him some Hero name or other. Something like Marco or Yuri.'

' "Hero name"?'

'Yes. You see, when people are growing up they often have heroes they would have liked to have been named after rather than some relative or other. I mean, when I was ten I wanted to be called Yuri, after Gagarin of course. Great man, great name. But I was stuck with dull old Simon.'

The mention of the name Yuri startled Maddie. The picture of Mikael Lomakin being pushed to the ground, stamped on and then shot flashed in front of her. Oh Jesus, she thought. They're going to do that to this one too if I say so. But maybe this one is innocent; perhaps we can let him go. Or perhaps he's just being clever. Watch it, Maddie, she told herself, this is just business. Don't get involved.

But Simon appeared not to have noticed her momentary confusion. 'Or,' he went on, 'I would have called him Buzz.'

'Buzz? You mean Buzz Aldrin, the moon man?' She

pushed her head on one side, her politely amused and interested smile firmly back in place.

'Yes. But not because he went to the moon but because of what he said when he landed.'

'You mean, "One small step"? But I thought that was Armstrong. I don't remember Aldrin saying anything special.'

Simon shook his head knowingly. 'Well, it didn't get in the papers but actually his was the better thing to say.'

'So?' she smiled. 'What was it?'

'You have to go back a bit,' he began, 'to when Buzz was about ten. Apparently he was playing in the yard behind his parents' house one Sunday afternoon. He was being an aeroplane, running around with his arms out and that sort of thing. Anyway, next door upstairs, the neighbours, Mr and Mrs Blumenstein were having a little rest after lunch. So Mr Blumenstein thinks its time to spice things up a bit so he tries to get his wife to join in a little, how shall I put it, oral sex actually.'

'What!' shrieked Maddie, beginning to laugh.

'Shhh! Yes. Well, she says to him, "Look, there is as much chance of you getting that as there is of that Aldrin boy next door walking on the moon." But what she didn't know was that Buzz was refuelling on the aircraft carrier right under their open window and he heard the whole thing. And what with said Buzz being of an impressionable age, it stayed with him.'

By now Maddie was rocking back and forth with laughter.

'So anyway,' went on Simon, beginning to laugh too, 'when he eventually got to the moon and stepped off the ladder he shouted out into his helmet "OK! Go for it, Mr Blumenstein!" '

When they eventually stopped laughing, Simon said, 'So? What do you think, good name or what?'

'I think it's another story and you made the whole thing up,' she replied and began laughing again. 'But what the hell did Ellen think when you suggested it?'

'What? Oral sex or the name?'

'The name you fool!'

'Oh, I'm afraid I never got round to asking her about it. It would never have got past the censors!'

'I should hope not!'

'Anyway,' he said, 'enough of all this Deep Space talk. I think it's time we went to Byron's Pool.'

'Yes, sir. Ready, sir!'

'Good, I'll just have to drop into the office on the way to the car. I think I have to pick up my mail.'

Outside in the brightness of the afternoon they turned right up King's Parade towards his office. The pavement was almost completely blocked by bicycles so he held out his hand to take her across the road.

Instead, she stepped closer to him and linked her arm in his.

'I see you don't know your Bob Dylan then,' he said.

'What?'

'It's in one of his songs. "I offered her my hand, but she took me by the arm. I knew that very instant, she meant to do me harm." '

179

She squeezed his arm gently. 'Yes, I do know that one. But no. I'm not going to do you any harm. You are quite safe here. And I don't think you really mind anyway.'

He smiled down at her. 'No. I quite like it actually.' He squeezed her arm in return.

They reached the entrance to his office. It was a small black door next to an off-licence. 'Look, you wait here,' he said. 'I'll only be a moment.'

Ginny was waiting for him as he came in. 'I thought you were dead,' she started. 'I was trying to reach you at home. But I guessed there must have been a miracle cure or something. I should have known.' She tipped her head to the window. 'Is that your Mother Teresa?'

'Thank you, Gin. And good afternoon to you too. Is there anything urgent for me?'

'Yes. Thousand. She needs you to ring her immediately.'

'What was the message?'

'No message. Just to ring her as soon as you could.'

'I'll do it later. Anything else?'

'Plenty. But with you being so ill, you won't be able to cope. But you have to be in tomorrow.'

'Definitely.'

'Good, because I've got you down for KK at ten. Wear a suit.'

'Thanks. Oh, wait on. Did Thousand say where she was?'

'No. In her eyrie presumably. But she did say she would be at the windows place later on. Whatever that means. But you were to ring her tonight regardless.'

'Windows? Oh yes. I know what she means. I can't stop now because I'm on the single yellow. But if Thousand rings again, say I promise to ring her later.'

Ginny smiled and leaned her chair back so she could see down to the street below. 'Single yellow? I should have thought that particular shade of yellow took at least two bottles.'

'No. It's natural. I swear to you.'

'Simon! I can practically see her roots from here. You be careful now. She looks like bad news.'

'What with me being so ill and everything?'

'No. With you being such a fool and everything.'

'Thanks. See you in the morning.'

Ginny looked after him wistfully as he went down the stairs. He really is a fool about women, she thought. Why doesn't he see what he really needs is right here in the office? He'd be much better off with someone quiet and reliable like me instead of that Yellow Peril outside.

She looked back to her desk and caught sight of herself in the small mirror next to her monitor. A little plain perhaps. A bit thin. But sensible and practical, which is what Simon needs to balance his altogether too relaxed style and tendency for too long lunches for example.

Lunches? She smiled to herself as she remembered how she and Simon had spent many a lunch together feeding the ducks down by the river, talking easily and setting the world to rights. She had thought that particularly during his divorce he had found her comforting and sensible.

Whenever he went abroad he always brought her back a small duck ornament or carving. Perhaps an elaborately painted one from the Far East or once even a real Copenhagen porcelain duck from that conference in Denmark.

If he couldn't find a duck he came back with a painted egg of some description. The eggs she kept in a wooden bowl on her office desk but the ducks held pride of place on a shelf in her bedroom at home. They formed a little procession next to the window and under each one she had stuck a paper label saying where it had come from.

Ginny had hoped that one day Simon would ask to see them but he never had. In fact, he never mentioned their 'duck' thing at all except to say 'I saw this and had to buy it for you,' when he came back with an addition to her collection.

She stared thoughtfully at the bowl of wooden eggs for a moment. Then she turned briskly to the pile of invoices and correspondence in front of her. Lots to get done this afternoon.

Maddie was standing with her back to the sun when he came down. He thought her hair looked marvellous.

'We'll just nip in here and get a bottle and borrow a couple of glasses.'

'A picnic,' she beamed. 'I like a picnic.'

When they came out of the shop she took his arm again. 'If I had known you were going to be so much fun I would have made Buddy introduce you to me ages ago.'

'Ah. But I was married then wasn't I?'

'Well, I would have made her lend you to me for picnics. Free afternoons.'

'There is no such thing as a free afternoon.'

'You're too glib, Simon. You are.'

'Probably. But you will remember me saying it.'

Oh, I will, she thought. I will.

Ten minutes later they were getting out of the car in the grass car park by the bridge near Byron's Pool. They walked along the path that led between the woods and the river. The air was still and warm. The sun caught the surface of the water where it swirled quietly around tree roots at the water's edge. White seeds of Willowherb landed and drifted gently on the river's surface. They walked without talking.

Presently the path opened out by the pool itself. They found a flat piece of grass near the edge of the water and sat down. The weir was making a quiet splashing sound away to their left. Simon picked up a stick and tossed it into the water. They watched the ripples spread out and subside.

Eventually he spoke. 'It was on an afternoon just like this when Buddy came here first. That must be five years ago now. I remember he couldn't get over how incredibly peaceful it was. An absolute island. I suppose it was at the height of his divorce so anything would have looked peaceful compared to what she was putting him through.'

'But he was right,' she said. 'It is peaceful. Divorce or not.'

'Yes. He often wanted to come here when he came over to Cambridge. He said it was a place apart from things.'

'You are talking about him in the past tense.'

'Oh, Christ. Am I? I don't mean to.'

'Never mind. And anyway his life will be very different from now on. He'll see everything differently now.'

'How do you know?' he asked.

'Someone told me about it once. I don't remember who.'

'But it won't change what he thinks about this place will it?'

'Not really. He'll like it even more is my guess. He will sort of count the times out more.'

'I'll try to remember that. I hope he will come here again.'

'I'm sure he will. Try not to worry. It won't help either of you.'

As they spoke a dragonfly darted out from the reeds by the side of the pool. It flashed blue and green as it darted first one way and then another over the water in front of them.

'The dragonfly. The messenger,' said Simon.

'Messenger?'

'Yes. It's a dragonfly right? And that is a very ancient group of insects indeed. That one there is practically identical to ones in the fossil record millions of years ago. Most things have evolved out of all recognition, but not the dragonfly. It goes on unaltered.'

'But how does that make it a messenger?'

'Well, say you wanted to send a message through time. You'd give it to a dragonfly. They go backwards and forwards through time. It could take a message for you.'

'You are funny, you know. Not at all what I imagined. One minute you are telling me all about Washington and the next you are telling me fairy tales about dragonflies. I don't know which is you and what to take seriously.'

'Both.' He smiled. 'Washington and all that is as important in the real world as the dragonfly is in this world. Our River World. You can choose what you want to remember but my money is on the dragonfly.'

She leant forward to see the insect more clearly. 'I don't think I've seen one so close before. Are they common here?'

'Quite. But earlier in the year. That one has waited for you in case you have a message for him to take.'

She smiled and leant back against him. He put his arm around her and they watched the sun play on the dragonfly's colours. Suddenly it vanished as quickly as it had appeared. Simon reached out his hand and turned her face towards him. He kissed her gently on the lips. They lay back and she rested her head on his shoulder.

'I wasn't sure if you wanted me to do that,' he said.

In reply she sat up so the sun was behind her head and shone through her hair. She smiled at him and put one hand each side of his face and leaned forward to kiss him again. 'There,' she said. 'You know now.'

She ran her hand through her hair and looked down at him. 'Actually, I don't think I have let anyone kiss me for a very long time. You seem to be changing the rules for me. And it must be this place. It's just so magic. I don't even know if it is real. I'm not sure I know what to think.'

'Whatever it is,' he said, 'I think it is real enough for me.'

She lay down next to him again. She felt the quiet of the afternoon wash over her. She closed her eyes. I'll relax just for a minute, she thought. Just for a minute.

Shortly, two little girls aged about nine or ten came splashing along the bed of the river by the corner towards them. 'We're famous explorers!' one of them shouted. 'We're on an expedition!' They climbed out of the water on the grass in front of Simon and Maddie and ran off towards the top pool shrieking and laughing. They jumped back into the water and swam out across the deeper water towards the other side. They played again in the shallows by the bank, throwing handfuls of water up into the air. Sparkling arcs rose and splashed back onto the surface. Then they climbed out onto the bank, turning to wave at Simon and Maddie before running back down the river path in the direction they had appeared from.

'The Children of the River,' said Simon. 'They were not real at all either. You were very lucky to see them. Hardly anybody does.'

'I think they were real for today. For us. Like now.'

He kissed her gently again. 'Yes. For today. Our children for today.'

He sat up and tossed another stick into the water. 'We have to go soon. Get back.'

'I'm not sure that I want to. I don't know if I will like what I find as much as I like it here. Can't I stay?'

'Yes. You can. You will always be here. Like the children. Like the dragonfly. Some things don't have time attached to them at all. You can be here whenever you want.'

'And will you be here too?'

'Perhaps. I expect so.'

Slowly they got up and walked back through the woods to the car. It is a perfect afternoon, he thought. As perfect as an afternoon can be.

He dropped Maddie off at the hotel and walked slowly into town to collect his mail from the office. He looked at his watch. Six already. He smiled at himself. It was a long time since an afternoon had passed so quickly. She had seemed so, well, friendly really. He couldn't remember Buddy telling him much about Maddie and he reminded himself to ask him why not. She was obviously attractive but it was more than that. She had seemed genuinely interested in him and what he did. No, it was more than that as well. She seemed to want to know how he *felt* about things – Buddy, Ellen, Cambridge. She had even wanted to know about his dealing program but he concluded that really must have been just politeness. It was pretty boring to anyone who didn't know what it could actually *do* and she certainly didn't have any inkling about that side of it. She seemed to have such an amusing lightness about her. And she certainly smiled a lot. So, friendly, amusing, attractive. There didn't seem much more one could ask of a first afternoon together. And he would pick her up dead on time tomorrow, he told himself, then drive out somewhere for lunch. She will like somewhere very English probably. How about the Tickell Arms? Perhaps they would see dragonflies again.

He walked slowly in the last of the low afternoon sun and let himself in to the office with his pass key and was surprised to see Ginny still typing away at her desk.

'Really exciting minutes from the board this afternoon,' she explained. 'Story of my life. But tell me how you got on.'

'What do you mean?'

'You know exactly what I mean Simon. So? Well?'

'Yes. If you must know she seems very nice. Very nice.'

'Is that all?' quizzed Ginny. 'When are you going to see her again?'

'Tomorrow as a matter of fact.'

'Fast worker!'

'Fast worker! Me?'

'No, Mr Dumb. Her. I should say she's got you fair and square in her sights by now.'

'Oh, don't be ridiculous. She's just a friend.'

'Not what I hear.'

'And what's that supposed to mean, Ginny?'

'Well,' she began, 'Thousand rang again and she told me all about your little friend.'

'Thousand? What the hell has it got to do with her?'

'Nothing really. But we women do talk amongst ourselves you know. It is allowed.'

'Oh. Anyway, how did Thousand know Maddie was in Cambridge?'

'The Washington grapevine apparently. She was ringing because she said she was trying to reach Buddy and wondered if Maddie would know where he was on walkabout.'

'But Maddie hardly sees Buddy. Why should she know where he is?'

'Beats me. But Thousand wants you to call her again anyway about some more data or other.'

'OK. But I wish everyone around here would mind their own business once in a while.'

'Oh, come on Simon. Just a bit of goss. And what's more, your Thousand says Maddie is a bit of a man eater. As sticky as a Venus fly trap, she said, and she hoped you would know what that meant.'

'Oh, for Christ's sake!'

'Sorry. Just passing it on.'

'Well, don't. If there aren't any more messages, I'm going now. See you in the morning.'

'Ten sharp,' she said. Then she wagged a finger at him, 'And give your shoes a good clean. You seem to have got some mud on them walking around the colleges.'

He gave her a friendly laugh. 'Just finish your typing and go home.'

'Yes, sir. Three bags full sir.'

Half an hour later, Maddie was taking a whisky from

the mini bar in her room out onto the balcony to decide what to do. She thought again about the two Englishmen. It had to be one of them. Nothing she had learned in Washington or Cambridge pointed to a third person. Yet neither of them really fitted the usual pattern. Of the two, Lessing looked the safer bet. Or was the fact that she actually liked Simon Northcott clouding her judgment? Surely not. She certainly wasn't 'involved' in the Warkowski definition of the word. She never became 'involved'. Yes, she had needed to get 'close' enough to him to find out what she needed but that was what she was supposed to do. That was as far as it went. Ever went.

Lessing had told her enough over dinner the night before for her to believe he was technically capable enough. Simon didn't think so but Lessing was hardly likely to let on to Simon that he, Lessing, had capitalised on the original idea and taken it to a profitable conclusion, was he? And she knew from her own cover work as a programmer that the access codes were nothing like as hard to crack as Warkowski thought. Besides, surely someone couldn't become a senior economist at Cambridge without being pretty good with computers? Lessing it had to be then.

She smiled to herself as she sipped her drink. Poor Simon, she thought. I bet people have been taking your good ideas over all your life. You're that type.

She looked down over the garden to the river. A noisy group of young people were punting by. The girls wore long old-fashioned dresses and the men had on brightly striped blazers and straw hats. One man had a wind-up gramophone with a large horn on his knees. The scratchy sound of a waltz floated up to Maddie. Laughter. Two large white swans glided unconcernedly by in the opposite direction.

In the water meadow beyond the river cows were sitting in the shade of willow trees. Maddie smiled to herself. She could see what Simon meant when he said he didn't ever want to live anywhere else.

One other thing, she told herself: even if Buddy suspected Simon, he would never turn his old friend over to the wolves because he would know what would have to follow. Surely the Department didn't really mean more to someone like Buddy than a best friend of ten years' standing? Another reason for it being Bell Lessing.

She had desperately wanted to talk to Buddy about it but had been completely unable to contact him. She had tried his home, the office, the Conference Centre in Chicago and the hotel Nocta said he was staying at. Nothing. And what exactly had he meant by 'interfering' with Foreign Exchange Dollar files? For those were the exact words quoted by Warkowski at the briefing.

She flicked the end of her cigarette over the balcony into the garden below and walked back into her room to the telephone.

She lay back on the bed and went over in her mind the picture she would paint for Warkowski. She knew of old he would be more interested in answers than reasons and on this occasion there could only be one of two answers, Lessing or Northcott. She had decided on Lessing and would just have to say she had done more footwork than she had in the unlikely event of Warkowski wanting details.

She lit another cigarette after dialling the codes and waiting for the scrambler to kick in and for Warkowski to come to the phone.

She blew out a puff of smoke. 'It's Professor Lessing, General. I've spent the afternoon with him at his college and there is no doubt that he is our man. God, he is so vain. I just had to sit there and listen. He looks on it as some sort of game. Hacking in. Forex trading. Hacking out. Quite sophisticated but not as clever as he thinks. He even thinks that if he was caught he would only be prosecuted under British Data Protection Law.'

'More fool him. He'll know differently tomorrow.'

'I imagine so sir. Do you want me involved?'

'No. I'll do it from here and talk to Mildenhall in the UK myself. They will contact you if they need anything.'

'Yes, sir. What about his files? I can do that best from here. I have full access to the University Mainframe that he uses.'

'No. We can do that from here. I'll get Rolands to look after the back-up tapes later.'

'Very good, General.'

'And nice work, Major. But one more thing. Northcott? Does he know anything about this at all?'

'Negative sir. He has no idea what Lessing has been doing. His part was only unwittingly to put Lessing in touch with my brother. It appears they met socially.

And you have all those contacts documented, I think.'

'Yes, Major. I spoke to Colonel Marlin this morning. He is very pleased that it is you in Cambridge. OK. Now I want you to stay there for another twenty-four hours. Watch Northcott's reaction as we take out Lessing. If he knows anything at all he will show himself then.'

'Yes, General. I will, but I'm sure he knows nothing.'

'But what about that credit card business?'

'Turns out not to be so difficult after all General. One or two of the undergraduates at the Computing Department found out how to do it. Quite a number of people here know about it. I think Amex have probably already shut the loophole sir, but I can check for you if you like.'

'Do that thing. Report back. I'd want Rolands to do it but I guess he will be pretty busy sewing things up here for the next week or so. Do you know who to contact?'

'Yes, sir.'

'That seems to wrap it up then. I'll see you back here for the de-brief in three days.'

Click. End.

Maddie replaced the receiver slowly. She took a full drag on her cigarette and blew a long plume of smoke to the middle of the room. She watched the smoke curl up and drift towards the open window.

Wrapped up? Sort of. All that remained now was to frighten Simon so badly that he would never go near his silly dealing files again. Shouldn't be difficult. He looked as though he would frighten pretty easily. Might even be quite fun.

Gavin Robertson

She took a long shower and changed before going down to dinner. The restaurant doors were open to the river and every now and then a punt would glide past on its way back to Cambridge. She heard the sound of the scratchy waltz again and looked out to see the same group of young people she had seen earlier. They must have been on the river about an hour. Was that long enough to reach Byron's Pool? Probably not. It was too far away. Another world away, she reflected. Fool that he was.

Later, on her way back to her room, she passed by the front desk and was surprised to see a message in her key slot. 'A gentleman left it for you half an hour ago, madam. I did call your room but I didn't know you were in the restaurant. If I had known I would have asked him to go through.'

She took the yellow envelope up to her room. She walked over to the open balcony and opened the envelope in the last of the evening sun. Inside was a small box about two inches square. The lid folded back to reveal what looked like a silver brooch made of fine silver wire. Slightly puzzled, she turned back into the room and switched on the light to see it better. She saw immediately how beautifully it was made. But it was not the workmanship that made her gasp. It was the shape. It was a silver dragonfly. Perfect in every detail.

As Maddie was standing in the middle of her room in Cambridge, Thousand leaned back in her chair in the State Department and linked her hands together on top of her head.

194

Jake Cohen walked in. 'Have you found those phone calls yet? I want to see the transcripts before Bradley, damn him. The little shit didn't even tell me he wanted them at all when I saw him yesterday. First I hear of it and it's six inches from the fan.'

'Yes, Jake. I've found them. They were only routine. I'm having them typed up now by secretarial. They will be on your desk by six.'

'Routine? Then why the hell was Buddy using the safe line?'

'Well. Routine yes. But sensitive. He and Northcott are discussing payments for Costa. He was right to scramble them.'

'Has the phone log been tampered with in any way? Copies taken? I have to know those are the original calls. I wouldn't put anything past Bradley.'

'No, Jake. I checked as part of the de-encryption. These are definitely the right calls and no copies have been taken.'

'OK. Just bring them to me as soon as they come up.'

'Yes. And don't worry Jake. I do know what I am doing.'

'I hope so, Major, there is no telling what the Chief could do in his present mood.'

'No sir.'

When Jake had left the room she ran her fingers through her hair and sat forward again. It had been a terrible day.

As soon as she heard the first tape she had realised what was happening. Her first reaction had been to panic. Call Buddy. Call Simon. Anything. But the damage had already been done.

She had forced herself to calm down. Then she had sat for a full hour with her fingers pressed against her chin trying to work out what to do.

For the next four hours she had worked without even stopping for coffee. An hour to access the phone log codes. An hour to substitute calls of approximately the same length from her own back logs. Another to edit them by adding and taking out individual words until the fit was perfect. Then the last hour to change the original entries and the back-up log again and to come out of the system so that no one could see what she had done.

I've done as much as I bloody can, she thought angrily. And now I have to find a way to stop them. It's total madness. I have to reach them and tell them. Have to. Why the hell didn't they return her calls? Where the hell were they?

She tried Buddy's hotel in Chicago three more times but failed to get through.

An hour later the transcripts came back from typing. She read them through very carefully, signed them as correct and took them along the corridor to Jake Cohen's office.

'What took so long?' he asked.

'I don't know,' she said. 'I sent them down after lunch. It would have been quicker to type them myself.'

Jake flicked through the sheets, reading the odd sentence here and there.

'Nothing here is there?' he said, looking up at her. 'I can't see what all the fuss is about, can you?'

'No. Bradley going off at one of his tangents I expect. The Chief goes along too easily with him.'

'Maybe. But there must be more to it because Rolands is involved too.'

'Rolands?' she asked quickly. 'What does he want?'

'Search me,' said Jake signing his name next to Thousand's on the cover. 'Word is that there is some kind of data leak somewhere and these calls took place at the same time as the data accesses.'

'Well, if that's all, I could have saved them a whole day. Buddy wouldn't know how to use an access code by himself. I have to show him every time, you know that.'

'As maybe, Thousand, but what about Northcott?'

'Simon? Hardly. He hacks about a bit but strictly commercial. He could never get into our system. He'd have to time key-stroke the code and he doesn't know the sequences.'

'I know that. But Buddy could get them for him.'

'Oh, come on Jake. You and I both know he wouldn't do that even if he knew what to give Simon.'

'Whatever,' said Jake, passing the file back to her. 'Take this lot down and hand it to Disley for the Chief. I guess you can go then. Quite a day.'

She took the file to the lift and on the long ride down to Warkowski's level she wondered again why she couldn't reach Buddy. She had left messages all over the place and it was unlike him not to call her back. Normally if she wanted to contact him when he was out of Washington it was because he had forgotten something important and so he always returned her call promptly. But not today.

The lift door opened and she stepped forward to the marine and handed him the file.

'Thank you, Major Nocta. The Chief said he wanted to see you in person when you came down.'

'Me?' she said, surprised. 'Are you sure?'

'Yes, ma'am. Follow me please.'

She felt distinctly uncomfortable as she walked down the bare concrete passage. She had only met General Warkowski twice before. Once when she had been appointed and once at a Washington reception for visiting security heads. On neither occasion did he give any indication he knew anything more about her than her name.

Disley entered the day code on the key pad and opened the heavy door for her to go in.

Warkowski was reading some papers spread out in front of him as she walked over to the table. 'Sit down Major Nocta. Do you have the transcripts?' he said without looking up.

'I have them here sir,' she said as she took a seat opposite him.

He gathered up the papers in front of him and put them in a folder next to him before looking up and taking the fresh file from her. 'Are these accurate? You've heard the tapes.'

'Yes, sir. They are. Brigadier Cohen has heard them too and he has countersigned.'

'And?' he asked.

'Sir?'

'What do they tell you, Major?' he asked in a mock-patient voice.

'They are commercial calls, sir. Mainly confirming shipping arrangements and dates for Mr da Costa.'

'Is that so?' he said. 'In that case why would Colonel Marlin need to use the scrambler line?'

'That would be Dr Northcott's request, sir. His company, United Machines, is sensitive about working with Mr da Costa and he asked for the added security I understand.'

'Is that so, Major? Sensitive?' He looked down and began to read the file.

She watched him uneasily as he read the sheets in front of her. Once or twice he turned back a page or so as if to check something. Her unease grew. She knew Warkowski would read them but she had not expected this level of scrutiny.

When he had finished he looked up at her expressionless. 'Do you know what this security alert is about Major?'

'No sir.'

'Then you must be the only person in this building who doesn't.'

She did not answer him but met him eye to eye without blinking. Two can play, she thought.

'It's about access codes. Someone has been tampering with my mainframe sequences. I don't like that.'

'I am in charge of the distribution of codes in my section sir. They are very restricted.'

'Then you know who gets what.'

'I do, sir. I can get into all the PCs and the floor mainframe. But only Colonel Marlin and Brigadier Cohen can use the main machine down here. Major Bradley brings the sealed codes to me each morning and we take them together to the senior officers who break the seals in front of us. After that we place them in an outer envelope, sign that seal and Major Bradley brings them back down.'

'Every time, Nocta?'

'Every time, sir.'

'Doesn't that seem like a lot of trouble to you?'

'No sir. I know how important they are. The Brigadier is very strict on security. We all have to be.'

'Good answer, Major. I hope it's accurate too.'

'Accurate, sir?'

Warkowski did not answer her but leaned back in his chair and fixed her with a cold stare.

'OK,' he said at length. 'How is your checking of Colonel Marlin going?'

'It's finished, sir. I was typing it up when I was asked to decrypt these calls sir. You will have the full report by mid-morning tomorrow.'

'Anything in it about this disaster with the containers between Lagos and Manila?'

'Yes, sir. I do know about that. There is a lot of e-mail correspondence.'

'And?'

'I think the mistake was in Lagos customs. They always get something or other wrong but not usually as badly as this.'

'And the warehouse deal for Puerto Rico. Do you cover that in your report?'

She hoped her expression did not change. 'Yes, sir. I was involved in that. Colonel Marlin asked me to accompany him to Mr da Costa with the initial payment.'

'Initial payment. Is that what he called it?'

'Yes, sir.'

'And in the paperwork. Is that what it's called there too?'

'Yes, sir.'

'And is it?'

'No, sir.'

'So what is it then?'

'Start-up money, sir. Da Costa wanted it to set up a deal chain. The Colonel said it was a loan and that it would be back in seven days.'

'But in the paperwork it's an "initial payment". Is that right?'

'Yes, sir. All of it.'

'All of it. Good. I look forward to reading your report tomorrow. Ask Disley to come in as you go out.'

Audience over. She stood up and started towards the door.

'One more thing, Major,' he called to her back. 'Could Northcott have got to the codes?'

She had been half expecting that question but was still glad it had come when her back was to him. She cleared her face and turned around.

'Dr Northcott? No. He could not have had the codes.'

Gavin Robertson

'You came back pretty quick on that.'

'Yes, sir. The only person he could have them from is Colonel Marlin and he would not pass them on to anyone. I know both men well sir.'

'Oh, yes. I heard about that.'

'Sir?'

'Northcott. Didn't he try it on with you a while back?'

For someone whom she thought only knew her name he seemed to know rather a lot. 'Yes.' She managed a small smile. 'It was several years ago. I dealt with it very quickly sir. I think it was only half-hearted and he was a little drunk. But I thought I should report it.'

'I'm glad you did,' said Warkowski. 'Fixed him with one of your famous "Ice Smiles" did you?'

'Something like that, General.' Was there anything he *didn't* know?

'That is all. Go now.' He opened the transcript file and began reading again.

Washington games, she told herself in the lift back to her office. Just Washington games. And it wasn't only Buddy who had grown to hate them.

202

Chapter Six

Kenneth King, 'KK', sat at his tidy desk at United Machines looking down at the pile of green print-outs. He half turned over one or two pages and then let them fall back again. He laid his hands flat at either side of the pile and looked up at Simon.

They had started out as young men in the company together. While Simon had risen slowly and was now falling, KK had always done well. When the first area manager's job had come up, they had both known KK would get it. By the time Simon was promoted to area manager, KK was moving up to the board. While KK had married young and had had four children, Simon had married late and had had no children until much later. While Simon was going through his divorce, KK had been planning his eldest's wedding.

Simon often wondered if he could have played things differently or how he could have done better for himself. He knew that KK was not actually cleverer than him or understood the projects better. It was just that, slowly and consistently, over the years KK had sold more.

Sometimes Simon told himself that some people were just lucky and some were not. But later he came to feel that it wasn't that. Some people were just successful and some were not. That was all.

And now it was all coming to a head again. Simon sat in the armchair against the far wall while KK lifted his hands and steepled his fingers under his chin.

'You must be as disappointed with these as I am,' said KK. 'I know you have worked hard but frankly there isn't much to show for it, is there?'

'It's been difficult. Very difficult.'

'And for everyone else too. But they seem to have done better. Campbell in Eastern Europe. McNally in the Pacific. They have more than made quota, but this is the fourth quarter in a row that you've not. It really is very bad. I don't think it can continue. I can't let it.'

'What are you saying, Ken?' His mouth was completely dry.

'I think you know. This is a commercial organisation. I have a board and a holding company to report to.'

'Yes.'

'Simon, I think we have to look at a parting of the ways.'

Not dressing it up, was he? 'Do I understand you correctly?'

'I'm afraid so. We agreed last quarter that there would have to be an improvement and there hasn't been one. I've got to give the territory to someone else. I'm very sorry. You can work out your three months if you like. It's the best I can do under the circumstances.'

'Perhaps I could come home. Take a market here. On the road.'

'No Simon. You don't know anything about the British market. We both know that. Don't make it difficult.'

Why the hell not? thought Simon. 'But my market. No one knows Aid like me. All the people. The contacts. Washington. I know US Aid better than anyone else. Anyone.'

'No, Simon. I don't have to spell it out. If you knew the patch as well as you say then you would have sold more and you haven't. Okido and Paris-Nord have both done more. You have seen the figures. I cannot go on. I have my own position to think of you know.'

Simon stared at the floor. KK stared at his desk. Neither man spoke.

Eventually KK looked up. 'Here is a letter from personnel in London. It explains all about the leaving terms. Pension and so on. And look, go to Washington as planned next week. Talk to your man Cohen. See if there is anything there for you. Consultancy. Something like that. You are not fifty yet. Still time to try something else.'

Simon stood up without speaking and took the letter from KK. He walked out of KK's office back to his own. He passed Ginny, who was suddenly examining some details on her desk. She did not look up.

He went into his office and shut the door.

It wasn't a surprise. He had known for some time

that it was going to happen. He had seen as clearly as anyone else his figures fall away. For some time he had been able to put it down to 'difficulties' in Washington. But the hoped-for big contracts had remained elusive. Buddy had been able to swing a few deals for him, but never in the markets that counted. Sometimes it had looked as though all he had done was set up territorial bases for Buddy's department. They sometimes laughed that all they had done was set up a 'pretty necklace' around the old Soviet Union.

There didn't seem much point in going over it all again. The job was finished. Out. And with it his trips to Washington to see Buddy. And Thousand.

Thousand. Well, it looked as though this really would put a full stop to all that. Not before time, he told himself. All that time spent waiting for things to spring to life. But she had been content for them to tick over as work colleagues. Yes, they had come closer over time but only because of work. Even that business at her flat the other evening. Perhaps that was just the equivalent of him and Buddy going out for a few beers to set the world to rights. Put it aside then. Still. He would miss her.

Suddenly there wasn't much left was there? Job out. Wife out. Thousand out.

Was anything left? Just the scam? No. That was ridiculous. No job, no Buddy and so no bank codes. It looked as though it was time for the dreamer to wake up. Be fifty not twenty.

Anyway, they would always have backed down before the big one. It was all right when it had been just a few hundred or even a few thousand. Just a game like the credit card trick and the airline tickets. It wasn't really worth the risks. Too much on the table to chance it all.

But suddenly there wasn't so much else at all on the table.

Perhaps if the scam worked other things might change. The job wouldn't matter any more. And Ellen was gone anyway and wasn't coming back. That only left Thousand. And perhaps with the money he might be able to go on seeing her.

Without the money that would not be an option. So was there a choice?

But he knew if it was going to work he was going to have to do it properly. And there would only be one go. He would need his final trip to Washington and Buddy to open more dropping accounts and then get ready to build a big enough Drifting Table to hold the interim deals in. Big enough tables would be difficult with his limited LNT but he would just have to do it. One, two, three ... Rich. Perhaps he could build a Drifting Table so big the edge effect wouldn't matter? Pity he didn't know anyone to ask how to do it.

He looked out of his window over King's Parade. 'The best view in Cambridge,' he had told Buddy. Well. No more of that. Was it possible? Had it actually happened?

He looked at the piles of papers on his desk. Service agreements. Invoices. Conference notes. Brochures. Exhibition plans.

He put his elbows on the desk and rested his

forehead on his fingertips. Shit.

I don't want to be here, he thought. I don't know where I *do* want to be but it isn't here.

He stood up and walked out of the office past Ginny, who still wouldn't meet his eye. Down the narrow stairs out into the noisy street. How different it felt compared to yesterday. Maddie? He realised he hadn't thought of her at all. Later.

He looked at his watch. Twelve. Time for a drink? But he didn't really feel like one. So he walked aimlessly across the road and through King's College towards the river.

At least he did not have to go back and face Ellen. He sat down on a bench and watched a group of schoolchildren stream past him towards the chapel. They look bored, he thought.

So who was there to tell? Buddy, yes. Thousand. And here in Cambridge, Bell. That was it really. Lewes could come later.

Perhaps he had better go and have a drink after all. He stood up and walked towards the town.

In Shades he took a glass of claret and sat at the same table he had sat at with Maddie the day before. He wondered what she would think. Probably hardly notice. Yesterday had been very nice but it probably would never have come to anything anyway. Brooch or no brooch.

Perhaps another glass might help.

He stayed in the wine bar for another hour. At first he had sat by himself but after three glasses he went over to the bar and had a rather adamant discussion with the barmaid about the relative merits of Australian and Spanish Chardonnay. And then wine generally. And then Spain and Australia generally. Quite interesting really.

When he eventually thought about the time again, he saw he was an hour late for meeting Maddie.

The brightness of the afternoon after the wine bar took him by surprise. How boringly sober everyone looked. It was a poor do if a man couldn't have a few glasses over lunch.

He made his way towards the Wallingford Hotel and waved at several people he thought he knew.

He went straight to the front desk and spoke to a uniformed concierge. 'I've come to see Dr Madeline Booker.'

'Yes, sir. Is she a guest here?'

'No. I imagine she has to pay.'

'I'll try her room for you, sir. Oh, I'm afraid that line is engaged. If you care to wait in the lounge I will bring you a telephone when the line is free.'

'Good idea. But I think I'll wait in the bar.' Simon leant over heavily on the counter and squinted at the concierge's name tag. 'What is your name?'

'Jackson, sir. Stanley Jackson.'

'Good. Well, Stanley Jackson. I'll be in the bar.'

'Very good, sir.'

Simon walked into the lounge. He saw he was in the wrong room and came out again. He waved at his new friend at the front desk and went into the bar.

'A bit dark in here isn't it?' he asked the barmaid.

'It is very bright outside today sir. What may I get you?'

'I'll have a glass of red please.'

'We only serve wine by the bottle, sir.'

'In that case I'll have a bottle of wine please. Red. And two glasses.' Simon leaned over. 'Are you his sister?'

'I'm sorry, sir?'

'That man. At the front desk. Jackson. Are you his sister?'

'No sir.'

'But you are very similar.'

'I don't know him sir.'

'Very similar.'

'Perhaps it's the uniform sir. We wear the same hotel uniform.'

'Ah, yes. Easy mistake.'

'Yes, sir. Would you like this here or in the garden.'

'Oh, why not? I'll take it in the garden. The green, green garden.'

'Yes, sir.'

Maddie came through to the garden ten minutes later. 'They said I had a visitor. I guessed it must be you.'

'I'm sorry I was late. One or two events. I went to Shades. I didn't notice the time.'

'Shades?'

'Yes. You see in front of you an ex-salesman. There it is.'

She sat down. 'I don't understand. What do you mean?'

'Should have thought it was clear. I've been sacked and went to discuss it with Lady Red Wine. When I woke up this morning I had a job and now I don't.'

'But that's awful. When did this happen?'

'This morning. As soon as I went in.'

'Oh, Simon. I'm so sorry. Why?'

Simon sighed. 'The parting of the ways. That's what he said. Like the Red Sea. So that is why I'm a bit late.'

'That doesn't matter. But it seems crazy. I thought you and Buddy were doing so well.'

'Apparently not. Not well enough anyway. But I'm not really surprised. I saw it coming.'

'But they can't just do that.' She looked at him, puzzled. Her mind racing but trying not to let it show. 'What will you do?'

He poured her a glass of wine.

'One or two things actually. I've been sort of head-hunted.'

'Another job? But I thought this only happened this morning?'

'It did. But I have headhunted myself.' He picked up his glass and held it against the light. 'And I am delighted to tell you that I have accepted the position on offer. The king is dead. Long live the king.'

'What?'

'English expression. Confirmation of the status quo. All change and no change.'

'I'm afraid you are not making much sense. How much have you had to drink?' She put her head on one side.

'Ah! I know that look. Been married too long not to. Yes, I have had a glass or two. But why not? You don't lose your job every day you know. At least I don't. Can't speak for the other three million of course. But I do understand jobs come and go. Like marriages. One minute they are there and the next they're not. What do you think, Maddie?'

'I don't think this is a very good time to talk about things is what I think. Shall we go for a walk or something?'

'Why walk when we can drive? Let's go to the Fens or something.'

'I don't know that you should be doing any driving just now.'

'Well. You can drive. Do you think you can stay on the wrong side of the road?'

'Well, I suppose so. What is the Fens?'

'Are. Not is. A state of mind really. Quite extraord-inary.'

She shook her head lightly. 'It might be better than staying here. I don't think you are making much sense today.'

They walked arm in arm to his car.

'It's all right this, isn't it. Feels good,' he said.

'What does?'

'This arm in arm business. Feels good.'

He sorted through his pockets for the keys to the car and gave them to her.

Maddie took the wheel and drove cautiously north out of Cambridge, following Simon's extravagantly waved directions.

She pointed at the cassette player. 'What's the music? It's rather good.'

'Ah, the famous Felix Mendelssohn Violin Concerto.'

'I didn't think you would like classical music. I had you down as a jazz man. Semi-modern, perhaps: Tubby Hayes, Brubeck even.'

'You don't get to know everything in one day.'

'I think there is quite a lot I don't know,' she said.

'And I'm not helping by being a bit pissed am I?'

'Pissed?'

'English pissed, meaning drunk. Not American pissed meaning pissed off.'

'Oh, well. As you say it's not every day you leave your job. I think you are entitled to a few drinks.'

'Yes. But only a few. It's wearing off now. I'll probably go into shock next or something.'

'I doubt it. And, besides, I thought you had another job to go to. Didn't you say something about that?'

'I'm not going to it. It's coming to me you might say. I told you about it yesterday.'

'What?'

'Well, that money thing you asked about. Now I'm running on empty, I think I have to put my money where my mouth is. I have to stop talking and do a bit of doing.'

'Try it out for real, you mean? I didn't think you were ready. And anyway you said the whole thing was dangerous and that only Bell could do it.'

'It isn't.'

'Well, that sounds more confident than yesterday.'

'I don't have to be confident. I just have to go to

213

America and press the right buttons.'

'America?'

'Where the big banks live. And the codes.'

'And Buddy?'

'And Buddy, yes.'

'The way you talked about it I thought you and Bell did it by yourselves. You didn't mention Buddy at all.'

'Like I said, you don't get to know all about someone in one day. Even on a picnic.'

'The picnic. And that reminds me. I didn't thank you for the brooch. I should have thanked you right away. It's really beautiful.'

'The Messenger. What did he have to say for himself?'

'He said days like that don't come around very often. That's what he said.'

'He was right. And we couldn't have had that day today.'

'Why?'

'This job thing. I don't feel much like sitting by a river today.'

'Of course not. I really am very sorry. And then I start pestering you about your next thing. You probably don't want any company at all.'

'No. If I'd been left to my own devices I would still be in Shades and in God knows what state by now. I barely made it to the Wallingford as it was.'

'I did notice actually,' she smiled.

'Sorry.'

'Never mind. Done now. And where are we going, by the way?'

'March. The Wooden Angels of March.'

'Another of your Simon-type tourist attractions?'

'Yes. It's about another half hour away. Is that all right? I never thought to ask. Don't you have a lecture to go to or something?'

'That was this morning. And I went. Just to take notes for my boss.'

'Couldn't he just send for a transcript?'

'You try to tell him. The transcript won't be out for at least a month and he has to know what is going on everywhere the moment it happens.'

'Is that it? Will you go home now?'

'Well, I wanted to stay here for at least a week and go and see some people in London but actually I have to go back to the States tomorrow. I had a phone call last night.'

'You didn't say.'

'I didn't have much chance did I? I was going to tell you.'

Simon ran his hands through his hair. 'This is all a bit funny, isn't it? There we were yesterday having a nice quiet afternoon by the river and now you've got to go home and I've lost my job.'

'Well. Better than not having had yesterday at all. But it's not all bad. My boss wants me in Washington for a few days so we could meet there next week if you like.'

'DC? That's a bit off your beat isn't it?'

'Not really. My boss, Erickson, sits on various committees there, and one is sitting next week. He rang to tell me to go because he still can't travel.'

'What's supposed to be the matter with him?'

'Flu or something. Nothing serious.'

'Oh well. That's nice. Where will you stay? With Buddy?'

'Yes. The three of us can meet up in the evenings or something.'

'Yes.'

'Buddy. We still haven't decided what to do there have we?'

'No. Any ideas?'

She turned to smile at him. 'We got a bit distracted didn't we?'

He leant back in his seat and ran his fingers through his hair again.

'Is there any other family? He only ever talks about you and the children.'

'Just his children. But you know they don't see him much. And Mum and Dad are long gone. Buddy went into the army straight from college and the next thing he knew he was flying helicopters in Vietnam. Then he married Sue and settled in Washington. I don't think he ever got to know many people, and most of those he met through Sue.'

'I liked her actually. Did you know her very well?'

'Quite well. I used to go to Washington much more in the seventies and I always stayed with them. The children were great. But I think she turned them against him. And then by the time they were old enough to see through that crap it was a bit late.'

'What were you doing in Washington?' he asked.

'Much the same as I am now. Programming and so on.'

Like hell, she thought. 'Countersurveillance', Warkowski had called it in the early days. Spying on friends really. Getting people to trust her. Then going further. Sleeping with them, taking secrets from them on trust and then handing them over like so many books going back to the library.

She had been shocked at how easy it had been. And it became easier each time she did it. She began to realise how good she was. She became absorbed by the technicalities of it. The people she was trading in lost identity and became simple stepping stones to ever more intricate and complicated assignments.

'Yes,' she said. 'Much the same sort of thing as now. Then when I got married I went to Washington less and less. I started coming back more two or three years ago. But by then things had started to go wrong for Buddy. He put it down to that man Costa but I don't think it was only that. It was the drinking as much as anything. But perhaps that was Costa's fault too. I'm not sure.'

'The famous Mr da Costa again,' said Simon. 'I think we should have known it was too good to be true. For just a little he could achieve things so fast it seemed a miracle. And he never asked for more than five per cent. Always there when we needed him. "Simoon, Buddee, of course. What can I do for you?" I mean we knew he wasn't completely legit but we took that as just par for the course. We really liked the man at first.'

He rubbed his hand back and forth on the dash-board as if rubbing off some dust. 'I think the turning point came about two years ago. Costa suddenly started telling less and less about what he was doing and at the same time asking us for more and more. We sort of woke up to what sort of dealer he really was. But by then it was too late. He was our only "main man". Without him we never achieved anything any more. He may have been becoming expensive but at least he kept the show on the road. And the amazing thing was that no one at Buddy's end seemed to mind. I asked Buddy to tell Jake a couple of times but the message came back for us to shut up and get on with it. We suddenly felt we were pawns in a game we didn't understand. It didn't seem to matter what we did so long as we didn't make waves. Well, that may have been all right for Buddy. We would set up a distribution depot and service depot and he would get credit for that but I had to shift the bloody pumps afterwards and that was never so easy. I had a boss and wife who weren't happy with us simply establish-ing a "presence" in some country or other. "Bottom Line" was all that counted. And results were frankly pretty dreadful even with Costa's help. I mean he only lived up to expectations at the very beginning. I think we each realised quite early on that we had backed the wrong horse, but there had never really been a choice. It had been Costa or nothing and he was better than nothing.'

'So, enter dream stage left.'

He smiled. 'Perhaps that's what it was. I'd always

messed about with hacking ever since I learnt how. Then gradually I began to see the possibilities. I mean with all that money floating about it seemed obvious that there had to be a way to take a bit as it bobbed by. But I don't think it became much more than a plaything until I saw I could never be caught. You see, the really nice thing about the scam is that it's not stoppable.'

'Oh, come on, Si. I'm sure you are good, but not stoppable? No way!'

'Well, I thought so too for a while. I tried to think of various ways of breaking it. But there aren't any really. It's because of what it is. It's not a virus and it doesn't use what are called "illegal hardware calls". It's bog standard really. To stop it properly they would have to change the way satellite communications work and I can't see anyone doing that.'

'You are missing something though aren't you?'

'I hope not.'

'Hope again then. Put it this way. If there is only one person, namely you, doing it then to stop it all they have to do is stop you.'

'But that's the point. They won't know who I am or how I did it. I tell you Maddie, there are no footprints. Nothing to go on.'

'Oh, come on! They will eventually find you. They'll set everything they have against you. They'll win. It's their game. And it's a game without shadows. When they come looking, there is no place to hide. Their ball.'

'That's a Buddy expression. Funny you should use it.'

'What?'

' "Game without shadows".'

'I must have heard him use it sometime.'

But he continued. 'I used to think that if we kept it small they wouldn't bother to look for us even if they could. But the real ace is that we could suddenly go so big so fast we would have enough money for ever. Clean away. No trace.'

'Yes, but how much does "for ever" cost?'

'Name it.'

'I mean are we talking one million? Two? If they really wanted to come looking they would pull out all the stops. Money no object.'

'One million? Two? You are way, way out. The actual overnight float on the Foreign Exchange is five hundred million.'

'Jesus! Are you serious?'

'Scary isn't it.'

'I don't believe it anyway.'

'You don't have to. It's not something that needs proving. If you knew about how it worked you would see that there isn't a practical limit.'

'Does Buddy know all this?'

'No, of course not. I tell him we can't go very big. Anyway he doesn't know how it works.'

'But you are telling me.'

'I'm not actually. I'm just telling you the "what", not the "how". Besides, any half-competent systems administrator, which incidentally they must have, would be aware by now of what's going on. At the very least they would know someone was going in and out of the system and playing with it. Maybe they even have an idea what is going to happen next, but they can't come looking because they don't know the nuts and bolts.'

'And say you're wrong? What if they do know where to look and find you in the system?'

'That's a maybe. And anyway I'll be long gone.'

'Simon, no.'

'Long gone,' he repeated. 'Wham. Bang. Out. Five million for me. Five for Buddy. And what shall we say for the girl with the dragonfly brooch? Another five? Ten?'

She opened her mouth to speak but he got in first.

'The game looks different from the inside doesn't it?'

'Five million,' she repeated quietly.

'Or ten. You choose,' he said. 'I talk too much don't I? You shouldn't listen, you know.'

Oh yes, she thought, you do talk too much. You all do.

Coming over a slight rise in the road, Ely cathedral appeared on the horizon.

'Is that where the angels are?' she asked.

'No. No angels there. At least I never saw any there. There were some in the stained glass windows but the locals threw stones at them.'

'Stones?'

'The sack of the monasteries. Or maybe Henry VIII. I don't know which. Anyway all the windows worth looking at were broken. Nothing there now but Americans and collecting boxes.'

'I'm American.'

'True. But you don't count. You're not a tourist. You are here on business aren't you?'

'Yes. Business.' Five million? The whole thing was ridiculous.

'We, my dear business visitor, are going to the real attraction of the Fens. The Wooden Angels of St Etheldreda. Actually, I have never seen them but I know where they are. At least they are meant to be wooden during the day. I think at night they fly around and do angelic deeds.'

'Perhaps we should go and see them at night then?'

'But they wouldn't be at St Etheldreda's then would they?' They both laughed.

The road took them out past Ely through a series of smaller and smaller villages. The land became flatter and the soil darker. Eventually they were on a long stretch of road with wide black fields stretching away on either side.

'Is this the Fens?' she asked.

'Sort of,' he smiled. 'They call it the Big Sky Country. It was all wetland around here. Swamps. Malaria even. Then they drained it and started farming. The soil turned out to be incredibly fertile. Absolutely anything grew. It was so easy. But they didn't look after the soil and so most of it blew away.'

A church appeared on the horizon. 'That's it. St Etheldreda. It's in a town called March. It used to be a big town but now it's rather forgotten its way and nobody goes there except to see the angels.'

'But it looks like a big church.'

'Yes. Most of the Fen churches are big. I think it's because when the farming was good they built big churches as an insurance policy for getting into heaven. Keeping on the right side of the Main Man. Worked too. Loads of top farmers up there. They don't have to do anything except sit about and count their blessings. A bit like farming down here really.'

She smiled and shook her head gently. 'I thought heaven was for nice people, not rich ones.'

'Well, of course that was the original idea but hardly any nice people qualified in the early days and so the Man had to let out whole Elysian Fields just to fill the place. And of course the highest bidders were the rich. It's a commonly mistaken belief that you can't buy your way into heaven.'

She laughed again. 'Where do you get such ridiculous stories from?'

'Nowhere really. It's just the storyteller in me. Rubbish really.'

'Maybe. But I like the stories you tell. Being with you is a whole series of stories isn't it? Angels, Dragonflies, Children of the River. I don't know how many of them you have told before. And I'm not sure what you are weaving. But I like them. Left of field, but I still like them.'

'I've never said any of them before. It's all new. Really.'

They were almost at the church. It did not look so large close-to. It stood in a rather untidy graveyard. They walked over the rough grass to the large wooden door set into the side. It was locked.

They peered in through the windows and could just make out the dark shapes of the angels' wings high up on the wall just below the ceiling.

'I thought they would be more impressive,' he said.

'Oh well. If you had only come at night. Then Sir would have seen them flying about. Sir would have been much more impressed then.'

'You see?' he laughed. 'You really do believe in the stories.'

She put her hands up and cupped his face with her fingers. 'Sometimes it's easier to believe things than others.'

He looked down at her. 'Do you really think so?'

'Trust me storyteller. Trust me.' She stood on tiptoes and kissed him.

Chapter Seven

Simon fell asleep as Maddie drove back to Cambridge. She was not sure where Simon normally parked and so she drove to the hotel.

She carefully checked her make-up in the driving mirror before gently shaking his arm to wake him.

'Oh God,' he said. 'Fallen asleep again.'

'Don't worry. It was a lovely drive and I hardly got lost at all.'

Simon blew into his hands and shook his head. 'That will teach me to drink at lunch. You would think I'd know better by now. I'm afraid I went on a bit.'

'No problem. Would you like some coffee?'

'No thanks. I should get home. Perhaps I could ring you later and we could have dinner. I mean if you have to go back tomorrow. I'll have a bath and get myself together.'

'That would be fine. Shall we say eight o'clock? I'll wait in the bar if you like.'

'Yes. And with any luck they'll have a different barmaid on by then.'

'Why? Does that make a difference?'

'Not really. It's just that I didn't conduct myself all that well at lunch.'

'Oh, never mind. I'm sure nobody noticed. Give me a ring later and tell me how you feel.'

He walked slowly back over the water meadows towards Trumpington trying to remember what he had said to her earlier. About the job? Yes. No reason not to. And about the scam? Not so good. Still, there was no reason to think she would believe him any more than anybody else.

Then he remembered he had promised her some money. But never mind. He could always play that down over dinner. Put it all down to being a dreamer.

Back at the cottage there were two messages on his answering machine waiting for him. The first one was from Thousand.

'Simon. Three o'clock and where are you? I need to talk to you. I called Ginny and she said you might be with Maddie. I do hope not. I really do. And, by the way, Ginny told me about the job. I'm really sorry but I think you knew it was going to happen. We can talk about it next week if you see what I mean. But I really need to talk to you about Maddie. Ring me at the office the minute you pick this up. Then I'll call you back on a quiet line. Things are going wrong here and we have to do something. But in the meantime remember what I told you. Bye.'

The second message was from Ginny.

'Simon. Four o'clock and where the hell are you? There has been a car accident. Bell Lessing. They've taken him to the hospital. I'm afraid he is very badly hurt. In intensive care or something. Lizzie rang me and she's in a hell of a state. Apparently the doctors won't let her see him or tell her anything. I think you need to get down there right away. I'll be here until six and after that you can call me at home. Let me know how he is. Bye.'

Simon cursed himself for leaving his car at the hotel and set off for the mile to the hospital on his bicycle.

He found Bell Lessing in a side room of the main accident and emergency ward. He was connected by a maze of wires to monitors above his head. A drip bag hung on a rack next to him. His head was bandaged over one side of his face. The other side of his face was ashen grey and his eye was closed. One arm was suspended in a traction sling and the other lay along the bed. Lizzie was holding it and crying. Her face was blotched and dark from where her make-up had run as she had cried.

She looked up when Simon came in. 'Thank you for coming. I didn't know who to call. He's just come back from surgery and the doctor says it's too early to know how he is.'

'What happened? Was he driving?'

'No. It's crazy. He was just crossing the road outside college and a car came up too fast on the wrong side of the road and went straight into him. The driver can't have been looking where he was going. He didn't stop or anything. In broad daylight. Look at what they did to him. Just look.'

Simon sat down next to her and put his arm around her. She turned her head to his shoulder and burst into tears again.

'Oh, Simon, look at him. I feel so bloody helpless. What can I do? Oh. I'm sorry. What can I do?'

Simon held her to him and looked up the bed at Bell. He was lying completely still and seemed to be hardly breathing. Only a green trace on the screen above his head and an intermittent tone matching his pulse showed any life at all.

'He'll be fine Lizzie. I'm sure he will. They are very good you know. Would you like me to call the girls? Do you know where they are? I don't know their London number.'

She stopped sobbing and looked up at him. 'Sorry to be so silly. I let myself go. I've called them but they are out somewhere. I've left a message for them to come as soon as they can. Should I have done that? Will you wait till they get here? Please wait.'

'Of course I'll wait Lizzie. But I'm sure he'll be fine. Let me go and find a doctor to see what's going on. I'll come straight back.'

There did not appear to be anyone at the ward reception desk, but he eventually found a doctor chatting to some nurses in a kitchen at the end of the corridor. He was a young man of about twenty wearing a Sydney Harbour Bridge T-shirt under his open white coat.

'Can you tell me about Dr Lessing please. I'm Dr Northcott.'

'No worry, doc. Let's go and take a butchers at his notes by the desk. He's not my patient. I've only just come on.'

The 'notes' turned out to be a single sheet of paper clipped to a board and hung on one of a series of hooks.

'Here we are. RTA. Male. Sixty years. Lessing, Bellman. Laceration to right side and upper abdomen. Sus sternal fracture. Sus fracture verts two and three. Dislocation right scapula. Sus rupture spleen. Sus subcranial haematoma. That's all so far.'

'I'm afraid that doesn't mean anything to me at all.'

'You said you were a doctor.'

'Not that type.'

'Oh, sorry. I shouldn't have said anything then. I thought you were his GP or something.'

'No. Just a friend of the family. How is he really?'

'Well, I'm not supposed to say anything but I'm afraid he is very badly injured. They will operate on him in about an hour as soon as he stabilises.'

'I thought he'd been operated on already.'

'No. He just went up to X-ray. I told the woman but I don't think she took much in. They don't.'

'Are you surprised? Look, I don't mean anything but are you the senior doctor here tonight?'

'Yes. The neuro has been beeped and should be here soon. There really isn't any more we can do at this point in time.'

'Neuro?'

'Neuro surgeon. Two of the bones at the top of his

neck are cracked. We don't know how much pressure there is on the soft tissue.'

'You mean his neck's broken?'

'Bit worse than that I'm afraid. He'll be fine if nothing is actually crushed. Can I ask how well you know the family, sir?'

'Well enough. Have you told Mrs Lessing how bad his injuries are?'

'Like I say, we don't really know ourselves yet. We have to wait for the neuro. It really is best not to tell her too much at this stage.'

' "This stage"? She has been here two hours and nobody seems to have told her anything at all do they?'

'I'm sorry, sir. We are very busy.'

'So I see. I'll go back and wait.'

Simon thought he saw one of the nurses making a face at the doctor as he went back to Lizzie.

'The doctor said Bell's neck is injured. They may want to operate soon to relieve some pressure.'

'Pressure? What pressure? He's going to be all right isn't he?'

'Of course. We just have to wait for the specialist to see him?'

'What specialist? Can't they do anything now?'

'As soon as he can Lizzie. He'll be here soon.'

At around midnight Bell was wheeled up to the operating theatre. He had not moved at all.

Two hours later a very tired looking surgeon came to explain things to Lizzie and Simon. 'We have done what we can now for your husband, Mrs

Lessing. He's been moved to the special recovery area where he will stay for the rest of the night. They will take him to the normal ward in the morning. He has a number of serious injuries but the most important is the one to his brain stem. Fortunately there is no break but a certain amount of crushing took place around the fracture lines of the vertebrae. You can go and sit with him if you like but I suggest you go home and try to get some rest. The nurse will give you something if you like. I will see him at about ten tomorrow and I'll be able to tell you more then. I'm very sorry not to be more helpful but it is very early days.'

Lizzie turned to Simon. 'What shall I do? Do you think I should stay?'

'No, Lizzie. I'll drive you home and wait until the girls come. You can come back here with them when you've had some sleep.'

She leant forward and put her hands behind her neck.

Simon looked up at the surgeon. 'Perhaps he will have woken up by then?'

The surgeon did not reply but shook his head at Simon very slightly.

Bell and Lizzie lived less than a mile from the hospital and so within a quarter of an hour Simon and Lizzie were in the sitting room waiting for the girls.

'Do you want some tea Lizzie? Or perhaps something to eat? I don't expect you had any supper.'

'No thanks. I don't need anything but you go

ahead. A drink if you like. There should be some Scotch in the kitchen.'

'Probably not a good idea. But I think I will have one. Sure you won't join me? It might help you sleep.'

The two grown-up daughters arrived as Simon was walking back to the sitting room from the kitchen.

Simon sat with them and he and Lizzie told them what little they could.

Simon felt completely drained and very tired. He knew he ought to go home and sleep. As he got up to go the older daughter, Nancy, followed him out into the hall. 'Have they found the car that did it? Do they know?'

'I don't think so, Nancy, but I don't know any of the details. I could ring the police station in the morning if you like and find out.'

'Please. I know it seems terrible to be talking like this, but whoever it was can't just get away with it. He might have been drunk or anything.'

While they were talking, the telephone rang on the hall table. Before he could pick it up, Lizzie had rushed out from the sitting room. 'I'll take it. It might be the hospital.'

She brushed her hair from her face and picked up the receiver. 'Hello. Yes. Yes. He's here. Wait.'

Lizzie looked up puzzled and put her hand over the mouthpiece. 'It's for you, Simon. That American woman.'

He took the receiver from her. 'Maddie. Is that you?'

'No, it's not Maddie. It's me, Thousand. Now listen very carefully. I haven't got long. I know exactly what's happened. I've just spoken to Ginny. I'm ringing from the windows but I must speak to you on a quiet line from the office. Go to your house and I'll ring you in one hour on the dot. Do you understand?'

'Frankly no. What are you on about? And what the hell were you doing ringing Ginny in the middle of the night? I'll bet she was pleased.'

'Never mind that now. I have to talk to you. Please do what I say.'

'If it's about Costa it can wait. I'm coming over next week anyway.'

'Costa? No it's not about Costa. And it won't wait. It's about the deal. Now do what I say.' The line went dead.

Nancy took the phone from him. 'What was all that about?'

'I don't honestly know. I'm half asleep but she wasn't making any sense at all. And I don't know how she knew I was here. She wants me to ring back tomorrow. Look, I really am half dead. It's been a long day. I really must go home, but I'll ring you first thing in the morning.'

The night was still and cold as Simon made his tired way the mile back to his own house. He had shut the door before he realised he didn't have his car and didn't feel he could ask to borrow Lizzie's.

A full moon lit up the streets and trees. Only one or two cars passed him. An ambulance with flashing lights but no siren. Good luck whoever you are, thought Simon. Perhaps you'll get the bed next to Bell.

When he was halfway he regretted not calling a taxi and he pulled his jacket collar up against the coolness. He scented a trace of autumn in the breeze and smiled when he remembered how Ellen had always said she liked this time of year best. 'I love that smell. It means the work of the summer is done and everything can start getting ready for winter.' He wondered if she was still saying it. Probably not. They had shared their love for autumn with its smells and colours and she would want to put shared things like that aside. She had said she wanted to move on completely and had done so rather better than him. Maybe that had been the problem. She was better than him at so many things. It must have been that as much as anything that had worn her down. Possibly she could have chosen someone different in the first place. Perhaps they both should have. But then there would have been no Lewes.

He realised he was going around all the old circles in his mind again, so made a conscious effort to think about something else. For instance, what could be important enough for Thousand to want to ring him up in the middle of the night? Him losing his job? Surely not. And anyway she knew about that when she had rung him earlier. Perhaps Bell's accident. But why would she want to ring about that?'

It was four o'clock when he finally turned up the lane to his house. He realised he hadn't eaten since breakfast and that all he had had to drink was the wine at lunch and the whisky at Bell's. No surprise then that he felt as tired and old as he could remember. He decided he needed to sleep more than he needed to talk to Thousand and went up to his room and lay straight down on his bed. He was asleep almost immediately.

It seemed to him that he was no sooner asleep than he was being woken up by an incessant ringing and knocking at his front door. It was six o'clock.

He swung his feet over the side of the bed and sat up. He immediately put his hands up to his head. This was going to be a mother of a headache. He opened his bedroom window and leaned out to see who it was. It was just beginning to get light and he could make out a policeman standing by the door.

'What is it?'

'Ah. At last. I've been trying to raise you for ten minutes. Could I have a word please sir?'

'What about?'

'Could I come in please sir? It won't take long.'

Simon went down and opened the door.

'If it's about the accident, I don't know anything. I only went to the hospital. I wasn't with him at the time.'

'I don't know about any accident. I've come about the break-in to your work premises. I wonder if I could ask you one or two questions.'

'Break-in? What break-in?'

'To your office sir. At approximately two this morning. I understand you have a key. There was no sign of forced entry but the alarm was activated. The attending officer contacted the registered key holder, a Mr King I believe. And he thought you might be able to throw some light onto the matter. That is with the nature of the items removed.'

'What items? I tell you I don't know about any break-in.'

'Quite sir. But it seems that the only items taken were those under your responsibility.'

'I don't have any "items" there. What do you mean?'

The policeman referred to his notebook. 'Two personal computers, one case of tape cartridges and one box of disks.'

'Oh, Christ. What is this? Two PCs taken. They go walkies from offices all the time for the chips. You know that. Why should I know anything?'

'I don't know what you know sir. That is what I am here to establish. I understand Mr King was certain you would be able to help. Perhaps you could come down to the office with me sir.'

'What? Now? Can't it wait until the morning? I'm not awake yet.'

'With respect sir. It is the morning. They are waiting for us to return.'

'Who is?'

'Mr King and our Inspector Morris of Commercial. I really don't want to have to insist.'

'This is ridiculous. Why should I know anything King doesn't? It's his bloody office, not mine.'

'Yes sir. But I understand there was something of a disagreement between the two of you yesterday afternoon. There is the question of the data on the cartridges and disks. Inspector Morris is particularly interested in data, sir.'

'Oh I get it. He thinks I went in and took my own PC. Frankly I can think of better things to do at two o'clock in the morning.'

'Can we go sir? The sooner we get there, the sooner you can come back.'

'Faultless logic, Constable. You'll go far.'

'Please, sir. And it's Sergeant, not Constable.'

'Oh, is it? I didn't notice. Very well. Just wait while I collect my deerstalker and magnifying glass.'

'Sir?'

'Joke, Sergeant. Let's go then.'

At the office, the sergeant waited by the front door and Simon went up. In the reception area Kenneth King and Inspector Morris were having coffee. Ginny was also there, sitting to one side.

'Is this your idea of a joke, Simon?' said King. 'I must say I think it in remarkably bad taste. I really do.'

The inspector held up his hand. 'Please Ken. Let me ask the questions.'

'Are you two old chums?' asked Simon.

'I am Inspector Morris of the Commercial and Data Protection Section. Are you Dr Simon Northcott?'

'Good guess.'

'Simon!' snapped King. 'You are in enough trouble as it is without being offensive as well. You can count yourself lucky that I happen to know Inspector Morris personally. I was able to persuade him to ask you to come down here rather than take you direct to the police station.'

'Wait a minute, Ken. The one downstairs told me that a couple of PCs and some disks have been taken. And you think it is something to do with me. And on the basis of that Inspector Morris here is going to whisk me off to the station? I don't think so. For your information I was at the hospital with Lizzie Lessing at two o'clock this morning. You can ask Dr Kildare if you like.'

The Inspector spoke. 'But you can see how it looked, sir. You can see why Mr King was concerned. He thought that you were perhaps harbouring some sort of grudge.'

'Oh, for God's sake,' said Simon.

'Sir. If I may continue. This sort of thing is not unknown. I appreciate that the machines in question have only moderate value but, as the disks and cartridges were also taken, Mr King was concerned with the commercial implications, and that is where I come in. He tells me that there was commercial data on them. Of value perhaps to a competitor. He further told me you left here considerably agitated yesterday afternoon. And so I thought it best to locate you in person before I took it further. After all, I understand you still have a key and the main lock was not forced. You can see how it looks. You say you can establish your whereabouts at the time of the incident? Very well. If that bears out we should not have to trouble you further at this stage of our enquiries.'

'I told you. I was at the hospital.'

'Your secretary here, sir, said you might be there as I understand she left a message on your answering machine about your friend's road traffic accident. On her advice my sergeant rang the hospital but they had no record of you being there. Only a Mrs Lessing, with her injured husband.'

'I'm not surprised,' said Simon. 'They can't even find a surgeon when they need one.'

'Sir?'

'Oh, never mind. Yes, I was there all night with Mrs Lessing. You can ask the doctor. I don't know his name.'

'We will check if you don't mind sir.'

KK looked at the inspector. 'Thank you for coming, Brian. Perhaps I acted too hastily. I can see now it wasn't Simon. But you can see what I thought. I do appreciate your coming over.'

'Not to worry, Ken. Glad to be able to sort things out. But we still have to establish who did gain entry. Still, I can leave that to my boys. There isn't anything here for me now. Perhaps I could give you a lift back to Grantchester?' He turned to Simon. 'If you could give the Sergeant the full list of the items taken I would be most grateful.'

'Yes,' said Simon. 'But I thought you said two PCs were taken. I had only one.'

'The other was Miss Webb's here sir. She was good enough to come in as soon as we contacted her.'

'And I wasn't? Point taken. Yes, I'll work out a list

for him from the paperwork. Can I go home to bed then?'

'Yes, of course.'

The inspector and KK went out, leaving Simon and Ginny alone.

Simon leant back in his chair.

'What a circus, Ginny. What a day. KK didn't honestly think it was me did he?'

'No. I don't expect so. But you heard the inspector chappie. It didn't look very good, did it? Not after yesterday.'

'No. I suppose not. I think I'd better go home and sleep it all off. Perhaps when I wake up yesterday won't have happened. The job. Bell. This. You know, I work here for fifteen years and sod all happens. Everything rock solid. Good old uncle Si. Then in one day I lose the job and get accused of grand larceny.'

She smiled at him. 'Hardly grand larceny. A couple of PCs, that's all. But I'm afraid there is no beddy byes for you yet. There is something else.'

'What?'

'Washington. You are on the eleven o'clock flight.'

'No. That's not right. I'm not going till next week.'

'I know. But KK was in a bit of a state after you went yesterday. I know he did say you could go over for one more trip but I thought he might change his mind so Thousand and I sort of got on with it.'

'But I can't go. Bell. Lizzie might need me.'

'No one is indispensable. Not even you. The girls can look after her. Even Lacrima might do something worthwhile for him for a change. And you do have to go to Washington. You know Jake Cohen is your best chance for another job. There isn't going to be anything here for you any more.'

'I suppose you're right. But I'd better go home. At least have a bath.'

'You've time for a coffee first. I'll make it while you talk to the nice policeman. Then we'll have a little goodbye ceremony. Fifteen years is a long time.' She looked down at her knees.

'Ginny?'

She did not look up. 'What?'

'Oh, come on. I am coming back you know.'

'Are you? But not to here. All this is finished isn't it? Done.'

Simon did not reply immediately. After a few moments he got up and stood in front of her. 'Don't be silly, Ginny. Not now. Look I'll go and make the coffee. You stay here.'

'Yes,' she said in a small voice. 'Good idea. I thought they might want a proper list. It's on my desk. I made it out when they went to get you.'

'Thanks.' He took the list and went down to give it to the policeman. When he returned Ginny had gone to make the coffee and he could hear her in the small kitchen at the end of the corridor.

He sat down, leant his head back and closed his eyes until she returned.

'Thank you,' he said. 'Anyway, you will see me. I'll still be based in Cambridge whatever Jake comes up with. I don't see any reason to move.'

'Probably.' She picked up her mug. 'Silly old me. What about your new friend? Where does she live?'

'Who?'

'The natural blonde. Is that where you went yesterday?'

'Maddie. Oh, Christ! I was meant to see her last night but completely forgot. The Bell thing. She was going back to America today. Perhaps I could ring her. What time is it?'

'Only seven. You can't ring yet.'

'No. Which reminds me. I've left my car at the Wallingford. Tell me to pick it up when I go. I'll leave it at home while I am away.'

'The Wallingford? Simon! I warned you about her. You didn't "actually" did you?'

'No, Ginny. I did not "actually". I left it there when I was pissed. That's all. And why is everyone warning me off Maddie?'

'Everyone?'

'Well, you and Thousand anyway.'

'Good for Thousand. You should listen to her more.'

'Possibly.' Simon sipped his coffee.

She looked up at him. 'Seriously though. What will you do for a job if Jake hasn't got anything for you?'

'I think he will have. Or Buddy.'

'Famous Buddy. I wouldn't have thought he was much of a bet.'

'He's all right.' He put his mug down and stood up. 'I'll go now. I'll see you when I get back.'

She stood up too. 'Put your arms around me, Simon. Say goodbye.'

He held her to him and kissed the top of her head. 'You look after yourself.'

'Yes. You too.' She stood back and brushed the side of her face. 'You too.' She bent down to gather up the mugs. 'Please go now.'

'Yes.' He turned and walked to the stairs.

She put the mugs back on the table and sat down again. She heard him go down and listened as the front door banged shut behind him. Then she began to cry.

PART THREE
Washington DC

Chapter Eight

When Simon arrived at Thousand's office the following morning she was standing looking out of the window with her arms folded.

She turned around when he came in and put her arms down. 'I was really sorry to hear about Bell. It must have been terrible.'

Simon sat down heavily in an armchair against the far wall. 'It was awful. I was having dinner with him just the day before. He was his normal lively self and the next time I saw him he was lying stock still all bandaged up. It was like a completely different person. And Lizzie. Just a nightmare.'

'How is he now?'

'I rang when I got in last night. He's still unconscious but stable. They can't say how long it will be. They won't even say how much of a recovery they expect him to make.'

'They would say if they knew. I'm afraid you can't expect any good news.'

'No. Lizzie is drugged up to the eyeballs of course. I don't think she knows what's going on.'

Thousand turned to look out of the window again. 'Ginny Webb says you've come to see Jake.'

'Yes. A bit of a long shot really. Do you think he'll have anything? He might know someone?'

Thousand walked back to her desk and sat down. She leaned back and looked at him. 'What do you think?'

'Thanks for the encouragement.'

'Anyway Jake's not here. He had to go to a meeting downstairs and he'll be there most of the day.'

'Downstairs? In Admin? Who has he gone to see?'

She smiled to herself. 'Downstairs plus plus. And Buddy's not due back till midnight, so that gives us all day to sort something out.'

'Sort out?'

'Yes. Despite appearances, all is not yet lost. But no thanks to you two clowns. Can we go somewhere to talk?'

'I've only just got here. What's the matter with here?'

She did not reply but stood up and picked up her jacket from the back of her chair. 'Come on, I'll buy you a coffee.'

'I said what's the matter with here? I don't want a coffee.'

'You will. Is your lap-top in your case? Good. Bring it. Chop chop.'

'Go easy Thousand. I've had a hell of a two days and practically no sleep. It wasn't my idea to come to Washington. I wanted to come next week.'

'No. It was my idea. I told Ginny that your man

KK might change his mind. Do you think he would have?'

'Yes. Probably. After the break-in.'

'Ah, yes. The mysterious break-in.'

'Not so mysterious. Just a break-in.'

'Possibly. Come on. Elevator time.' She led the way briskly down the corridor to the lifts.

Once outside the building she crossed the main road opposite. She did not take his hand.

He turned to her. 'Something tells me you're not in Famous Day Part II mood.'

Without looking at him she said, 'Maybe not. But I can tell you one thing. You are going to remember this day for the rest of your life. It's up to you what you call it.'

Simon expected her to turn right to the little coffee shop on the corner they normally went to. Instead she went left and set off up the hill towards the main shops.

'Where are we going? What's the matter with Donuts and Co?'

'We are going to Buchan Music 'n' Tapes. They've opened a coffee thing on the top floor. Besides, Harvey rang earlier to say a book I've ordered is in. So I thought, why not? Birds and stones.'

'Perhaps you will make more sense when you are sitting down.'

'Oh, I will Simon. Don't worry about that. Here we are.' She pushed open the heavy glass door of the shop and went in before him.

'Hi, Harvey,' she called. 'How are you doing?'

'Hey, Thousand! Fine. Got my message then? Your book's right here. But the way you were playing last week I don't think you are going to need it long.'

'Last week?' asked Simon.

'She didn't tell you yet? She made top Go Dojo in straight games up the ladder. And no one, but no one, has ever done that before.'

She smiled at him. 'It's not so hard, Harvey. Like I say, you just have to concentrate.'

She took the book. 'On my account.' She opened it and began walking to the open spiral staircase in the middle of the shop.

'Coffee Shop's not open until ten,' called Harvey. 'But I can put some music on if you like. Any preferences?'

Without looking up she said, 'Thanks. The Mendelssohn.'

'Coming up.'

Simon shrugged at Harvey and followed Thousand up the stairs.

She walked over to an alcove by the window and sat down, putting the book neatly on the table in front of her. Then she leant back and folded her arms as the first bars of the Mendelssohn began.

'What do you want to talk about?' asked Simon. 'This place doesn't look particularly private.'

'It's not bad. No one will hear us over the music and there are no bugs.'

'Don't tell me you checked.'

She smiled. 'Trust me.'

'People are always asking me to do that.'

She unfolded her arms and brushed some imaginary crumbs off the table in front of her. 'The point is this Simon. I know what you and Buddy have been up to.'

'Oh, really?'

'Yes, really. But that doesn't matter. But what *does* matter is that I don't know if I'm the *only* one.'

'Sorry, Thousand. Lost me.' He sat back, put his hands behind his head and looked up at the ceiling.

She ignored him. 'Yesterday morning, Washington time, I was given five telephone calls to scan. All from Buddy. All to you. Each one exactly five minutes in duration and each one starting at four minutes to midnight. Have I got your attention yet?'

He did not move but said, 'Oh. I remember those. About Costa. Too bad we made them on the quiet line or you could actually have found out what we were talking about as well.'

'I think we can leave the good Mr da Costa out of this for the moment. Now are you going to tell me exactly what's going on or are you going to make me piece it together bit by bit? Do it my way and we just might make some progress and get you and Buddy out from the rock and the hard place. Do it your way and we run out of sand in the top half of the hourglass and then I can't even begin to help you.'

He moved his hands from behind his head to the top. He blew out his cheeks and stared at her. Eventually he said, 'Have you ever heard of the rule of ten per cent?'

'That's just a myth. But give me your version anyway.'

'OK,' he said. 'I've been a salesman of one sort or another for the best part of twenty-five years. Out on the road. Away from home for six, maybe eight months a year. It's very boring but the only compensation is that it's all on expenses. I've filled in more expense forms than you've had hot dinners. So has Buddy. You should know. He passes them via you to Jake.'

'Yes, but it's only after he met you that they became works of art.'

'OK. So I passed on a few tips. But never once, and I mean never once, was ever more than ten per cent unaccounted for. Nobody minds that. Not Jake. Not KK. Not anyone. It's par for the course. The ten per cent rule. All agreed.'

'If you say so.'

'I say so. Now what Buddy and I were doing the times you are on about was nothing more than ten per centing. A little bit here. A little bit there. Nothing to lose any sleep over.'

'Yes, but this wasn't expenses, Simon. Buddy was giving you bank access codes. It was money straight out of the till without touching the sides. Now I don't know where it went but I know *exactly* where that money came from. Nothing to do with expenses. Nothing to do with Buddy's department or anyone else's come to that. It was overnight bank money and you went and took it. Ten per cent? Ten per cent of what, Simon?' She held out her hands palms up.

She went on, 'Now I know you play about with accounts all over the place. Airline tickets, hotel bills, restaurants and whatever. It's a game and you're good at it. And, as you say, nobody really minds. They can see what you are doing. It's cat and mouse. You see one thing and they try to stop you. So you try something else. And so on. Everyone knows how much has been taken and where it's gone. But what you are doing now is different. A whole new ball game. I'll be frank with you, I don't think they have *any* idea how you do it and I don't think they have *any* idea where the money goes. Now that may make you very happy but how do you think it makes them feel. What do you think they actually *feel*?'

'Not my problem.'

'Yes it bloody is. And I'll tell you why. Because even if they don't know the *"how"* they have a good idea about the *"who"*. And they are mad as all hell.'

'Rubbish. No trace.'

'What about the phone calls?'

'I told you. Scrambled. Washington secure codes. No way to break them.'

'Well, I unscrambled them.'

'No way. Some of it maybe. Not all. You're bluffing.'

'Would I be here otherwise? I broke the calls because I have the same access set as Buddy. He should have used a higher level, and probably told you he was, but you know how hopeless he is. Have I got your attention yet?'

'A bit.'

'Good. At last. Now so far as I can tell I'm the only one who knows. I think they accepted the version I gave them. But it won't hold them for long. They are right on your tail and the sooner you realise it the better. Now I agree with you that they are some way off the "how", but the "who" will do them just fine for now.'

'Fantasy.'

'Fantasy! I'll give you fantasy. Get out your lap-top and look in Bell Lessing's files in Cambridge.'

'What the hell has this got to do with Bell?'

'Just do it, that's all. You'll see what I mean.'

He reluctantly took out his lap-top and opened a modem link to the Cambridge mainframe. 'This is a complete waste of time Thousand. I know Bell's files. And he has got nothing whatever to do with anything. Anyway, his files are all protected. Ten digits. Timed key-strokes. Footprinted. No way in or out without being logged.'

'Well, you don't seem to be having much trouble getting in do you?'

'No, of course not. I've got his Ident. He gave it to me because we work on some things together. I help him with stuff. You know that.'

'Are you in yet?'

'Yes. And all normal.' He was reading off the screen. 'Two directories for the book he's writing. Two of spreadsheets. Two of lecture notes. Normal. Normal. Normal.'

'What about your stuff in there?'

'Yes, all right. In with the spreadsheets. But it's

nothing special. I'm not a complete bloody fool you know.'

'Well, I'm glad to hear that, Simon. And you say that only you and Bell have the Ident?'

'Yes.'

'Are you sure?'

'Pretty much. It's Cambridge. They have to make it hackproof in a place like that. Students are into everything.'

'Perhaps Bell gave the Ident to one of his students?'

'Not Bell. It was all I could do to get him to let me have it. He's pretty slack about a lot of things but it's more than his job is worth to have students crawling all over his files.'

'Well, then. When was the last file access?'

Simon returned to the keyboard.

'Twelve hours ago. One local modem access. Five minutes. No, wait. That's a zero. Fifty minutes. But read only. No file changes. No download. That's bloody odd.' He looked up at her, puzzled.

She leant back and folded her arms. 'And where exactly was your friend Bell twelve hours ago? At his keyboard tap-tapping away? I don't think so. I think you'll find he was where he is now. Flat on his back and out like a light. Hackproof you say? Apparently not.'

Simon held his hands palm up. 'I admit it's odd. I didn't think anyone could get in. There has to be a simple explanation though.'

'Oh, yes. There's a perfectly simple explanation all right. It's just that I don't think you are going to like it very much.'

'Try me.'

'How about someone with massive resources behind them. Who could go in and out of any bloody file anywhere they chose? How about someone five foot six, pouted lips and bottle blonde hair?'

'What's that supposed to mean? It's absurd.'

'Absurd is it? Don't you think it's just a teeny bit odd that she suddenly crawls out of the woodwork after all these years in the very week that yours and Buddy's little experiment comes to light? And in the same week that your office is broken into and Bell's files are opened? And moreover in the selfsame week that Buddy is whisked off to somewhere we can't even telephone him? Let alone me being given five scrambled calls to decipher?'

'She had nothing to do with any of that. Look, I agree that someone is looking at what Buddy and I were doing, but Maddie just happened to be in Cambridge last week. And anyway, she didn't "crawl out of the woodwork", as you so charmingly put it. She's Buddy's sister and she's been around for years. You probably even know her yourself.'

'Oh, yes. I know her all right. And I know what she does. Do you?'

'More or less. She teaches at some university or other. Ohio State I think.'

'Is that what she said?' Thousand put both of her hands flat on the table in front of her and leant forwards. 'Simon, listen to me. She is not a teacher. She does not live in Ohio. She works here in Washington. For the government. And the reason you never see her is because Buddy can't stand her. And why not? Because she's a Sticky Trap. A Goddamn Sticky. Do you know what that is? Do you?'

'Oh, for God's sake Thousand. What world do you live in? Sticky Trap? She's nothing of the sort. She is just someone I met last week. Buddy's sister, yes, but nothing to do with you or Washington or anything. My business. And I'll tell you another thing. In a bad week she was the only decent thing. Leave it.'

'Crap. I tell you, she is the worst thing that has ever happened to you. This week or any week. Walking bad news.'

'Look, Thousand. I don't have to listen to this. I came to see Jake, that's all. Then you march me off here and tell me time's up for Buddy's and my little game. OK. Bad news I admit. But I can live with that. Thank you. But you don't leave it there. You spin off into some fantasy world of file hacking, break-ins and Stickies. Do you want me to call the van and men in white coats now or later?'

Thousand put her hands to the sides of her head and said, 'I should have known better than to try to get through to you. If it wasn't so important I would say I was wasting my time and just walk away. Now stop messing about and tell me what you've told her and when you are seeing her again.'

'Mind your own business on both counts. Nothing whatsoever to do with you. End of conversation.' He leant back and turned his head sideways to look out of the window.

Harvey appeared at the top of the stairs. 'You two

OK? The girl who works the coffee shop says she's not coming in today so I'm not opening up. But I made you a couple of cups downstairs anyway.'

Thousand stood up and took the cups from him. 'Thanks Harvey. That's really sweet of you.'

She returned to the table and sat down.

'I didn't mean to start a row,' she said.

'It's my fault too. I shouldn't have raised my voice.'

'Perhaps it doesn't matter. I tried. I mean you either believe me or you don't.'

'And I'm afraid I don't.'

'I can see that. But there is one other thing I want to say.'

'Fire away.'

'It's just about the people who I think know about you.'

'The mysterious "they".'

'Yes,' she said. 'Well, they're not at all nice. They don't just go around slapping people's wrists. They've got virtually limitless resources. Carte Blanche to do whatever they like. If they want to break in somewhere, they just do it. If they want money, they can have it. And if they want to wreck someone's life, they can do that too.'

Simon put his hands behind his head again. 'Oh yes. That sounds very real world. I can practically hear the film themes in the background. The next thing you're going to say is that it's a Game Without Shadows. Nowhere to Hide. And perhaps one or two of them have a double "O" prefix and are licensed to kill.'

'You wouldn't say that about them if you'd seen what they can do. And what you say is upside down anyway. It doesn't work like that.'

'What doesn't?'

'The last bit. Nobody has a "Licence to Kill". It's just that some people are senior enough for no one to care *what* they do. They are trusted enough to go and get on with things. If a few people fall by the wayside, well, that's all in a day's work isn't it? And before you make another of your glib remarks and dismiss the whole thing, just ask yourself what happened to your friend Bell Lessing.'

'You know that was just an ordinary accident. Hit by a car crossing the road. Not exactly the signature of a top hit squad was it? No. Give me a poison umbrella tip every time if you want to impress me.'

'Perhaps they got it right though. Even his best friend thought it was an accident.'

'Look. He's not dead anyway. He's in hospital. He's coming out.'

She fell quiet and looked out of the window. 'Is he? We'll see.'

Simon looked at his watch. 'Are we done here?'

'I guess so. Finished. I hope you liked the coffee. I hope you like the music. Finito. You are free to go.'

'I'll call by to see Jake in the morning. Can you make me an appointment for about ten?'

'I can try. But it won't do you any good. I told you.'

'And I'll talk to Buddy too. He'll be in the office tomorrow as well.'

'Will he? I think that rather depends on how much

he has to drink tonight, don't you?'

He stood up. 'I don't want us to finish like this Thousand.'

'Well. We'll meet tomorrow then. Let's all have a Goodbye Lunch. You. Me. Buddy. And perhaps you can bring your new girlfriend too?'

He suddenly leant forward and banged his hand on the table. 'And if you ever want to know why all you've got to do in the evening is stand and look out of your bloody windows, well, you play the tape of that last remark again. After all, you're good at tapes aren't you?'

He turned and went down the stairs without looking back.

She sat staring straight ahead in front of her without moving.

Harvey came hesitantly up the staircase. 'Are you all right Thousand? I could hear you two hammering away from downstairs.'

'I'm sorry Harvey. Just a minor disagreement, that's all.'

'I hope so. He's the one you told me about isn't he? He seems a really nice guy. The way you talked about him, I had hopes for you there.'

She smiled at him. 'Yes. He is a very nice guy. But I doubt I'm his type. Blue eyes you see.'

'OK,' said Harvey. 'None of my business. But how about the book? I had a look at it when it came in but it's real propeller head stuff. Way above me.'

She picked up the book and read the title, '*The Application of Large Number Theory to the Game of*

Computer Go.' She smiled again. 'It was just an idea I had.'

'You just have to concentrate. Right?'

'Maybe. But I think my best chance for understanding it just went out the door.'

Harvey picked up the empty cups. 'I got to go. Maybe catch you later on the net. And I hope you two guys patch it up between you. Bye.' He walked over and went down the stairs.

Chapter Nine

Simon had arranged to meet Maddie at the Navy and Marine Memorial at the South end of Columbia Island on the Virginia side of the river. He drove over the Arlington Memorial Bridge and turned left down the slip road to the car park. He left the car and went to sit on a low stone wall overlooking the river.

Colourful dinghies were sailing in and out of the Pentagon Lagoon Yacht Basin behind him. Some turned left past him going upstream towards Roosevelt Island and some made their way across the river to the tidal basin beyond the Riverside Drive bridge.

In the three days he had been away autumn had begun. The trees on the island and the ones across the river in Potomac Park had begun to change colour. The end of summer dark greens were changing to the deep reds and bright yellows of the American fall.

It was his favourite time of year in Washington and he was just beginning to wonder what Ellen would have made of it when he heard Maddie behind him.

The dragonfly brooch was pinned to the lapel of her jacket.

'Hi Simon. You found it OK then?' She was carrying a brown paper bag which she put on the ground between them as she sat down next to him on the wall.

'Not difficult. I've often seen this place from the bridge and wondered what it was. Buddy and I often go up to Arlington when we've had enough of the office.'

'It's not quite Byron's Pool but I guess it's as close as we'll find in Washington.'

'It's fine,' he smiled. 'What's in the bag?'

'A picnic. I thought I owed you one. I hope you haven't had lunch?'

'No. That would be great.'

'All-American. Pizza takeout and a can of Bud.'

'Fine. Food courtesy of Italy. Beer courtesy of Czechoslovakia.'

'Like I said, All-American. And the advantage to you is that I didn't cook it.'

'Are you such a bad cook?'

'Well, let's say I assemble rather than cook. I do a great chocolate mousse. But I'm not sure that would have been right for a picnic!'

'Point taken.'

Maddie grinned. 'I shouldn't have told you that. Rule one, never tell a man you can't cook.'

She passed a can of beer to him and opened one for herself. 'Did you have any luck with your Jake Cohen this morning?'

'I haven't seen him yet. And I don't hold out much hope. Even Thousand thinks I'm wasting my time.'

'What does she know? From what Buddy told me, she's a real misery guts at the best of times.'

'Maybe.'

'Anyway,' she smiled, 'I haven't come to talk about her. I want to ask you a favour.'

Simon took a sip from his can. 'OK.'

'Well. It's to do with that thing you told me about.'

'What thing?'

'You know. The dealing program.'

She drank from her can and put it down between them. 'The thing is this,' she said taking a piece of pizza out of the bag. 'Well, it doesn't sound such a good idea to me.'

'Oh. Why?'

'Correct me if I'm wrong but the bottom line is that it's hacking for profit isn't it?'

'It's a bit more complicated than that.'

'But that's what it comes down to isn't it? You've got some way to take money that isn't yours. Isn't that what it comes to?'

'Well, put like that I suppose you're right.'

She held up her hand and pointed the pizza at him. 'Don't complicate or justify it. In American terms it's putting your hand into someone else's cookie jar. Right?'

'So?'

'So my favour to ask you is this. Just drop it, that's all. Drop it.'

'I can't do that, Maddie. It's not that simple.'

'It is you know. I've been thinking about it. And if you don't stop yourself then someone else will. And if they stop you they'll want their money back. And being American and full of shit, they will get it back.'

'Not if I'm careful.'

'You couldn't be careful enough. I know it sounds possible in theory but, when push comes to shove, you are playing on away turf. You said it was to do with the banks. Hardly a group of kiss-and-make-uppers. I say you are better off without it. Well out.'

'You sounded keen enough back in England. Why the change of heart?'

'I was amazed rather than interested. The way you told me about it at first it seemed quite practical, but I've been putting it in context. It would be dangerous and anyway you don't need the money.'

'Everyone needs money. Particularly me. You forget that, as of now, I don't have a job.'

'Jobs for people like you are not so hard to come by. At least not in America.'

'I wouldn't know that. I live in England.'

'Yes, but you don't have to. Tell me why.'

'Well, I just do. I have a house there. Everything is there. And Lewes is there too, don't forget that. I'm English. We both are.'

'You told me Lewes was at university and you only get to see him in vacations. If you lived over here it would just be a bit further for him to come.'

She took out a cigarette and lit it. 'So,' she went on, 'I think you should consider it. You won't get many more chances. And England, even your precious

Cambridge, is not exactly a roaring success for you just now is it? Come to America and there's lots of opportunities. You could come to Ohio. It's a good university and I know a load of people there. There's a good Agriculture Faculty and I am sure you could get a teaching post.'

He held up his hands. 'Now, slow down, Maddie. It's just not that easy.'

'Yes it is. You've got a Cambridge PhD which is more than any of them. It's a degree to die for here. With that, your experience of irrigation schemes, and a nice reference from Jake, you'd be in.'

'You're crazy. You say Ohio. Frankly I don't even know where Ohio is. I know you live there but that's all I do know.'

'Ohio's OK. That's the name of the state. My university is in Columbus. Now you have heard of that?'

'Yes. But it doesn't mean anything to me. They didn't teach us about America in school and you can only learn so much from Alistair Cooke.'

'Who? Oh, never mind. Well, you can take it from me that it's a nice city and university. Actually, I live about ten miles out. And despite what you've seen on your detective thing, Alistair Cooke or whoever, America's not full of people shooting each other all the time. You think about it now.'

He finished his beer. 'You're a funny girl, Maddie. You know that?'

'You wouldn't even have to sell your house straight away. Let it out for a year. Give it a go. And more important, give yourself a go. Anyway, how am I going to cook you a chocolate mousse if you're the other side of the Atlantic?'

Simon took out a slice of pizza and took a bite. 'Why are you saying all this? You know it's really not on.'

She looked at him seriously. 'It probably does sound unrealistic. But what you were proposing was just as unrealistic wasn't it? Your dealing thing. At least my idea has a bit of substance to it. At our age we're running out of options. If a boxcar with an open door comes by then we have to jump in.'

'But my dealing thing . . . It really is feasible. It's even had a couple of trial runs. It works. I could make some money from it. Your idea is completely off the wall. And I thought I was supposed to be the dreamer.'

'You wouldn't have to leave your thing completely behind. Doing things my way would give you time to finish it and then maybe do it when you were really ready. It's not an either or situation.'

'I only have to do it once,' he said. 'For all you know I could be planning to do it tonight.'

'But you're not are you?'

'No. I have to talk it out with Buddy and I shan't see him until tomorrow. Did you tell him I was coming by the way?'

'No. By the time I tracked his hotel to ground he had checked out. The girl said he was going to the last day of the conference and then flying back. He won't be in till about one, so don't bank on him being in first thing.'

'I won't. And you? How many more days will you be here?'

'None. The last session I have to go to is at three. I'll go direct to the airport and take the five o'clock shuttle to Columbus. Home by eight. What are you doing this afternoon?'

'I hadn't thought. Probably go back and sleep. I think I'll go home tomorrow night.'

She reached out and put her hand on his sleeve. 'Don't just whizz off. Take a couple of days' leave or something. They probably owe you.'

'They do. But I can't just sit around in Washington.'

'I wasn't thinking of Washington. I was thinking of Columbus.'

She saw him look at her. 'Well,' she went on, 'why not? It's all done here isn't it? And maybe I could get Buddy to take a few days too. He likes Columbus and the two of you could get some time together. Look around.'

'One thing at a time, Maddie. I'm just getting used to having no job and I'm not ready to think about anything else.'

'I wasn't suggesting "anything else". Just a few days off. That's all.'

'Besides, I ought to get back. There's still Bell.'

'Bell Lessing? But you can't do much for him can you?'

'Not Bell of course. But Lizzie. I've known them a long time. When something like this happens it throws everybody out. People have to rally round. A bit like you and me for Buddy. They still don't know the details of the accident anyway.'

'What do you mean? I thought he was knocked down by a car.'

'He was. But it doesn't just stop there. They have to find out who did it. Because if he's left incapacitated or he can't go back to work then it's an insurance job. It could be a lot of money. I could help sort out that side of things. I should.'

'Why you?' she asked.

'Because I'm his friend. Lizzie won't know what to do and she'll know she can rely on me to help.'

'I hadn't thought of that. I suppose it's because I don't know him. I only met him the once and actually I didn't like him very much.'

'He's all right really. A bit much at first perhaps. But, as I said, it's not just for him. There's Lizzie and the girls.'

'Girls?'

'Yes. They've got two grown-up daughters. They came up from London the night of the accident. At least one of them will stay there until I get home.'

'I understand.'

'Do you?'

'What's that supposed to mean?'

'Well, do you? He's not just an accident, a statistic. He's part of a family. He has a group of friends and it affects us first-hand. If nothing is the same for Bell again then all our lives are changed too.'

'Yes. But don't be too gloomy. Perhaps he'll be all right. I believe the first few days are crucial.'

Simon and Maddie watched the boats going by

without talking for some time. In the distance a helicopter came in to land on the White House lawn about a mile away. A large airliner passed overhead coming in to land at the airport.

She moved to him and took his hand. 'Do you think you'll miss all this? Washington?'

'I don't know. I haven't had a chance to think about it really. I'm finding out that when you lose your job it's pretty traumatic. Whole slices of your life go with it but you don't notice until the next time you look for them. I think Washington's like that. It's been part of my life for so long now that it's hard to imagine things without it. But places are only the people who live there and, outside of work, I don't really know anybody here. There's only Buddy I suppose.'

'And Jake. And Thousand,' she added.

He smiled. 'I hardly know them. Hardly at all. They'll soon recruit a new Simon. And if Buddy has to go, then a new one of him too. Water closes over your head pretty fast you know. Business as usual.'

'And Costa? What about him?'

'Well. He is one person I definitely won't miss. In fact, I get some comfort from the fact that I never even have to see him or his crew again.'

'Crew?'

'Yes. His entourage. Minders. He never goes anywhere alone. There are always two or three of them with him all the time. Even when we go to a restaurant they have to come along and sit at the next table. Anyone would think we were going to take a pot shot at him any minute.'

'Even if you're not going to, there must be all sorts of people who might. You told me he's into all sorts of things.'

'He is. But if Buddy and I leave, that's Jake's problem. And Thousand's.'

'The Ice Queen. What does she think of your leaving, by the way?'

'Polite disappointment I should say. Not more. She doesn't like you, you know. She said I should be careful of you. Made quite a point of it actually.'

'I've never even met the woman. She doesn't know anything about me.'

Simon looked across at Maddie. 'Well. She says she does. She says she knows all about you.'

'I shouldn't have thought there was all that much to know.'

'She says she looked you up. She says you work for the government. The Agency. Look, I'm just telling you what she said.'

Maddie took out another cigarette and lit it. 'Looked me up did she? On one of her computers? Freedom of Information was it?'

'Well. Do you? Do you work for the government? Tell me.'

'Once. I did once. But it was a long time ago. Twenty years. But government people are all bureaucrats at heart. Once they write something down, it stays written down. He told me at the time they would keep track in case there were any comebacks or anything. He said he didn't think there would be but better to be sure. You see, I was a bit scared at the time it all happened. I thought he said it to comfort me as much as anything. To show Uncle Sam cared.'

Simon looked at her. 'He? I don't know who you mean.'

'Buddy. I mean Buddy,' she said. 'I did it for him. He asked me. Oh, not Buddy as he is now in International Aid, but as he was then. Still in the army. It never came up between you and me so there wasn't any reason to tell you. But, if the Ice Queen has dragged it up, I'll tell you. She may not have much time for me but by the end of what I've got to tell you, you'll understand why I'm not exactly wild about her and her lot either.'

She blew a plume of smoke up into the air.

'Buddy had just come back from Vietnam,' she began. 'I was a student at Columbus. He was in helicopters as you know. And not all regular flights either. His commander at the time, some man with a foreign name, was also responsible for some covert stuff so Buddy had to fly some of that too. I don't know the details and Buddy never told me but I don't think it was very nice. So he couldn't wait to get out of the army. But when Buddy got back to America, this man hauled him in and said he couldn't go yet as there was something else he wanted done. The man said Buddy would get a last-minute promotion out of it and get a bigger pension so Buddy agreed. He thought it would be more flying. It wasn't. The Chief told him to recruit me for a "special operation".'

'The Chief?'

'The man with the funny name. Polish sounding, but he was American.'

'Go on.'

'So Buddy brought me to Washington and they took me down to some underground room or other and sat me at a long wooden table and told me what they wanted me to do. I tell you, it was really creepy. They knew all about me before they started. What I did. Where I lived. Who my friends were. All that sort of thing.'

She flicked her cigarette away and lit another one.

'At Columbus there was a guy in the same class as me they wanted me to get to. A Russian exchange student. Basically they wanted to know what he was up to. Remember it was Reds Under the Beds time and they thought he was some sort of spy or other. He wasn't of course. He was only nineteen for God's sake.'

'So what was he?'

'Ordinary engineer really,' she continued. 'He worked for the power station division of some mega-ministry or other. He was going back to be a software safety engineer. His English was pretty terrible but he spoke French. I'd done French at school so I knew him a bit. I think he was rather lonely. So what they wanted was for me to get to know him better. Go out with him.'

'And you did?'

'Yes. He was called Andrei Gorov. He was nice. I just had to smile at him a couple of times.'

'And was he up to anything?'

'Of course not. Well, only in a way. You see, Andrei knew that when he went home he would have to write software for the safety systems on their reactors. Nothing very secret. They didn't have many computers in those days and the ones they did have were only cobbled together from chips imported illegally or stolen from the West. The chips were all right but he said the computers were unreliable and slow because they didn't have proper operating systems. What he wanted to do was find a fast and reliable operating system. He said if he could do that it could be used as safety software to shut down the reactors if anything went wrong. Without it they would have to rely on mechanical shut-off, which he said was dangerously slow.

'He talked quite openly about it,' she went on. 'It wasn't a secret as far as he was concerned. Not a government thing. Just one of the things he wanted to get from his course at Columbus.'

'So what happened?'

'Nothing, I thought. I spent some time with him. I might have gone out with him anyway. Then one day I was called to Washington to report. I told them more or less what I've told you. I don't think the committee, or whatever it was, knew much about computers so I'm not sure they even understood what I said. I thought that would be it. But when I got back to Columbus the next day, Andrei was gone.'

'Gone?'

'Yes. It was a weekend and so I thought he'd just gone sightseeing or something while I was away, but

275

they said he'd gone on some canoe trip. He'd never done anything like that before but I didn't really think about it until I heard about the accident when the others came back on Sunday night. Apparently they'd all been horsing around at the end of the second day and had had a few beers. They dared each other to go down a particular set of difficult rapids. They all came through all right except Andrei. His body was found two hours later.

'I rang Buddy straight away to tell him about the accident because he'd met Andrei. But he already knew. He said it was all taken care of and not to worry. I asked what he meant and he said that what I'd told them about Andrei backed up what they already knew. He said they were very pleased with me. He said it wasn't an accident. I didn't believe him at first. I mean, no arrest. No trial. Nothing. One day, Andrei. The next, no Andrei. I honestly don't know how I got through. I was as near going mad as I ever want to go. They never told me what they were going to do. Never. Perhaps they knew I would never have agreed. Christ, he was just a student like me. And Andrei was a good person. He just believed in something a bit different, that was all. And do you know what the really sick thing is? It's where he was meant to be going when he got home. Chernobyl. Yes. All he was going to do with his so-called secret operating system was to put in a faster emergency shut-down to the reactors they were trying to build.'

She dropped her cigarette on the ground and pressed it out with her foot.

'So that's it,' she said. 'Maddie's little secret. Now that may make me look some "Agency Person" to Eagle Woman but I think you should make your own mind up.'

'I didn't know Maddie. Of course I didn't.'

'No reason why you should. I was just someone you met. We were just getting to know each other when that witch screams at you to watch out. But it's all right. It's only Washington. Everybody is everybody's business. No shadows. I don't know how Buddy sticks it.'

'I'm sorry, Maddie. I didn't know what it was.'

'Never mind.' She took out another cigarette. Looked at it and then put it away again. 'Well. I didn't see Buddy for a long time after that. I think he was ashamed. And I drifted. Went a bit wild. Then I met Henry and he was older and more sensible. He seemed something to hold on to. We got married and I gradually learnt to block the Andrei thing out. When Buddy and I met up again we didn't talk much about it. He said he'd been as horrified as I had been and he had managed to leave the Army soon afterwards. It never went away altogether but became a sort of nightmare that lived on somewhere in the back of my mind.'

She ran her fingers back through her hair and turned to look out over the river. 'That was all I've ever had to do with the Military. War and that sort of thing. I don't think anything good came from it. But perhaps I understand better how others feel when they come back from war. Nobody wants to ask them

what it was like and they don't want to tell anyone.
Like Buddy and what he did in Vietnam. There is a
whole layer of so many people's lives they try to
forget. At least I know about that now.'

She smiled and turned back to Simon. 'Jake Cohen
was in Washington. Buddy knew him from before
because they'd both been KAs and Jake managed to
wangle Buddy a job in Aid.'

'KAs?' asked Simon.

'Kappa Alphas. It's a sort of club people join at
university. I think it's mainly social but they help each
other get jobs afterwards. Perhaps you've got the
same sort of thing in England.'

'I don't really know. I've never been much of a one
for clubs or societies.'

'Well, as I said, it's a long time ago. I didn't think
anyone would ever hear about it again. Don't forget it
wasn't me that brought it up.'

'No. It was Thousand. She wanted to put me off
you.'

'Did she say why? Probably jealous.'

'Hardly.'

'Why? She's got designs on you hasn't she?'

He laughed. 'I don't think so. You wouldn't say that
if you knew her. She isn't the type to have designs on
anyone.'

'Garbage. Everyone is. Anyway she can't have you.
She's had her chances for long enough. My turn now.'
She leaned across and kissed him on the cheek.

He put his arm around her and she rested her head
on his shoulder.

'And you told me I was the dreamer,' he said.

'It's catching. Oh, I know you are going to say it's going a bit fast but when you get to our age you do have to make your mind up fast. One of the things I did learn from being young is that chances don't go on forever.'

'But you can get hurt that way too. That's another lesson you should have learned.'

She turned her face up with a serious expression on it. 'That's my risk. I thought as I drove down here that if I didn't say or do anything the best thing to happen to me in years would just get on an aeroplane and not come back. It's not easy saying you want to see someone again at the best of times, but bloody impossible over the other side of the world.'

He squeezed her gently and she said, 'So say you'll come to Columbus instead of going home.'

'So you can "have a go"?'

She grinned up and pecked him on the cheek. 'We'll see.'

She looked at her watch. 'Time to go. Out with the notebook and serious expression again.'

She stood up and he held on to her hand. 'Why don't you ring me when you get home. We'll talk about it. If I'm going to Columbus I'll have to change tickets and things.'

'Good. And it'll give me something to look forward to on the boring flight.'

He stood up and put his hands on either side of her face and kissed her. Once on the lips, once on the forehead and once again on the lips. 'Safe journey, little one. See you soon.'

279

When Maddie had gone, Simon sat down on the low wall again. He looked over his shoulder back at Arlington Cemetery as it rose up behind him. The headstones fanned out in neat white rows over the uneven hillside. In the distance he could see the row of seats where he and Buddy had sat at the top. Was it really only three days since he was there? He turned back to the dinghies on the river. They were organising themselves together to get ready for a race. Marker buoys had been set out and soon the boats were streaming up towards Roosevelt Island. He watched as they zigzagged and tacked against the gentle afternoon breeze.

He could see the Lincoln Memorial and the Washington Monument opposite him. Behind them the land rose up towards Mount Pleasant and the Columbia Heights. Thousand Country. They had looked down this way from her flat after visiting Costa. An age ago. Another world. Yes, Maddie was right, chances didn't last for ever. His chances with Thousand had gone a long time ago. Not admitting it to himself had only made her grow to be more important than she should have been. As Maddie said, it was 'her go' now. He smiled to himself at her apparently simple approach to things. Perhaps she was right about that too.

He walked back to his car and drove back to the Arlington Memorial Bridge. As he crossed, he could just see the colourful dinghies below him making their way back to the yacht basin on the second leg of their race.

Chapter Ten

Simon returned to his hotel to find Thousand waiting for him in the lobby.

'Can I see you, Simon? It won't take long. It's about tomorrow.'

'I thought we had said just about everything already.'

'Please.'

'Sure,' he shrugged. 'Shall we have a drink?'

Without waiting for her he walked into the bar. He went directly to a table by the window and sat down overlooking the river. She sat down beside him and neither spoke.

A waiter came. She asked for a glass of orange juice and he ordered a whisky.

'Well?' he said.

'It's not easy. You are not making it easy.'

'I haven't said anything yet. You should see me when I get going.'

'Look, Simon, we've had our row for today. I wasn't looking forward to this but you've got to meet me halfway.'

He shrugged again.

She drew in her breath fully and then breathed out slowly. 'The first bit's easy. I've spoken to Jake and he's meeting Buddy at half ten tomorrow. He thinks that will take about an hour and so he can see you at half eleven. He'll give you about fifteen minutes.'

'Did you tell him what it was about?'

'He already knew. Or guessed. I don't know. I don't think you can expect too much.'

'You said that this morning.'

'Have you got a proposal or something to put to him?'

'I haven't had much time have I? If I had come next week, as I wanted, I might have been able to put something together. As it is I'll just have to do the old seat of the pants trick.'

She put her hand up. 'Don't blame me for that. If KK changed his mind there wouldn't have been any next week.'

'I'm not blaming you. I'm just telling you.'

The drinks came. He stirred his with the plastic stick that came with it. I used to collect these for Lewes, he thought.

He looked out of the window towards Roosevelt Island. Some of the dinghies from the yacht basin were gathering for another race. He picked up his glass and turned back to Thousand. 'Anything else?'

'We won't see each other any more will we? Not after tomorrow,' she said. 'And I won't get a chance to talk to you tomorrow. Not properly.'

THOUSAND

'If you say so. Are we having a goodbye drink? Is that what this is?'

'Yes, Simon. That is what it is. Why have you put up a wall against me? I'll never see you again and you are batting me away.'

She picked up her glass and swirled the ice around. 'Just look at it from my side for a moment,' she said. 'I know you've had a very strange three days. Costa, your job, Bell, the break-in. I don't have to give you a list. Well, I've had a pretty crappy three days too. Costa and Buddy the other night weren't exactly routine for me you know. And then there was the business with the phone calls. I had to deal with all that by myself. And when you and I finally get together to talk, you just push me away. Presumably because of Maddie Booker. Then I try to tell you what I know about her and you knock me away again. Now, she may well be the reason you don't believe a single word I say but I don't think that means you can just flick me off the table. Ask yourself why I should go out of my way like this. Ask yourself why.'

'I am sure you will tell me anyway.'

'Yes. I will then. Once. Once only.' She put her drink carefully down. 'The other night. After we'd been to Costa and went back to my apartment. You remember how we stood looking out of the window over the city? You were different then. I thought we were making progress and I was looking forward to seeing you again. I thought, well, we're not young and we haven't got it all in front of us but there might be something. For us. Despite things. And what you said about "reasons against". That was the nicest thing anyone has ever said to me. But when I had the phone calls to decipher and I heard Maddie was going to see you I began to panic. I wasn't sure what to do. I knew as soon as she was involved, what might eventually happen. You see, she's pretty senior at what she does. They don't wheel her out for something trivial. Maddie Booker means big time. She's like some falcon. They send her out and expect her to come back with blood on her claws and to tell them where it came from. So when I heard she was in Cambridge, I was sick to my stomach. I knew it was *you* she was after. Then came the Bell thing and I thought you would be next. Close. That close. So I had to get you back here as soon as I could. I can't do much to help you but I can do a damn sight more than in Europe. And that's why you are here. Nothing to do with KK or Ginny. To do with me. My idea. And now you won't believe me. So why don't you stop thinking about yourself for a minute and tell me what am I to do? Or even think come to that? But you just sit there with a "not my problem" expression on your face.'

He picked up his glass, took a drink and looked at her for some time before answering.

'Look, Thousand,' he began, 'we can't go over and over this. You and I had our chance a long time ago. Famous Day and all that. And for whatever reason it didn't work out, it just didn't. And I know I spent a lot of time afterwards thinking about it and perhaps you did too. Perhaps we shouldn't have done. Chances don't come round again and again. We had one and we blew it. The only result was that we knew each other better. We had to go on working together which wasn't easy for me at the time but I did it. And, because we know each other so well, we can still call on each other if we have to. You had to call on me for the Costa thing and I was there for you. I would be again. But that's all it is really. Not more. And we can't pretend it was more because, if we were going to come to anything together, we should have done so by now. We haven't.'

He took another sip from his glass. 'Then I meet someone new,' he went on. 'Now it turns out you don't approve of her and so you start on about you and me again. Can't you leave it alone? I've lost my job and I don't think I'll come to Washington again. I'm going to miss Buddy but perhaps I'll see him if he comes to London. And I'll miss you too. But then I always have. I can't do anything about any of it. Sorry. Going round and round it like this isn't helping anyone. Goodbyes are never easy, but that is what this is for us. You are a special person and I hope everything works out for you. I'm sure it will. Look after yourself.'

'You are right,' she said. 'You usually are.'

She stood up to go. 'And thank you for the other night,' she added. 'I owe you one. If you ever need anything you can always find me. I mean that.'

'I know you do. Same here. Can I walk you to your car?'

'No. Please don't. I'll go now.'

He stood up and watched as she walked across the

room. He wondered if she would turn to look at him before she went out. She did, waved, and was gone.

He sat down to finish his whisky. Out on the river behind him the boats were all sailing back to the yacht harbour. The light was beginning to fade and one or two lights were coming on in the tall buildings along the riverfront. Another day in Washington was beginning to close.

Ten floors below street level in the State Department General Warkowski was sitting at the head of the wooden table in the Long Room. He was reading a single sheet of paper when Maddie came in and sat down. Without looking up he said, 'You're late, Major.'

'I had an appointment to meet Northcott and couldn't cancel.'

'I told you to see him as soon as possible after the Lessing incident to gauge his reaction. Why did you disobey?'

'He returned to Washington before I could see him sir. My first chance was this afternoon.'

'Chance, Major? I don't like chance.'

'Opportunity, sir. Opportunity.'

'What did he tell you?'

'As far as he is concerned it was an accident, sir. Dr Northcott has known Lessing for many years and was visibly disturbed but he does accept it was an accident.'

'How many years is "many"?'

'Twenty-two, sir.'

'Better. And it damn near was an accident too. I tell Mildenhall to do a simple take out and the best they can think of is to knock him down with a hire car. I don't know what the fuck they think they are playing at. I have to fly in my own sweep team to finish it.'

'I appreciate that, General, but it's very difficult in England. Cambridge is a very quiet place. I think anything more than a car hit would cause more problems than it would solve. They have very strict gun control laws there.'

'That's their problem. Now give me the rest of your report on Northcott.'

She folded her hands in front of her. 'He's not involved, sir. Lessing was acting alone.'

'How can you be sure?'

'Northcott has neither the aptitude nor the application for anything more than party-trick hacking, sir. Lessing on the other hand has an established academic reputation for complex financial analysis. He wouldn't need an accomplice. I have spoken to Colonel Rolands and he can confirm there were no files of any interest on the disks or PCs we took from Northcott's office. Northcott has not posed a data integrity threat to us at any time. I am sure my brother, Colonel Marlin, would have alerted us if he suspected otherwise.'

'Have you spoken to your brother about this?'

'No, sir. I'm basing my analysis on Major Bradley's work. My brother has been out of Washington.'

'Yes. Good. Well that's it for this time Major. Please stay in Washington for two more days in case we need you. After that you can return to Columbus and resume cover.'

'Thank you. But there is one other thing. Northcott has asked to see me again.'

'What about?'

'Socially, sir. Socially. He wants to visit Columbus with my brother on vacation.'

'The answer's no. This is a security section, not some dating game. Put him off.'

'Yes, sir. But he will ask again.'

'Put him off. Did you hear me? Dismissed.'

'Very good, sir.'

Maddie stood up and Warkowski returned to studying his file. As she reached the door, he looked up. 'One more thing, Major.'

She turned. 'Yes, sir?'

'Nice work Major. Difficult one.'

'Thank you, sir.'

When she had gone a door opened on the opposite side of the room and Rolands and Bradley came in and took seats two down from the General on opposite sides of the table.

Warkowski looked up. 'Did you get all that?'

The two men nodded.

Warkowski turned towards Rolands. 'Your thoughts first, Colonel.'

'From the technical point of view she is correct. There was nothing non-commercial in the data from Northcott's office. We also checked his machine at home and modem-checked his lap-top. All clear. The only files of any interest we found were on Lessing's personal stack in the University mainframe. I want to talk about Lessing's files but I think we can rule out Northcott.'

Warkowski looked across at Bradley. 'Is that what you say? Is it?'

'I would have to agree, sir. I spoke to Major Nocta today sir, and she agrees also. Northcott would not have the ability.'

'Good. What did she come up with on Colonel Marlin?'

'She hasn't found any data anomalies, sir. But that is just from the computer side. She has not made a behavioural approach to the situation.'

'And you have I suppose?'

'Yes, sir. I've studied all his reports, checked his overseas visits for the past two years. Also his Medical files.'

'And?'

'He has a deteriorating record, sir. His private and department spending are more and more erratic. I feel we do have a problem, sir. One that can only become worse.'

'Bradley, do you remember what I told you last week?'

'Sir?'

'Initiative, Major. Initiative. Do you have a problem with that?'

'No, sir.'

'Good. Then show some. Do something about him.'

The General turned back to Rolands. 'So what was

in the Cambridge files? Make it simple so even Bradley here can follow.'

'Very well, General. But I am afraid it *is* a little complicated.'

'I said make it simple. Is that clear?'

'Very good, sir. I have prepared a number of flow diagrams for you,' said Rolands, producing several sheets of paper.

'No diagrams,' interrupted Warkowski. 'If you can't explain something without pictures then you don't understand it and we certainly won't. I keep telling people, this isn't a TV show.'

'Yes, sir. Well, the first thing to know is that the version, or set of procedures we have, may not be the latest ones. Nothing on the files we looked at has a date stamp more recent than six months ago. There may have been developments since then but I think all the fundamentals are in place.'

'Get the up-to-date files,' said Warkowski. 'I don't believe this is a time for speculation.'

'We have looked for them, sir. But I think we are out of time. We have to go on what we have and what we can anticipate.'

'This is beginning to sound as though I'm not going to like what I hear. I hate that.'

'It is not good, sir. I have to say that.'

'Get on with it then.'

'Yes, sir,' began Rolands, pushing his glasses onto the bridge of his nose. 'The first point is an understanding of how the Foreign Exchange, Forex, computer trading works. Now this market, like all others, consists of prices that rise and fall with external pressures. Profit is made by buying at a low price and selling at a higher price. The commodities, in this case, are the twenty-five currencies used for world trade. The principle is the same whatever the market but the chief difference between the Forex and other markets is the speed at which it can operate. That and the fact that nothing physical ever has to change hands.'

Rolands rubbed his hands nervously together in front of him. 'The main players,' he went on, 'are governments, banks and the transnationals. This is because the actual price swings on the markets are small in percentage terms so individual transactions have to be large for there to be any significant profit. Only these big players have sufficient funds. The other users of Forex are much smaller. Say, companies changing money to trade with or even individuals changing money for travel purposes. The fundamental difference between them is that the small players cannot really choose when they trade. It's a service for them and they expect to pay for it. But the big players don't really need the currency changes. They deal simply for profit. When they see a currency move up they buy it and sell it again when it is higher. Their constraint is that if they buy too much at once they will affect the very prices they hope to profit from.'

Warkowski turned to Bradley. 'You getting all this?'

'Yes, sir.'

Rolands tried to ignore the distraction. He knew how much ground he had to cover before the General became bored. Five minutes at most.

He continued. 'At the end of each working day, say six o'clock, the big players have cash in their accounts they cannot use for business until the beginning of the following working day. This "float" money is put on the international Forex markets. Out-of-hours trading takes place mainly by computer. If a price rises, a currency is bought automatically. A sale is made if a price begins to fall. Each of the traders sets a slightly different band for his machine and so the overall market fluctuates around a narrow band of prices.'

Rolands felt he was doing well. He tapped his fingertips together. 'The computers are constantly monitored and they cut out if there is a large market change. The same is true of day trading of course but on the overnight markets this hardly happens and trading is pretty quiet. The players are always the same, the swings are small and everyone is happy.'

He adjusted his glasses before going on. 'This is happening in each of the main markets around the world. London, New York, Tokyo and so on. Now at midnight on each of these markets there is a technical changeover from one day's trading to the next. The markets do not actually close but there is a sort of pause or blip as accounts are settled and a new trading period begins. Now at this point all the big players put their money into one of the big currencies, Dollar, Mark, Yen or Sterling, to "box" it as they say.'

Rolands made the shape of a square in front of him with his fingers.

'I think I remember what shape a box is,' said Warkowski.

'They do this,' Rolands went on, 'because it is possible for a government to close its national bank and players do not want to be caught in a weak currency should this happen. And, if a bank is going to be closed, it will happen at midnight. The end of the trading day.'

Warkowski asked, 'But why would a government close its banks?'

'Two reasons,' replied Rolands. 'Either scheduled closures such as national holidays or for internal political reasons. To hide instability, prevent a commodity crash or sometimes just to make a point. In the more industrialised countries this second type of closure is pretty rare but it happens much more in the smaller countries. On average there is a scheduled or unscheduled bank closure somewhere in the world once every ten or twelve days. So, as I said, the big players "box" their currencies at close of trading. Just in case.

'The net effect of this boxing is a false "popularity" of the big currencies as everyone buys into them all at once at the end of the day. This always causes a fraction of a one per cent rise in the currencies just as the market closes. Not much. But it always happens. Always. Everyone knows about it but they can't take advantage of it because it happens at the very moment the market is actually closing. They can see it but they can't touch it. For some reason they call it the pressed meat in the wrapper.'

'What reason?'

'I believe it is a reference to an incident in a book

about the Chicago Police, sir.'

'What book?'

'I'm not sure,' lied Rolands.

'Well, if you're not sure, don't distract me. Get on.'

'Yes. But the point about the currency boxing is that Lessing found a way to exploit it. He found a way to go into the currencies, strike deals at the boxing and come out again just as the market was closing. Profit every single time and one hundred per cent reliable. No matter what he staked he could always come out ahead because the market was always rising.'

'How? Seems the obvious thing to do. Why can't they all do it?'

'Timing sir. No one else could do it fast enough. He needed several separate but interlocking procedures. All illegal and all quite frankly brilliant.'

Bradley began to chew at some loose skin on one of his thumbs.

'First, sir, he has to enter the dealing system,' said Rolands.

'Hack in?'

'In crude terms, yes. But in a very clever way. Now the actual trading takes place inside the computers of course and he uses side files to gain access.'

'You're getting complicated Rolands.'

'I'm sorry, sir.' He drew in his breath and blew out his cheeks. There was still a way to go.

'A side file,' he continued, 'is like a computer virus, sir. But while a virus uses code to corrupt or alter a program, a side file runs alongside the main program and does not actually alter the main program at all.

The side file "shadows" the main program and whatever it is doing. If the main program is moving files, which is what the Forex computers are essentially doing, the side files can piggy back on this and move a similar set of files. These "passenger" files will end up in the same place as the main files. These side files cannot be detected because they don't impinge on the main program at all. The possible existence of side files has been known for some time and I've read a lot about them but this is the first time they have ever actually been seen. It's a world first, sir.'

Warkowski stretched. 'Got to admire him, haven't you?'

'Lessing, sir?' asked Rolands.

'No. Bradley. You describe a world first and he sits there chewing his nails as if nothing had happened.'

Bradley put his hands back on the table.

Rolands tried to get back to the point. 'Now, his actual dealing is quite simple. Repetitive buying and selling as the currencies rise. But he has to make a massive number of individual deals to make a significant profit and he has to hide all these transactions or he would trip the mainframes.'

'Side files again.'

'No sir. Ring files.'

'Rolands, you are getting complicated again.'

'Sir, if a short file is moved between two computers, say via a satellite link, then there is a time when it has left one computer and not yet arrived at the other one. Like a ball being tossed in the air. The file is in the air just like the ball. What our man Lessing does is to bounce his files from one satellite to another all around the globe back to the first one and then off around the circuit again. These files are not on any computer, sir. These are his transaction files and they repeat his dealing instructions. Buy sell. Buy sell. Buy sell. This ring file quite literally fills up with money as it goes round and round without touching any of the main computers.'

Warkowski looked at Bradley. 'Did you know about all this?'

'No sir. It's very advanced.'

'I'm nearly finished, General,' said Rolands. 'So when the ring file is full he simply drops the money back to bank accounts using another set of side files. There is no way to interrupt any of the three stages. He knows we can't catch him.'

'How much money are we talking about?'

'It's difficult to be sure, sir.'

'You're stalling me.'

'Well, sir. The total overnight float on Forex is five hundred million dollars.'

'Say that again.'

'Five hundred million.'

'I heard you the first time. And how much of this amount is accessible to these ring files?'

Now it was Rolands' turn to pick some skin from one of his fingers.

'I asked how much Rolands, how much?' repeated Warkowski.

'It's difficult to put a precise figure on it, General.'

'I don't pay you to do easy things. Tell me.'

'Well, sir.' Rolands shifted in his chair. 'The point is that there may not be a limit. I'm afraid he could take as much as he wanted.'

Warkowski sat back. 'Good job he's in hospital then isn't it?'

'Sir?'

'Lessing. A good job he's so ill. You can learn from this Bradley. If there's a risk, don't take it. Act.'

'Yes, General.'

Warkowski turned his attention back to Rolands. 'How long have you known all this?'

'Only since this morning, sir.'

'But you told me last week that this was going on. Never more than a few thousand and only on five occasions you said. And now you tell me he can take a stagecoach through your entire system and load it up with five hundred million dollars and go home without you stopping him. Is that right?'

'It does appear that way, sir.'

'Well, you tell me why he didn't do it last time then. Why take a few thousand when he could have taken millions?'

'I have given that some thought, General.'

'Oh good. I'm glad someone has.'

'He may have some technical difficulties with his files, sir. He may not be able to build sufficiently large Drifting Tables to hold all the deals.'

'You didn't mention any Drifting Tables just now.'

'No, sir. But in order to carry out his deals he has to have some place to store the data as it comes off the satellites. He does this in special arrays or tables of numbers. They consist of rows and columns that move in sequence behind and in front of each other. They pass backwards and forwards like the threads in a sheet of cloth. As they move the rows and columns make patterns that store the special large numbers involved. It's like a weaver's loom, sir. But a large Drifting Table is very unstable and I think our man has a limit so he has to restrict his dealing, which is why we've never seen more than a few thousand traded.'

'Any way around?'

'One, sir. The construction of the Drifting Table requires a branch of mathematics called Large Number Theory. Unless he really masters that, the big sums of money remain inaccessible.'

'So are we safe? It doesn't look like he can do it.'

'Unfortunately not. I said at the beginning that the Lessing files from Cambridge are not recent. He may have progressed in six months. My bet is that he has used the time to learn how to float up bigger Drifting Tables.'

'And do you think we caught him in time?'

'There is no way of knowing that, General.'

'Could anyone else do it?'

'Apart from Lessing?'

'That *is* who we are talking about, Colonel.'

'Yes. Well, that is entirely possible. The design and construction I have described is a pretty extraordinary intellectual feat but it just needs a good university-level mathematician to build a big Drifting Table. Once done, the actual execution of the entire sequence is pretty straightforward. It could be done by anyone.'

'So, if Lessing has told anyone else what to do, they could do it without him?'

'It is possible, sir.'

'When could they do it?'

'Once he has the bank access codes? Any time sir. Any midnight market close.'

'And where does he get the bank codes from?'

'If he is as good as I think he is, hacking in to get them would not be a problem for him.'

'Can you stop him? Now you know what is happening?'

Rolands shifted in his chair again. 'As I said, sir, we do know what is happening but we still can't detect it fully. Remember that all this takes place in the last minute of trading. Perhaps less than thirty seconds. We could develop safety software for it but until it is in place we do remain vulnerable.'

'This safety software. How soon could you have it?'

'It's never been tried in this context, sir. An existing system developed for something else would have to be reconfigured and put in the core code of each of the computers controlling the ring of satellites.'

'I didn't ask how. I asked when.'

'Two days sir. My team can have a workable system in two days. I put them on it as soon as I had defragmented the Cambridge files and saw what they could do. Our first version would be pretty crude but it would work. A properly tested system would take a month but in two days I'd say we'd be safe enough.'

'Two days. That takes us over two midnights. Why so long?'

'It's because of the complexity of safety software, sir. It's very elaborate and we don't have an expert. It relies on a specially fast operating system named after the man who developed it. It's called a Gorov system. It was originally designed to protect Soviet nuclear reactors overheating and to shut the reactors off in cases of an emergency. I don't know what happened to the original research but it was never completed. We only have the initial equations to work from but in two days we should have enough to build something.'

Warkowski drummed his fingers on the table in front of him. 'OK,' he said. 'Two days to be safe. What about until then?'

'The ring files,' Rolands resumed. 'We can't ever see them but they *do* draw power from the satellites. I believe we could monitor this power drain and shut it off if the draw is more than the legitimate trading calls for. It would be pretty radical but I am sure it would work.'

'Sounds good to me. What do you say, Bradley?'

'I would have to know if there was a downside before I commented, sir.'

'Would you now?' Warkowski turned back to Rolands. 'Is there one?'

'Unfortunately yes, sir. All the data in transit at the time of power cut-off would be lost. All the normal satellite trading files would go down along with the ring files. They would become corrupted.'

'English, Rolands. English.'

Rolands cupped his hand on either side of his face and put his elbows on the table. 'What I am saying is that all the normal trading at that time would be lost. Whatever banking was going on would be minced. The transactions would be invalidated.'

'Lost? You're saying that money would be lost?'

'Yes.'

'How much?'

'Worst case scenario, General?'

'Worst case.'

'A fifteen-second shut-off in the last minute of trading? It could be up to ten per cent of the total overnight float. That would be twenty-five million lost, sir.'

'Lost as in can't find. Or lost as in lost.'

'Trashed, sir. The net effect of a complete shut-down would be to lose all the files. We might be able to get some of them back but I wouldn't bet on it.'

'And a planned shut-down? If you told the banks in advance?'

'If we went public on this? No file loss sir. But it would be our liability and we would have to compensate them for loss of trading. Just as expensive as the sudden cut-off. But if we do it my way, pull the plug, the insurance companies would have to pay.'

'Do it then. Can you have it in place by tonight? Six hours?'

'Affirmative. I will operate it myself today and tomorrow. After that we should have the Gorov software in place and we're home.'

'I would say this was a close call, Rolands. Wouldn't you?'

'Yes General. Very close.'

'As close as I ever want to be. Do you understand?'

Rolands looked down at his papers.

Bradley spoke. 'But what would you tell the media, sir? If you had to cut off the power unannounced? It would cause chaos. It would be very embarrassing and they would want to know what had happened.'

'Bradley,' said the General patiently, 'I'd say it was an accident. That's what insurance is for. And anyway it wouldn't be me talking to the media. It would be you. You've got a television face.'

'Perhaps it won't come to that, sir.'

'Maybe. But accidents can happen. Gorov himself should have known that.'

'Sir?'

'Before your time, Bradley. Way before.'

Chapter Eleven

After the meeting with Thousand he went up to his room. He showered and took a beer from the fridge over to the window to look out and then draw the curtains for the night. In front of him the Theodore Roosevelt Island lay matt black in front of the Fort Myers and Radnor Heights districts. To their left, and almost out of view, were the rolling slopes of Arlington.

He looked at his watch. Eight o'clock.

The telephone rang. He walked over to the telephone by the bed and sat down before picking up the receiver.

'Simon, it's Ginny. KK wants to know how you are getting on. Can you ring him at home please?'

'Yes,' he answered quietly. 'Anything else?'

'No. Just that. Are you all right?'

'Just tired. But I'll be fine. I've got a couple of meetings tomorrow and I'll check out after that. I may stay on and take a few days' leave so remind KK that I have an open ticket and it won't cost him any extra.'

'But where will you stay? He won't want it on expenses you know.'

'Tell him not to panic. There won't be any bills.'

'Who are you staying with? Not that woman?'

'No, Ginny. With Buddy. OK? Look, I'm very tired. I'll call you in a couple of days.'

He put the telephone back on the bedside table and lay back on the bed holding the beer to his side. He thought he would just have a short nap before Maddie rang.

He fell asleep almost immediately and the beer can rolled off the bed and spilt on the floor.

He did not wake up again until nine o'clock the next morning. The telephone by the bed had rung twice during the night. Once at three o'clock and then again at six. He had not heard it either time.

At about the same time Simon was waking up, Buddy was leaving his house to drive into Washington.

The car following Buddy must have been waiting just north of where the Great Falls Road joined the Leesburg Road at Elkins. Certainly it had not been following from his house at Great Falls, but as he joined the morning traffic he became aware of it three cars behind. A grey Buick Riviera with out-of-state plates. He would not have noticed it at all except that he was driving too fast himself and it was matching him three cars behind. When he thought he was being followed he slowed down and the grey car matched his speed again.

He called the office. 'Thousand, run me a check on a grey Buick, Ohio plates, 317884. And while you're at it ask Jake if he knows anything about a training tail on me.'

'Good morning to you too Buddy. How are we today?'

'Cut it Thousand. Just do it now.'

'Yes Mr Cross. Wrong side of bed today was it?'

'I said cut it and do it.'

'OK. Five minutes.'

'One.'

'OK. OK. I'm doing it now,' she said.

'Good. I'll stay open.'

He was past Swinks Mill now on the long stretch to the Langley Farms junction. He pulled his speed up and down several times. Still three cars behind. Actually they were quite good. Thousand came back on. 'It's a Hire Car, rented in DC last night. Name of Baigent by American Express.'

'Check the card.'

'I'm already on it. No, wait. There is a problem. I'm denied access. Unusual. No. Clear now. And not so good. Card reported stolen at 2 a.m. this morning. Further transactions cancelled.'

'OK. See if it was used at all between the hiring of the car and the report.'

'No. I've got that on screen now. Not used.'

'Shit. Who steals a card and uses it once? It should have been used dozens of times.'

'It may not have been stolen at all. The hirer could be Baigent himself.'

'Like hell. Check the signature.'

'That's not on screen. I'll have to call Amex direct and then need Jake's authorisation.'

'Can you get it?'

'No. He's gone into a meeting. No calls. I can't disturb him.'

'Like hell you can't.'

'Not for this. Buddy, you know I can't. He'd go wild. Particularly after last week.'

'He'd go a lot wilder if he thought I was being followed by someone we don't know in a stolen card car. Just ask him.'

'I can try.'

'Good. Meanwhile check out this Baigent character. Can you screen his Amex references?'

'What do you want me to do first? Baigent or Jake?'

'I don't know. Yes. Stuff Jake. He'd probably say no anyway. Just get me something on Baigent.'

'It's coming now. Baigent. George. Age 48. Address 187 Sidney Heights, Huntington, Fairfax County.'

'That's near here isn't it?'

'Not far. Your side of the river. South of Alexandria just over the Southern Railway yards. But it's not a residential area. Must be a business address. Don't go there Buddy. Stay in traffic.'

'Why?'

'You don't know what they want.'

'So?'

'Well, don't lead them onto their own ground. Stay safe.'

'Safe? What the hell do you mean?'

'Buddy. Think. If they know you well enough to know where you live then they know where you work. So they're not following you to see where you go. And they already know you know they are follow-ing you.'

'So what's the point in following me if they know where I am going?'

'Try to get a look at them. Who is it?'

'OK then.' He suddenly pulled out well into the middle of the road, braked hard and cut into the traffic one behind the Buick. It immediately tried to pull away but not before Buddy had looked in.

'One guy now. The one in the back must have ducked down.'

'This is weird. I think you should try to lose them. Where are you?'

'I'm coming out of Shrewdly.'

'OK. Go over the Key Bridge towards Pennsylvania Avenue. Then right down twenty-third. I think that's your normal route to the Department.'

'Yes, but where does that get us?'

'Just do what I say. Where is the car now?'

'Back to three cars behind. You know we really should hire this one, he's pretty good.'

'Many a true word. Are you on the bridge yet?'

'Just coming on.'

'OK. There's more stuff coming on Baigent now. Yes, 48, Fairfax County. Born Illinois. Married. No children. Business is called Fairfax Timber. Regular Tax returns. Three credit cards. Amex. Diners. Visa. Joint loan on a house with his wife but 90 per cent in her name. No police record. Regular guy.'

'Check his other cards. Where were they last used. And I'm coming off the bridge now.'

'Right. Now keep to the river till you get to the Memorial Bridge, then go back over the river and back up Lee Highway to Key Bridge again. Go round a few times. It'll buy us time. Right, card details coming up. Never uses Diners and hardly ever Amex. All Visa. Gas, shops, that sort of thing.'

'But he took out the car with Amex. I don't think I'm going to like this.'

'Me neither. And there is something else not nice. Apart from the hiring of the car there has been no card use for three months.'

'Did he book the car in person or by phone?'

'Wait.'

Buddy turned back over Arlington Bridge.'

'Phone, Buddy. Sorry.'

'You know what to check next.'

'Hospitals. Doing it now. Here it comes. Bad news. Baigent, George, admitted Illinois Memorial ten days ago. Stroke. Sorry.'

'Forget it. Check the hire car again. See if it has a phone, then patch me in. I want to know what's going on.'

'It's on the screen. There is a phone but I can't get the number. Restricted access.'

'Use a higher priority.'

'I'm on yours as it is.'

'Thanks for asking. Try Jake's.'

'I don't know the Ident.'

'You didn't know mine till you needed it. Just do it.'

'All right. All right.'

Back over Key Bridge.

THOUSAND

Thousand spoke again: 'I've got the number but I can't patch it from here. You'll have to dial it yourself.'

'Better still,' he said, 'you call them. Find out what you can. And while he's on the phone I'll try to lose him.'

'You wish.'

'I wish. Shit. Missed the turn. I'll have to go East on Independence then back West along Constitution.'

'It's engaged.'

'Great. Then I want the log on all calls in DC. Yes all. I want to know who is calling him and from where. All lines.'

'I'll book the log. But I won't get it yet. There is no way I can scan it now. It'll have to wait.'

'I don't think I have till the tenth of never. And while you're at it get the entry log from the State Department in the last twelve hours. Get security to hold the tapes. I want nothing wiped since midnight. And now I'm going back west on Constitution. I'll go over Highway Bridge and try to lose them in Clarendon or Ballston. It's hopeless on these big roads.'

'OK. I've booked the logs but what for I don't know.'

'Look, you're sitting this one out, I'm on the dance floor with these people. And they're good enough to be ours. I just want to know if they are. Now listen, I'm on Washington Boulevard. I'll follow it all the way to Ballston and then cut right into Waverley Hills. Then I'll lose them.'

'With you. Do you want me to try for a road block anywhere?'

'No time, sweetie is there?'

'No.'

'Thanks anyway.'

Buddy accelerated as the wide curve of the Washington Boulevard began. By the time he passed Columbia Pike he was doing ninety. Still the Grey Buick matched him.

'He's still engaged Buddy.'

'So what do you think clever girl?'

'You first.'

'OK. Well he doesn't need to follow me to know where I'm going because he already knows. But then if they know that they know my car phone so he could call if he wanted to talk.'

'Yes, I'm afraid so.'

'So it's not talkie talkie for them today is it? They want one to one and then one to none don't they?'

'So what are you carrying?'

'The Walther P37. It's in my case on the back seat.'

'Loaded?'

'Yes. But still on the back seat.'

'Can you reach it?'

'Thousand darling, I'm doing ninety.'

'Sorry. Then you'll just have to grab it as best you can in Ballston or Clarendon.'

'Maybe. But I've seen the needle and I'm practically out of gas. I'll have to go round the circle to take the Jefferson Davis to the rail yards.'

'Why for God's sake?'

'If I go there they'll know I know about the Baigent thing. It'll force them to do something before they want to.'

'I thought you wanted to lose them.'

'I did.'

'And now?'

'Look, it would only be till the next time. And that time they might be more careful. I have once to find out what this is about. Who they are. OK, I'm going down the highway now. Only about five minutes from the yards. I might even get there before I run out of gas. I can see them again now. I can see him! It's Bradley! The one in the back who ducked down. It's Bradley.'

'Buddy are you sure? You have to be sure.'

'Yes. It was him. I know it was him.'

'Then it's bad. Lose them. For Christ's sake lose him. Just lose him.'

'Jesus. Call Jake. Ask him what the hell's going on.'

'Done it. Log's on line now. Bradley came in at eight this morning. The system says he's still in the Department. Look, are you sure it's him?'

'Don't waste my time Thousand.'

'Well, look at the driver. Describe him. Do you know him?'

'No. Tall guy. Dark. Creole? Too pale but still looks it. Pocky face. Ugly bugger.'

'Could be Buller. New in with Bradley. Same office. Wait. Their line is open now. Who calls?'

'I do. Give me the number.'

He punched it out as soon as she gave it to him. It rang twice and he saw the driver pick up the handset.

Buddy shouted. 'Buller, you shit, I've got your fucking number!' He saw the driver react visibly and call over his shoulder. Buddy immediately redialled Thousand.

'Yup. It's them. Chips are all down. They're trying to draw level now. The game bit's over. I'll have to do what I can in the yard. I'll take the Walther and leg it. Maybe I can lose them in the trains.'

'Don't be a fool. Stay in traffic. I'll get a chopper to you. They won't try anything in traffic. You're safest there.'

As she spoke the rear window of Buddy's car crazed over except for a neat hole in the middle.

'Like shit, Thousand. If this is safe, I'll go risk it in the train yard.'

'If you have to. But the chopper is on its way. I'll send it riverside. Try to make it to there. It'll find you.'

'I wish.'

'Me too.'

Buddy pulled off the highway and slid down an embankment towards the rail yard. The car crashed through a wire fence and began to move over the train tracks. The Buick followed. Buddy's car bumped over the first set of rails. His case fell off the back seat onto the floor. No reaching it now.

Then the gas ran out. The Buick drew level and the side window was lowered.

Buddy lay flat and opened the opposite door and slid out. He crouched around to the back of the car and then ran doubled up towards the waiting shelter of a row of boxcars. An impossible hundred yards away.

Bradley stepped unhurriedly out of the Buick and

pointed towards the running man for the driver. The dark man climbed out of the car and smiled. He raised a pistol at arm's length between both hands and fired. Buddy's right leg gave out and he fell immediately, not even halfway to the train.

Bradley leaned into Buddy's car and picked up the handset and put it to his face. 'Sorry, caller. Connection closed.' Then he hung it back on its cradle and began walking to where Buddy lay clutching his knee and trying to crawl away. Bradley took his own gun out of his pocket. And smiled. He was going to get to see the expression on Buddy's face after all.

In the office Thousand heard Bradley speak and the line go dead. She stared dumbly at the screens in front of her without moving.

Jake Cohen burst into Thousand's office. 'What the hell's going on, Nocta? I've just had a panic call from Rolands in Central Data. He says you've got four level-six datastreams open and two of them are on my Ident. Now you tell me what this is about and you tell me now!'

She turned very slowly around and looked up at him. 'Officer down, Jake. Officer down.'

The helicopter found Buddy about ten minutes later. But the grey Buick was gone. The pilot spotted Buddy's car first and then the body about fifty yards away. It was lying on its back. Arms wide. At first the pilot thought the head was lying in a pool of oil. But no, not oil. Too pale. Not the right colour at all.

By then Simon had had another bath to wake himself

up properly and was standing by the bed about to dial room service for some fresh coffee when he noticed the small winking light on the telephone. Messages.

He called the switchboard and asked the girl to play the calls back for him.

First was Maddie, 'Hi there! My flight was held up for four miserable hours in miserable Chicago. I could have practically walked here in that time. Anyway, I'm here now but you're not. Perhaps you and Buddy are out on the town? I hope not! Anyway, ring me in the morning and we can work out flights and things. Looking forward to it. Bye.'

The second caller was a voice he didn't recognise immediately. 'Hello? Is that a message machine? It's me. Nancy. Nancy Lessing. Cambridge. Can you ring me back? It's daddy. It's about Daddy.'

He sat down on the bed and dialled Bell Lessing's home number. Nancy answered.

'Simon here. Is everything all right?'

'No. No it's not.'

He could tell from her voice what she was going to say next. He put his hand over his forehead. 'Has he gone?' he could hear himself asking.

'Yes. Last night. I tried to ring you at about one o'clock. But Simon it was awful. Just awful.' She was beginning to cry.

'Oh, I'm so sorry, darling,' he said. 'I'm so very sorry. He was so badly hurt. He could never have mended himself.'

'But that isn't the awful part. It's what happened before he died. We didn't know what was going on.

We would never have agreed to him being moved. And now they won't tell us anything at all.'

'I don't understand. What are you saying?'

'It all happened about eleven o'clock. Mummy had come home to rest but couldn't and said she would be better just sitting with him. She says she doesn't remember exactly what happened because of all the pills she is on but she says she does remember the men coming. Two doctors. They said they were American, she remembers that. And they had come in an ambulance to take him somewhere for specialist treatment. She remembers telling them that he wasn't to be moved at all but they said it was all right because they had spoken to the college and she was to go to the nurses' station and sign some papers. It had all been agreed, they said. So she went to talk to the nurse but she wasn't there and Mummy couldn't find her. So she went to the next ward and the nurse there said she didn't know anything about any transfer and went with Mummy back to where Daddy was. She said he looked the same but the machine above his head had stopped beeping and the nurse called a crash team and they came but it was too late. Mummy says she doesn't remember much about what happened after that. The proper nurse came back and said she had just been in the side ward and why hadn't Mummy seen her? Then the other nurse rang me and of course I went straight down. But they had taken him away by then and wouldn't let me see him.'

Simon stood up and looked numbly out into the grey morning light.

'So Mummy and I came back here and tried to call the college,' Nancy was saying. 'We couldn't get through to anyone except the manciple for ages and when we did they said they didn't know anything about any Americans transferring Daddy anywhere.'

Simon ran his fingers through his hair and gripped a bunch of it on the top of his head.

'I don't know what's happened,' she said, beginning to cry. 'Do you think it is one of those terrible mix-ups you read about?'

'I'm sure it wasn't, Nancy. You know he had the best possible care but I'll come straight back to help you sort things out. If I take an afternoon flight I should be with you tomorrow sometime.'

'Would you, Simon? I don't know what to do.'

'Don't worry,' he said, trying to comfort her. 'That's the important thing. I'm sure there is a perfectly simple explanation. You just look after your mother and ring the rest of the family if you can. I'll come back as soon as I can, darling.'

He put the phone down. He could hear himself saying the words again to Nancy: 'A perfectly simple explanation.' And what was it Thousand had said? 'Oh, yes. There is a perfectly simple explanation. It's just that you're not going to like it much.'

He dialled Buddy's number. Buddy would know what to do. No reply.

Simon then called the airline and converted his open ticket to a confirmed seat on the five o'clock flight to London.

He was about to ring the office but decided he had

better go in and talk to Buddy in person. And Thousand. Thousand. Christ, what a mess.

He had just put the telephone down and had stood up when it rang again. It was Jake Cohen.

'Simon. Jake. I have some bad news. Buddy Marlin has been shot. I think you had better come in. Help see to Thousand. Hello? Are you there? Simon?'

'I'm here, Jake. Yes. I'm here. What happened? Costa?'

'Just come in.'

'Ten minutes.'

Chapter Twelve

When Simon arrived at the State Department, he went straight to Thousand's office. She was sitting at her desk reading a file.

'I came as soon as I could,' he said. 'Were you here when it happened?'

'Yes. He was driving in from home. They were following him. I don't think he had a chance.'

'Costa? Was it Costa?'

'No. I thought that at first, but it wasn't them.'

'Who then?'

'Later, Simon.'

'Someone like Costa then? Perhaps there are others.'

'No. I said, later.'

Simon sat down in the armchair against the wall. 'But I have bad news for you too. Bell. They got Bell Lessing.'

She did not look surprised. 'In the hospital?'

'Yes. You were right. You know, I don't think I can take all of this in. Bell and Buddy in one day. It doesn't seem possible.'

She put the file in a desk drawer. 'It's all too

possible, I'm afraid. They were part of the same sequence. I did tell you what these people were like.'

'Well, I want none of it. I don't want to hear about "sequences" or "quite simple explanations". I want to go home. I'm done here. Completely.'

'Just go back to Cambridge, you mean?'

'Not "just". I live there. Home base. I belong there, not here.'

She locked the drawer and looked up at him. 'I don't think you should do that. It's not finished. You can't go until it's finished.'

'Yes it is,' he said. 'Look, these two men were my friends. It is finished for them, then it's finished for me too. I think they were both killed because they knew me. So it was my fault. I have to go home and decide what to do.'

'No,' she began, 'I don't think you can do that until you know what's been going on. When you know it all, you won't feel so bad. Believe me, none of this is your fault. You can't blame yourself. It's part of something else. You have to go on.'

'Like hell I do. It's not some sort of bloody game. Now, I have no idea what this "something else" is that you talk about. All I know is that last week two good men were alive and now they are not. I can't just stand up and dust myself off after something like that. In four days I've lost just about everything. Remember, I used to have a job as well.'

'I think you are feeling sorry for yourself and not them.'

'Not true,' he returned. 'I have a lot to do. Bell's

family need me. I can try to make it up to them. I'm going to wrap things up here and go out on a flight this evening. Is Jake here?'

'No. And he won't be. The shit really hit the fan with this Buddy thing. It's going to take a hell of a lot of work. But of course that's nothing to do with you is it? Your best friend is shot but you can leave it to good old Jake and Thousand to sort out can't you? It must be nice to be able to pick up sticks and walk out. You can go home and make yourself a pot of tea if you like. But I have to stay here. Sort out the mess. And maybe I can deal with Costa too. That would be nice for you wouldn't it? And Maddie Booker. Why don't I tidy that up for you too? Meanwhile, you go off and have a good old cry. Perhaps you'll feel better. Opt out, Simon. Go on, opt out.'

Simon stood up and walked over to the window without speaking before he turned to face her.

'I'm not opting out, Thousand. I was never in. All sorts of things have been going on but I didn't know about any of it. And whatever it was, it seems to have got my two best friends killed. And that's hardly an advertisement for wanting to know more. For all I know, I could be next. Not attractive.'

'And me,' she said holding her hands out. 'What if I were killed? Again because of you? Would you just walk away from that too? Tell me how many people you want shot before you take any notice. Just so I know.'

'Nobody is going to shoot you.'

'Why not? If the sole criterion for being shot is

knowing you, then I must be pretty far up the line.'

'Well, that's only another reason for me going. To put distance between us.'

'Distance? Didn't do your friend Bell much good. What could be further away than being a university teacher in Cambridge? No. I think I'm in line. And what's more, you are too. Now, you can either walk away and wait for them to come and find you or you can stay and help me. And they will come. Not one day. But real soon. For you and me both. So what are you going to do about it?'

Simon stood up and looked at her. 'I need a drink. Has Buddy got a bottle in his desk?'

'You don't need a drink. And as far as his desk is concerned I think you should go and take a look. It will help you make your mind up.'

'What do you mean?'

'Go and look. That's all.'

Simon walked through the door between Thousand's and Buddy's office. 'He always keeps a bottle in his desk. Used to anyway.'

But Buddy's desk drawers were all empty. The top of his desk was clear also.

'What's happened?' he called. 'Where is all his stuff?'

'Well,' she said, 'someone whirled in here ten minutes after he was shot and stuffed it all into a plastic sack and whirled out again. And not just his desk. All his disks and back-up tapes. I don't know why she didn't take the bloody filing cabinet. Perhaps she'll be back.'

'She? Who?'

'Oh, didn't I say? His ever-loving sister, you know the one with blood up to her elbows.'

'What the hell has she got to do with this? She may have had something to do with Bell, but it's lunacy to say she had anything to do with Buddy's death. She was his sister for God's sake. Family.'

' "Family"?' said Thousand calling through to him. 'Funny. That's more or less what she said when I asked what the hell she was doing, who she was acting for. "I don't act for anyone", she spat. "You lot have had all you're going to get from my brother. He may be going to Arlington with the rest of them, but everything else comes home with me. And if that bastard in the cellar wants it back, tell him to come looking for Maddie Booker, OK?" '

Simon came quietly back into the office and sat down again.

'So, Simon,' began Thousand, 'it seems your new friend has become a bit of a self-appointed wild card. And I don't think that will be particularly popular.'

'I didn't know she was in Washington,' he said quietly. 'She rang me last night from Columbus.'

Thousand quickly picked up a telephone in front of her and spoke into it without dialling, ' "Hello, Simon, Maddie here. I'm in Columbus. Byee." Just like that was it? Very convincing.' She put the phone down.

'I didn't have any reason to think she was here. Look, I admit I was wrong about her. Big mistake. OK. But there isn't very much I can do about it is there? On this week's disaster scale of nought to ten, she only rates a four.'

'Don't feel bad about it, Simon. She's the best they have at what she does. Take it as a compliment that they sent her after you and not some bimbo. But as you say, she can wait. We have more important things to do.'

'We?'

'Yes. You and me. I can't go on asking you. Will you help me or not?'

'What exactly do you want to do?'

She stood up and went over to take her favourite position with her back to the window and arms folded.

'I'll tell you what I want to do. I want to hit them so hard they will never know what hit them. I want to bang their fucking heads together so hard they never wake up. I want to do it today. And I want you to help. For Buddy. For Bell. For all the others. Now are you in or are you out?'

He leaned back and matched her by folding his arms. 'In,' he said. 'In up to my neck.'

'Good,' she said briskly. 'Let's get going then. But first, I've some explaining to do. Can we get out of here?'

'Sure. Why not? The bookshop for coffee again?'

'No. Arlington.'

'Why there?'

'It's where you and Buddy went isn't it? And it's Buddy I want to talk about. And me. Come on, I'll drive.'

They took the car from the basement car park and drove without talking further until she had parked in the bottom car park and they were walking up to the top of the cemetery by Roosevelt and William Drive.

She took his hand and said, 'Buddy used to love coming here with you. He always said it was a place apart. I think he used it as a sort of yardstick to measure his life by.'

She smiled at Simon and continued, 'He said that decisions made here were usually right and his mistakes all happened back in the office.'

'We both liked it,' said Simon. 'We came here first because of Kennedy and then when that wore off we just kept on coming. I think some of his people from Vietnam are here but he never said.'

'They are. I know that. But the one person in the world he most wanted six feet down isn't here.'

'Warkowski.'

'Yes,' she said, surprised. 'Do you know him?'

'No. But we saw him here last week. Buddy said he was his commander in Saigon. He thought he had retired but we saw him at a funeral of someone or other.'

They came to the Canadian Memorial and sat down on the grass looking towards the river.

'Janislav Freeman Warkowski,' she said. 'That's his full name. He was head of covert operations during the fall of Saigon. When he came back here, he was given a security job at the Pentagon.'

'Buddy couldn't get a job when he came back,' she continued, 'so Warkowski persuaded him to stay on and work for him. I think Warkowski was a bit too extreme even for the Pentagon types so they set him up with Jake in the State Department and told him to get on with things.'

'What sort of things?'

'It's called General Security now. Basically its role is to gather and filter as much information about all Externals as it can.'

'External whats?'

'Governments, oppositions, governments in exile. Terrorist groups. Stuff like that.' She waved her hand generally. 'They have to place agents in various countries and then take their data and filter it for the Politicals in the State Department.'

'How long did it last? I don't think they do anything like that now.'

She smiled. 'Oh, yes. I'm afraid they do. Your General Warkowski is a very busy man and Jake very much still reports to him.'

'And Buddy? But Buddy hated the Military. And that was mainly because of Warkowski himself from what I remember.'

'Well. That's true,' she continued. 'But he still had to work for him. Remember he didn't have many options. There wasn't much call for someone whose main claim to fame was that he could fly a helicopter backwards through a hail of bullets. So Buddy and Jake began setting up listening posts in various countries.'

She leant her head backwards and looked up at the clouds. 'And then you came along. It seemed too good to be true. Genuine cover. Someone already known in their target countries. They could follow you into dozens of places and set up depots and fill them with Americans and tame nationals.'

'But we did proper work,' he said. 'I mean the schemes. They were real enough. In the early years we did pretty well. Thailand, Pakistan. Quite a lot actually.'

'Oh, yes,' she replied. 'That part of it was real enough. You were good cover. The best.'

'You know what you are saying don't you? That I've been making a complete fool of myself for ten years. I worked jolly hard at those schemes and now you are telling me it was just a charade for their benefit.'

'Sorry.'

'But some good came of it. The schemes we set up are still in operation. Please don't say it was a complete waste of time. Not on top of everything else.'

She put her hands in front of her mouth and blew through her fingers before replying. 'Well, it wasn't a complete waste. You and your "Fighting for Strangers" was something Buddy could appreciate. I guess that working with you made him think that in some small way he was making up for the whole Vietnam thing. And sure, the projects you set up together were real enough. The money spent on them was genuine US Aid money but I'm just saying the main reason Buddy and you set up where you did was so that Jake could put in *his* people afterwards. From your point of view it all worked just as it would have done under a genuine set-up. I don't think you need feel bad about it. As you say, in the early years you did pretty well.'

'And what was your role in all this? Do you work for Warkowski too?'

'Oh yes. We all do. I had to help you and Buddy get things going but the main thing is helping Jake with all the data processing afterwards. You once asked what Jake did all day. Now you know. He's not at all the idle man he pretends to be.

'Don't get me wrong,' she went on. 'I liked working on the pumps with you and Buddy. And he did too. Much more than the other business. It made it worth-while for him. And for me too. Did you really have no idea what was going on?'

'No. None. You must think I'm particularly stupid.'

'Not at all. You are your own man, which is more than the rest of us can say. Warkowski, Jake, Buddy. Me even. We all belong to someone else. We have to live and act within what other people want. We go along. Don't ask questions. But you are self-contained and can be what you want. The rest of us can't be that. Everyone admires a free man.'

'Didn't get me very far though, did it?' he mused. 'I haven't got around me the things you are meant to at my age. Family. Job. And now my good friends are blown away. Free? Perhaps. But the price has been pretty high.'

'You only pay for freedom once, Simon. Captivity costs you something every day. You see, when you are done with all of this, you can at least say, "I did what I thought was best at the time", but the rest of us have to say, "I knew what I was doing was wrong but I went on doing it". Given the choice again, I know what I'd choose.'

She sat forwards and put her arms around her knees. 'Would you have gone on working for us if you had known what we did?'

'No. I don't think so. But tell me, is that why you wouldn't go out with me? Because of what you did?'

'Yes. I wanted to. Of course I did. But I couldn't have ever told you what I did and couldn't have gone on and on with a double life. And I did want to go out with you. More than you know.'

He sat up and put his arm around her. 'I wish you had. Even if it hadn't lasted we would have had some time together. And, when you look back, it's only the special times that mean anything. An hour here or there. That's all. Not many people get more.'

She turned her face to him. 'But it's not really about time is it? The very few times we've had together. Like this. They seem outside time. Not slower or faster, but just different. I think you are a special person. I'm glad I know you.'

He kissed her gently on the forehead. 'It's the same for me. I remember each hour I have spent with you. And should I grow old, then I could never be poor, counting those hours again and again.'

She smiled at him and kissed him briefly on the lips. 'We could sit here all day, Simon. But you and I have work to do. And I'm not finished telling you things yet.'

'What's left now?'

'Maddie.'

'Oh. I'm not sure I want to know any more.'

'Well let me ask you something about her. It's this. Does she know?'

'Know what?'

'About your scam?'

'Well, enough to finger Bell Lessing. Of course she knows.'

'But your involvement. Or does she think it was Bell's baby?'

'It was for all you know,' he said.

'No it wasn't. It was your idea, all along. I saw the files Warkowski had fished in from Cambridge. Bell's parts were rubbish. The only good parts were yours.'

'I didn't think Bell had a proper copy of anything. Nothing recent anyway.'

'Recent or not. It was on there. The procedures. The side files, ring files, Drifting Tables. The lot. Didn't you know?'

'No. No, I didn't. He must have poached them from my PC by modem when I used to keep them there. Or even my lap-top. I don't have it keyed in anywhere now because I know it all. I didn't think there were any copies left.'

'Well, he had one. And now so does Rolands.'

'Who's he? Another of Warkowski's people?'

'Yes. He's Head of Data. He's pretty good and I think he's put together what you did from the Bell files. Sorry. The cat's out of the bag.'

Simon picked a blade of grass and began rolling it backwards and forwards between his fingers.

'Oh, well. It doesn't really matter,' he said.

'Why?'

'Well, Bell Lessing was killed because of it and Buddy too. I think I get the message.'

'Bell, yes. But you don't know that was why Buddy was shot.'

'Oh, come on!'

'No. I know why Buddy was taken out and that's not it. And you haven't even asked me who did it yet.'

'OK. Who was it then?' he asked.

'Right. Just assume for a moment it was Costa.'

'I thought you said it wasn't him.'

'It wasn't. But if it had been, you wouldn't have been surprised would you? You'd think Buddy had crossed him one too many times. Say, something you didn't know about.'

'That's right. I wouldn't have been surprised. I've seen enough of Costa over the last couple of years to know he does more or less as he pleases regardless of people. You can't get where he is otherwise.'

She leaned forward and hugged her knees again.

'Well, Warkowski's like that,' she said. 'He does what he wants to as well. Always has.'

'But he's Military. Government. He wouldn't do stuff like that. Besides, Buddy was one of his own people for God's sake.'

'But it's true. Buddy was becoming a liability. Drinking. Erratic. And that business the other night was the last straw.'

'So he just had him shot?'

'More or less.'

'There is no more or less about shooting people.'

'Perhaps there is. I think Warkowski told one of his people that Buddy was beginning to be a real problem and that someone went off and did something about it.'

'What kind of person would do a thing like that?'

She looked directly at Simon. 'Someone like Bradley.'

'Oh, no. That's too much.'

'Is it? That file I was reading when you came in this morning. It was Bradley's so-called appraisal of Buddy. You should read it sometime.'

'God, Thousand, you paint a pretty bleak picture of Warkowski and his merry men. How can you bear to be a part of it? And Buddy? How did he stick it?'

'He found a way around it.'

'What?'

'He drank. A lot.'

'And you? What do you do?'

She did not answer immediately but stood up and started walking down the slope.

'Come with me,' she said. 'There is something I want to show you.'

They crossed down to the part of the cemetery Simon recognised as where Buddy had pointed out Warkowski. There was a row of recent graves forming a row away from the path. She pointed to the space beyond the last one.

'That's where Buddy will go. There. And over there,' she pointed up the hill, 'is where his crew from Vietnam are. Six of them. He told me about them one night when he was very drunk. I don't know what really happened but he blamed himself for their deaths. He said he felt guilty that he came back and they didn't. He always though the Vietnam thing was completely pointless but he said he owed it to them to stay on in case he could ever do something useful. Make it up to them in some way.'

'And he thought working with Warkowski was the way to do it?'

'No. He thought working with you was the way to do it.'

'Me? Why me?'

'Because he believed you thought what you were doing was for the best. He never found anything right and fair in his own life and so he settled for doing it secondhand through you.'

'And you?' he asked.

'The same I guess.'

'I'm sorry. I would have worked harder if I'd known. You make me feel guilty I didn't do more work. I think I've been a bit idle really.'

'I didn't tell you to make you feel guilty. I told you so you would know how I feel about Warkowski now that Buddy has gone.'

'I think I do understand. But you still have to work for him.'

'Do I?' she asked. 'If ever I needed an excuse to quit, then today is it. At the very least they'd expect me to take some leave. I've been making noises to Jake that I wanted to go for some time. I've stuck it longer than anyone.'

'And Jake himself? What will he do?'

'Go on. For a while anyway. He's only eighteen months off retirement. It rather depends on whether they replace Buddy. And that probably depends if United replace you.'

Simon smiled to himself. 'I'm not sure that they will. Not right away anyway.'

'Well. The listening posts are just about all in place. Someone just has to monitor them and replace them if they break down. Boring housework really. With any luck they'll make Bradley do it.'

'But can he stay? After this?'

'Sure. Why not? Buddy isn't the first person he's taken out. I know personally of at least two others. One was a Spanish journalist in El Salvador and the other was a West Coast law professor with views on immigration Warkowski didn't like. I'm not sure if you want to know but that one was one of Maddie Booker's pulls.'

'Thanks. But I've already got the message.'

He took her hand and started back up McKinley Drive towards the amphitheatre. 'Let's go to the Kennedy Memorial,' he said. 'It was his favourite place.'

They walked quietly along an avenue of trees. The red and yellow leaves of the maples and birches were beginning to fall. He squeezed her hand gently and asked, 'What will the official line be on Buddy?'

She swung their hands forwards and then backwards and scuffed some leaves with her feet.

'Costa,' she said. 'They'll say it was someone like

that. That Buddy was involved in some illegal shipments or other. That despite an exemplary early career
he had become corrupt in the ten years since he left
the Army and had gone in too deep.'

'Not much to make his family proud.'

'There isn't much family. Maddie. And she knows
all about him.'

'His children I meant.'

'Oh. Well, it's not so good is it? But we can explain
what really happened to him when they are older.'

Simon quickly turned his head to look at her. She
had said 'We'. But Thousand was looking intently at
the path ahead of her.

They stood at the Kennedy Memorial watching the
Eternal Flame. 'You know,' said Simon, smiling to
himself, 'I once made the mistake of asking Buddy
where he was the day Kennedy was shot. Everyone is
supposed to know. So anyway, he said he had been
sitting eating sandwiches with his kid sister on the
Grassy Knoll. Said he didn't notice a thing.'

'Dear Buddy,' she smiled. 'We are going to miss him
very much.'

'Every day, Thousand, every day.'

They walked slowly back to the car and Simon sat
in behind the wheel.

'We'll go to my place,' she said. 'But can you stop
off at the mall by Belmont and Thirteenth? I can pick
up some stuff for a stir fry and there are one or two
other things I have to get.'

'Are we having lunch? I don't know I feel much like
that.'

'Sure we are. I'm just about through with my explaining things and now it's your turn. It could take us some time.'

'What about?'

'You'll see,' she said, pointing at the road. 'Just concentrate on your driving and remember to stay on the wrong side of the road.'

When he had parked by the small group of shops, he said, 'You don't have to cook anything. Take away would be fine.'

'Nonsense. Too much junk food will give you spots. But I'll let you go to that German shop and buy two ring doughnuts. The big ones.'

'OK. Then I'll come back to the car and wait for you.'

'No. Then I want you to go to the drugstore and get me a big bottle of sun oil. Factor six.'

'For your holiday?'

'Yes. On second thoughts, make that two bottles. And factor fifteen.'

'Whatever you say.'

He was back in the car by the time she returned with a brown paper bag of groceries and what looked like a magazine.

'Reading matter for your flight?'

'Not quite. But you can't look at it yet,' she said, slipping the magazine into the bag.

Back at her flat, Thousand opened the curtains in front of the long windows. Simon stood there looking out over the city while Thousand busied herself in the kitchen area. The day was clear and bright and he was looking down at the Capitol Dome and the White House to the right with a splash of autumn colours around the lawns. Further away was the quiet sweep of the Potomac. He thought he could just make out bright yellow and purple dots on the surface. Perhaps there was another regatta today.

'It really is some view, Thou. Night or day.'

'I know,' she called above the tonk tonk of the wok. 'I took a time-lapse photograph of it once over a full twenty-four hours. I won a prize in a local competition can you believe.'

He laughed. 'A lady of many talents. Any beer?'

'In the fridge. We're nearly ready here.'

He took two cans and a small table over to the window so they could enjoy the view over lunch.

She brought the plates over to him. 'Chopsticks only. No cheating!'

'No problem. Buddy showed me the right way. More scoop than pick. Saigon style.'

'Me too.'

After a mouthful or two he said, 'Not bad this. Who taught you to cook?'

'Nobody really. I sort of picked it up from books and TV. Can you cook?'

'A bit. Delia taught me all I know.'

'Who's she? One of your women?'

'No such luck. Not bad looking. Blue eyes but dark hair.'

'And gentlemen prefer?'

'So they say.'

She pointed with her chopsticks. 'Down there about ten miles away is Andrews Air Force Base. And just outside the gate is a little place called Morningside. Warkowski has a house there because he says he likes to wake up to the sound of jets.'

Simon laughed. 'Good luck to him. What sound do you like in the morning?'

She looked serious for a moment. 'I'm not sure. What sound do you think a fishing boat makes being pulled up a beach at first light?'

He smiled. 'A gentle sort of hiss I expect. And there would be the sound of sea birds too. Perhaps the fishermen calling out to each other as they pulled the ropes and secured the boats.'

'Well, that's the sound I would like,' she said.

When they had finished eating she made some of Costa's coffee and brought it back to the small table with the two ring doughnuts.

'Back to work,' she said. 'My turn to ask questions now.'

'Fire away.'

'First. How up-to-date is the version of the scam Rolands has?'

'Scam?' he said. 'I never did like that word.'

'Call it something else then. I said how recent?'

Simon picked up his coffee and took a sip. 'His will be six months old. Not more. I've made a few changes but not many. If he can unravel the files and put the procedures in order I would say he has a running version.'

'That's what I thought. What changes have you made though?'

'Nothing significant. I take it you know as much as he does from the way you are asking?'

'Nearly. I hacked in to what he was doing this morning. No, don't worry. He didn't see me.'

'Well the only change really is to make the Drifting Tables larger. But only by a factor of two. But why do you want to know? Basically it's blown. If he knows enough to put it together then he knows enough to stop it.'

'You told Buddy it couldn't be stopped.'

'Did I now? Well, that was before. And I was right. It can't actually be stopped. But Rolands sure as hell can follow it every step of the way. Doing it now would be like holding up a bank and telling the police in advance so they could be waiting for you outside. I'm afraid it's back to the drawing board as far as get-rich-quick schemes are concerned.'

'Don't be so negative. There are three ways to stop Rolands. One you should have thought of yourself and two of my own. Ready?'

He pulled his ears out from the side of his head. 'Ready as I can be!'

She ignored him. 'Your Drifting Tables. I think the reason you can't build bigger ones is because of the edge effect?'

'Right.'

'Just like the Go board. Or chess. Do you remember me asking you about them?'

He shrugged. 'I remember and I guessed why, but I could hardly tell you could I? And yes, it is the edge effect. I tried a hundred ways but always came up

339

against the same stability problems when I went above sixty by sixty.'

'Well, that's still an improvement on Rolands. He's still using your ten by ten.'

'But going up to sixty doesn't really help much. You have to go to several hundred before you can shift really big numbers. I toyed with the idea of stacked tables but I couldn't cope with more than one surface.'

'Well. Here is idea number one.' She picked up one of the doughnuts and held it out in front of her. 'This is a ring, yes? So. Look at its surface. One continuous curved plane. No edge. So I think you should use a doughnut surface to build the Drifting Table on. Its real name is a torus. A Genus One Solid to be precise.'

She put out her tongue and licked off some sugar. 'Mmm. Good. And then use the torus to form your ring file as well. You cut out one whole step in your procedure if you can double up like that. And what's more, the geometry of the torus, the doughnut, is inherently stable so your size limit goes out of the window.'

He stared at her open-mouthed. 'That's brilliant. I would never have thought of that.'

She pretended not to look pleased. 'Well, you should have. So far we are one step ahead of Rolands because he won't have thought of it either. Now to step two. Clock speed.'

'You have to use the mainframe clock. It's just about the fastest there is anyway.'

'Not so. Do you know what an Interference Clock is? I thought not. Well, perhaps you know that wavy pattern effect you get on silk depending on the angle of light?'

'Moire banding I think?'

'Yes,' she said enthusiastically. 'You get the same effect if you take two grids and run one in front of the other. The lines you get are called "beats" and come about because of the interference between the two grids. Now the number of "beats" you get in a given length of time depends on the size of the grids and how fast you run them over each other.'

'Just about with you so far,' said Simon taking a sip of his coffee.

'Instead of grids,' she went on, 'you can use spoked wheels. You would see what I meant if you looked at one bicycle wheel spinning in front of another one. But in the case of wheels, the "beats" don't go round evenly. Some parts slow right down and other parts speed up. That's the effect anyway.'

'So?'

'So use the mainframe clock to handle the equations for two spinning spoked wheels. Then use the result from the fastest part of the spin to drive another clock. I've done the numbers and it's a speed increase of about two hundred at best. One hundred at worst.'

'Not stable,' he said. 'Always changing. The waft and weave on the Drifting Table wouldn't know what sequence to run in.'

'Not so. Stable as the mainframe clock. And better, out of phase and so undetectable to the operating system. It's a free ride. Put that together with the torus file and I should say we were really beginning to cook.'

He leaned back in his chair and blew out his cheeks. 'Wow. That's what I say. You really are pretty good aren't you?'

'Only standing on your shoulders, Simon. Yours was the difficult part. But now we come to step three. When we've got that, we really will have blue water between us and Rolands. It has to do with where you drop the money down at the end.'

She took a bite from her doughnut. 'End of ring,' she smiled. 'Now, on the five times you've got it to work I think you've dropped the money down into waiting accounts, right?'

'Yes. But they don't have to be part of the procedure. They can be set up in advance.'

'That's a weakness. Too risky if they know where to look. Let me tell you a little trick I learned from our good friend Mr da Costa. Now, do you know what a Dry Account is?'

'No. And I don't like the sound of Costa.'

'Don't worry. I just saw him use one once. So a normal bank account is one that accepts deposits and lets you take funds out, right?'

'That is why they are called bank accounts, yes.'

'Cut the glib. A Dry Account doesn't have to be set up in advance. If you just send money to a bank you don't have an account with, they will open one for you as the money arrives to hold the money in until you tell them how you want it placed. So a holding account is set up for each amount of money received.

They call them "dry" accounts because they are held separately from the normal accounts and you can't get at the money until you "wet" them by giving the bank the authorisation details as proof of ownership. At which point these accounts become like any other normal bank account. Now, these Dry Accounts are not very popular because they never earn any interest but, on the other hand, are *very* useful if you want to drop a very large sum of money into your bank without making a big splash. Another reason for the name I think. Anyway, from our point of view the most interesting thing is that they never show up on the transaction logs. So, I say drop the ring file money into Dry Accounts and pick it up at leisure. Rolands won't know where to look because there won't *be* anywhere *to* look.'

'But don't you have to tell the banks in advance at all?'

'No. At least not if you use an offshore one because they are used to opening dry accounts for clients all the time.'

'But where could you do this? It sounds as though you are going to need an awful lot of accounts. Dry or not.'

She stood up and went over to the kitchen counter.

'Do you know where George Town is?' she asked.

'Yes, of course, it's the bit of Washington between here and the river. Where the restaurants and museums are.'

'Not Georgetown. George Town, two words,' she corrected. 'It's the capital of the British Cayman

Islands. Where the turtles and the banks are. Big holiday place too.'

'Sounds nice. But so what?'

'I hope sc.' She took the magazine she had bought at the mall from the bag and came back to the table with it.

'In the Cayman Islands,' she went on, 'there are six thousand registered banks. All offshore. And every one of them knows all about Dry Accounts. Very private. Just what we need.'

'You're serious aren't you? I really think you're serious.'

'Oh, yes. That would describe it. Now have a look at this.'

She put the magazine in front of him. It wasn't a magazine at all, but a brochure from a travel agent called 'Grand Cayman. The Dream Destination.'

He threw his head back and laughed. 'You are a lot of fun, Thousand. You really are a lot of fun.'

She laughed too. 'You haven't seen the best bit,' she said. 'Open it up.'

He turned the pages. White beaches lined with palm trees. Blue skies, windsurfers, a boy holding up a huge turtle by its front legs.

He looked back up at her. Her whole face was smiling at him. 'One more page to go,' she beamed.

He turned it over. On this page was a smaller picture of the boy. Next to it was a list of hotels. One of them was underlined in pencil.

'The Turtle Beach Hotel,' he read. 'This holiday village is new and is one mile from the capital. Visitors can enjoy all the facilities of a modern five star hotel with the added pleasure of beachside chalet suites that lead straight onto the famous Turtle Beach. Early risers can join the fishermen at dawn as they haul their boats up the sand with the overnight catch.'

He looked up quizzically.

She reached out and took his hands in hers. 'I've booked us in. Tomorrow. Best cabin at the top of the beach. Name of Felix.'

He moved his hands on top of hers and squeezed gently. 'Well, you certainly know how to focus things. I'll give you that.'

She took her hands away and looked at her watch. 'Shit. It's one o'clock already. Only eleven hours to go. I have to start now. The dishes can wait.'

'Hold on. Thousand. Don't you think we should talk about this a bit first? Maybe there are risks you don't know about. Have you thought of that?'

She sat down. 'Talking? What else have we been doing all day? And, yes, there may be risks I haven't thought of, but it's today or not at all. We will never be this far ahead again.'

'Now, calm down,' he said. 'You may not know what problems are left but I do. Unless we can deal with them, we are dead in the water. Sorry.'

She looked at her watch again. 'Be quick then.'

'OK.' He held out the thumb and first two fingers of his left hand and counted them off.

'One. The bank codes. Only Buddy had them and he's gone. Two. The fickle finger of fate. With both Bell and Buddy gone, it's not going to take Warkowski long to work out whose hand is in the cookie jar. And Three. Sad news. But I have no idea how to build a doughnut-shaped Drifting Table. And even if I did, my Large Number Theory just isn't up to it. One, two, three. Out.'

She leaned back and folded her arms. 'Is that it?'

'I'm always careful when you do that.'

'What?'

'Never mind.'

'I said is that it?'

'The three things. Yes.'

'Right, then,' she began. 'Number one. I can get the bank codes. Straight level-four hack. No problem. Two. They probably will come after us anyway but at least this way, we can have a head start and we may even get time to cover our tracks. And Three. Don't worry about the Drifting Tables. It's covered. I can do it. It's all in the book.'

'I don't remember any book.'

'You do.' She stood up and went over to her desk and returned to sit down with the book she had bought from Harvey the day before. She read the title to him. *'The Application of Large Number Theory to the Game of Computer Go*. Not perfect, but good enough.'

She stared at him. 'Anything else, Mr Negative?'

He put his hands on his face and wiped them over the top of his head and locked his fingers. 'Shit, Thousand. I don't know. In a week of total mayhem at all levels you come up with yet another explosion. How can I know if it's sensible or not? It's not sensible. I know it's not.'

She leant forward. 'Look at me,' she said.

He unlocked his fingers and sat up.

She reached her hands out and put them either side of his face. 'I agree,' she began. 'We can go around the houses again and again until we talk each other out of it. We can talk till goodbye comes. We can even go home and never see each other again. I don't know how long all this would give us before they came looking. A day? A week? But you and I know there is a real chance it would be a lot longer. An always. Now, I let you slip through my fingers once before and I don't intend to do that again. This is me here. Thousand. Not some far-off person you nearly got to know once. I want you. I need you. This is Reality Checkpoint for both of us. Do this for me and I'll be yours for ever. Promise.'

She sat back. 'There,' she said. 'Done it.'

He looked down to the brochure in front of him and turned a couple more pages. More white beaches. A green and purple beach umbrella over a table. Another picture of the little boy, this time holding up two giant lobsters.

'A day?' he said. 'A week? It's still more than most people get isn't it?'

He looked back up at her. 'Yes. The answer's yes. OK?'

'You won't regret this. I promise you.'

He turned back to the brochure. 'Two bottles of sun oil? You must have been pretty certain I would say yes.'

She stood up and smiled. 'Maybe. But now I want

you to do your airline trick for me.'

'What? Four gins in ten minutes? My favourite.'

'Not that one. The ticket one.' She walked back over to the desk and switched her computer on. 'I know you can hack in and change reservations but can you fool the system into thinking you were on a flight you didn't go on?'

'I should think so.'

'Good. And then can you actually go as a passenger on a flight without appearing on the seat list.'

'Same principle.'

'OK. Put me on a morning flight to Los Angeles and then not on one to the Caymans. But in reverse if you see what I mean.'

He walked across and sat down at the keyboard. Within thirty seconds he was in to Galileo, the International Airline Reservation System.

She laughed. 'You're fast. I bet they don't know you can do that.'

'Not yet. But it's only a matter of time. Those flights? When did you say you wanted to travel? Or not as the case may be.'

She told him again and he began to key in the sequences.

'But what about your passport?' he asked. 'Even if you can bluff Galileo here, there is still passport control.'

'You leave the government computers to me. I can do that bit. Just you concentrate on your own Special Subject.'

She stood behind him and put her hands on his

shoulders and pressed lightly down. ' "If I have seen further it is by standing on the shoulders of giants". Do you know who said that?'

'Yes. Newton. I like to think that one of the giants was our friend on the screen here, Galileo.'

'That's right. It's nice that you know. They have always been two heroes of mine.'

He completed the flight changes. 'That's done then for you. The same for me now.'

'No. Confirm yourself on the London flight you were going to take this afternoon. Leave your "shadow" on it but take the five o'clock shuttle to New York and the eight o'clock to George Town.'

He took his hand off the keyboard. 'But that's today. I can't go until after midnight can I?'

'Why not?'

'Because I have to be here to run the scam. It's not going to run itself.'

'You don't have to be here. I can do it. You can be waiting for me at Turtle Beach. Book us a table for lunch.'

'You can't operate the system yourself. It needs two.'

She leant forward and ran her hand down his chest. 'No. It doesn't. You know that. I can get the codes and I am a big girl.'

'It's too dangerous. Let me do it. You go on ahead.'

'Nope. My call. And don't ring.'

'What if your ring file breaks down? Do you know how to exit the system?'

'No. But it won't.'

'And what do you do if the side files lock up. Do you know what to do?'

'No idea. I'll think of something.'

'In two seconds? I don't think so. You have to face it. I'd be much better. You can help if you want but it must be me who runs the actual sequence.'

'No. I will know all the details of the codes, the ring and the Interference Clock. You don't know any of them. You only know things I know already. No contest.'

He did not reply.

'Besides,' she said, standing up again, 'there is one really big "what if" neither of us has talked about.' She placed her fingers lightly around his neck.

'Ready?' she asked. 'Then what if Rolands plays his ace?'

'What ace?'

'The Big One. Come on. You've only got two seconds.'

'What ace?'

'Time's up,' she said and momentarily tightened her hands around his neck before letting go.

She walked away from him back to the little table and poured herself another coffee. 'Because, you see,' she said, 'if I were Rolands and I thought someone was messing around on the Forex computers, I'd pull the plug out. Shut the lot down.'

'He can't do that,' countered Simon. 'It would crash the whole banking network. The whole thing would come grinding to a halt for hours. No way would he ever do that.'

'You've forgotten this morning already haven't you?' she said looking at him over her cup, 'Warkowski. The lovely Janislav. He does exactly what he wants and if he wants to crash the international banking system, then crash it he will.'

'Well. If they really do that we're stuffed. Well and truly. Along with everyone else on the system at the time. It would be total data wipeout. Chaos.'

'Well. Let's hope he doesn't do it then. But it's the one thing we can do absolutely nothing about and so I don't propose to worry about it.'

She picked up her coffee and returned to Simon.

'So, you finish up with Galileo there before he thinks you've died. Exit the system. And then go and pack. I'll see you for lunch tomorrow. Lobster. Mmm. My favourite.'

Simon resumed at the keyboard. When he had finished he stood up and faced her. 'If you're sure then?'

She shrugged. 'The clock's running.'

He cupped her face with his hands and kissed her. Then he held his head away till they were six inches apart. 'Good luck, Big Eyes.'

When he had gone she did not sit down immediately but walked over to the window and leant over to see him go out of the front lobby and start looking for a cab.

'Oh, Simon,' she said to herself. 'You are a nice man but you do rather believe what people tell you. All that saying "yes" and you missed the real "reason against".'

351

She returned to the keyboard and opened a line to the State Department mainframe. Five access codes later she was into the personnel files and she had found the record she was looking for. She enlarged the photograph at the top of the sheet and sent it to the printer at her side. Ten seconds later the printer hummed into life and began printing. A single sheet of paper fed into the tray face-down. She picked it up and turned it over. Maddie Booker. 'Hello, problem,' she said out loud.

She folded the photograph in half, went over to her handbag on the kitchen counter and put the photograph inside.

Back at the computer again, she looked up at the wall clock above her. One fifteen. Ten and three-quarter hours left. There should just be time if she worked fast.

Chapter Thirteen

Simon collected his key from the front desk of his hotel and took the lift to his floor. On the way up he began to plan the telephone call he would have to make to Nancy Lessing.

He was surprised to see the door to his room ajar. Immediately cautious he pushed it slowly fully open before going into the room. Maddie was sitting on his bed looking up at him.

'Hello, Simon.'

'How did you get in? No. Don't bother to answer. Just go.'

'Please.'

'Go. I said "Go". I do not want to even talk to you. Go.'

She stood up but walked away from the door to the window end of the room. She lit a cigarette before turning around to face him. 'You're going with Thousand aren't you? You mustn't trust her. Don't go.'

'No. I am not going anywhere with anyone. Least of all anyone from here. I am simply going home. I have a funeral to arrange in case you've forgotten. And now I have to pack, so please leave.'

'She's clever. I'll give her that. And she is too clever for you. I know what she's like.'

'Oh. Surprise, surprise! You do know her after all. We've come a long way from "Isn't there some woman who works with you and Buddy?" haven't we?'

'That was before. What do you expect me to have said?'

'Before? Before what? Bell? The break-in? Before your own brother was shot?'

'No. Before this.' She reached her hand up to the dragonfly brooch on her lapel. 'Before Byron's.'

He did not reply but opened a cupboard, took out a suitcase and put it on the bed. He began filling it with clothes.

She sat down in the armchair. 'They don't have any idea that you are anything to do with it. I didn't tell them anything. You are completely clear.'

She stood up and stubbed her cigarette out. Then she sat down again and took out another one.

'I don't know what she's got planned but I think she wants to trick you,' she began again. 'If you so much as move an inch towards it they will hit you like an express train. You won't even have time to look up and see her fold her arms. Believe me.'

He put a shirt down. 'Believe you? Why should I believe you? I can't think of a single thing you ever said to me that was true.'

'Columbus was true. I want you to come there. Just us.'

'Oh, yes. Columbus. Isn't that where you rang me from at one o'clock last night? You disgust me, Maddie Booker.'

'I wanted to say sorry to you Simon. Am I too late even for that?'

'Just a little. Yes.'

'And I came to see you. To say goodbye. And so that afterwards I can at least tell myself that I tried to warn you.'

'Thank you. I'll be careful. Particularly when I am crossing the road in my own town. Particularly when sitting by rivers. I think I'll be very careful for ever now.'

She stood up again. 'I'll go now. But just promise me you won't try to operate your scheme again.'

'Scam. It's not a scheme, it's a scam. Plain and simple.'

She began to walk towards the door. 'Scam isn't the right word and you know it. It's much more than that. I don't know how long it took you to build properly. Years I should think. So give it a proper name. Say what it really is. When I think about it I think of it as your weaver's dream. I think you should call it The Weave.'

She reached the door and turned before she went out. 'Goodbye. Thank you anyway.'

He finished packing and then stood looking at the telephone. Calls to make.

General Warkowski and Major Bradley were waiting in Rolands' office at ten minutes to midnight.

The office was four floors below street level in the State Department and so did not have any windows. Where the windows might have been, Rolands had pasted up posters from travel companies which gave the office a cheerful if confusing feel. One picture was an alpine scene of a snowy mountain and a wooded valley. Another poster was a wide-lens view of San Francisco and the Golden Gate Bridge. A third picture was a tropical beach scene of a laughing boy holding up a large turtle.

Above the desk were three head-and-shoulder portraits. One of Steve Jobs, one of Steve Wozniak and the third one of Bill Gates. The picture of Bill Gates was hanging upside down.

Warkowski pointed. 'Bradley, why is that picture upside down?'

'I don't know General. Perhaps Colonel Rolands hasn't noticed.'

Warkowski gave Bradley his most withering stare.

Rolands came hurrying back into his office.

'Where have you been, Colonel? It's nine minutes to twelve,' snapped Warkowski.

'I went to relieve myself, sir,' said Rolands as he sat at his desk in front of five large monitor screens.

'Show me,' said Warkowski.

Rolands pushed his glasses up to the bridge of his nose and began: 'The two outside screens on each side are the dealing screens. They show the transactions logging, taking place, on all the Forex computers linked to the eight satellites.'

Warkowski leaned forward to look at one of them.

The screen was divided into a grid with each cell containing a number. The numbers were constantly changing which gave the whole screen a flickering appearance.

'And this central screen,' continued Rolands, 'shows the power call to each of the satellites from their solar panels.'

Warkowski and Bradley examined the middle screen.

There was a row of eight green columns like thermometer bars. The top of each of the columns was rising and falling gently.

'Now, if the demand for power exceeds the deals by the legitimate traders, we will see a red area appear above each of the green columns. How much red will show how much illegal trading is taking place, how much power the ring file is calling.'

Rolands pointed to one of the outside screens again. 'As soon as that happens we will see activity in the lower part of the dealing screens here, sir.' Rolands ran his finger along the bottom of the screen. 'A blue number will put a dollar value on the illegal trade up to the moment power is cut from the satellites.'

'And is that going to happen automatically or will you have to do it?'

Rolands smiled at the general and looked very pleased with himself. 'Automatically, sir. I am happy to say I was able to assemble a working version of the Gorov software in time. It's not perfect and will be better tomorrow but it is already eight times faster than a manual system.'

Warkowski looked again across the screens. He did not like charts and columns of numbers.

'I can see all this is pretty colourful, Colonel, but does it work?'

'I believe so, sir.'

'Did it work last night?'

'We didn't have this in place yesterday Wall Street midnight but there were no illegal transaction calls to the system.'

'So how do you know it will work if you need it tonight?'

'It's been tested, sir. We tried it four times earlier this evening. It worked every time.'

'But you didn't shut off the satellites?'

'Of course not, sir.'

'Then it wasn't a test. It was a simulation. You don't know if it will actually work.'

'It works, sir.'

'What do you think, Bradley?'

'It's very impressive, sir. I have every confidence in Colonel Rolands.'

Warkowski stood up and walked to and fro across the office a few times. He stood in front of the alpine scene. 'Alaska?' he asked.

'No, sir. Austria.'

'Nothing the matter with Alaska, Colonel. Alaska's American.'

'Yes, sir.'

The general turned back to the desk and pointed at the middle screen. 'You said yesterday that it would take you two days to build a computer shut-off system. Does this mean you've got a proper lock-out for the Lessing thing working for today?'

'Not fully, sir. This is only what we have so far. By tomorrow night we will have this duplicated fully and on the control software for each of the satellites with failsafe mechanisms. For today we only have a manual back-up.'

'Which is?'

'Me, sir.'

Rolands spoke again quickly before the general could comment. 'But we may not need it sir. As you say, Dr Lessing is no longer with us so we are only guarding against him having passed on the procedures to a third party.'

'Are you saying all this may be a waste of money, Rolands?'

'Not at all sir. Sooner or later someone else would have the same idea. This way we will be ready for them. Ahead, sir.'

The general resumed his pacing backwards and forwards. 'The value of forward planning, Major. Forward planning.'

Rolands turned to the screens. 'One minute to midnight, sir. Perhaps you and Major Bradley would care to take a seat.'

Bradley drew up a chair and Warkowski stood behind the two men.

Rolands spoke again. 'If anything is going to happen, sir, it will be between thirty and five seconds to midnight.'

At one minute before midnight the dealing screens

began to stop flickering as the numbers stopped changing one by one.

'Boxing, sir. The currencies are boxing.'

When all four screens were still the green columns on the middle screen ceased moving too.

'Power all level.'

At twenty seconds to the hour, Rolands began to sit back and relax. 'Clear, sir. No power calls. We're safe.'

But as he spoke, a fine red line appeared at the top of the eight green power columns. The red lines thickened rapidly.

'Shit! It's up! There it goes! It's flying!' shouted Rolands.

Within two seconds the eight red lines had reached the top of the screen. 'He's fast. My God he's fast!'

Suddenly the central screen went blank and Rolands spun his head to look at the nearest dealing screen. The grid of numbers began to fall away and spaces appeared all over the screen. Soon the main part of the screens were blank, leaving only a row of blue numbers across the bottom.

At five seconds past the hour the green columns appeared on the central screen again and the dealing grid filled again with flickering numbers.

General Warkowski raised himself to his full height, 'Well, Colonel. How much?'

Rolands ran his finger across the bottom of all four dealing screens.

'He was fast, sir. I don't know how he was so fast.'

'I asked how much, Colonel.'

Rolands checked again. 'Fifty, sir. Fifty million dollars down sir. But none to him. The power break cut him out. Whoever he was, our man didn't take a cent.'

Warkowski smiled. 'Go and telephone your mother, Bradley. You are going to be on breakfast television.'

Thousand was sitting back in her chair looking at one of the same dealing screens as at the State Department.

Rolands had been quick. Much quicker than she had expected.

But not quick enough. In the two seconds before she had been cut off, she had built the ring file, opened and shut ten thousand deals and dropped the money down into two thousand separate accounts. All Dry. Bone Dry. A take of fifty million dollars in less than two seconds.

Thousand reached forward and shut off the computer before picking up her coffee cup and walking over to the sink where she placed it in with the dirty dishes from lunch.

She made her way over to the windows and looked out briefly at the night skyline before drawing the curtains.

She returned to the kitchen area and stood in front of the telephone, hesitated momentarily before picking it up and dialling.

Someone answered the other end. 'Yes, good evening,' she said. 'Could I speak to Mr da Costa please. It is very urgent. Thank you.'

San Antonio da Costa was sitting in front of the

glass-topped table when Thousand was shown into his room. He stood up when he saw her and extended his hand.

'Miss Nocta, what a delightful surprise.'

'Thank you for seeing me so late. I hope I did not disturb you.'

He waved for her to sit down.

'Always a delight to see a beautiful woman. Never an inconvenience. Some coffee perhaps? Even something a little stronger?'

'Nothing thank you.'

She sat down opposite him with her hands in her lap.

'Have you come about Mr Marlin? I am very sorry for your loss. He was a good friend of many years' standing to me and Raõl here.'

'No. It's not that. But thank you.'

'What then? A social call? I think not so.'

She opened her bag. 'I have something to ask you. Something I want you to do.'

'A favour. Anything for a friend of Mr Marlin's. Don't hesitate to ask.'

She took the folded photograph from the bag. 'Not a favour. Business. But something we have not asked you before.'

She opened out the photograph of Maddie and put it on the table between them.

'Do you know who this is?' she asked.

Da Costa hesitated. 'As a businessman in Washington I have to know many things. Perhaps I have seen this person before.'

He picked up the piece of paper and held it up for Raõl to see. Raõl nodded.

Da Costa placed the photograph delicately back on the table and looked up at Thousand with a questioning expression on his face.

Thousand lowered her eyes.

'Please,' she said. 'Do you know where she is now? Tonight.'

Da Costa leant back and put his hands on his knees. Raõl leant forward and whispered in his ear. Da Costa sat forward again and nodded to Thousand.

'Very well. Are you trying to find her? She is staying at her brother's house. Is that all?'

'No. I know where she is.'

Da Costa held his hands up. 'Then what? What else is to know?'

Thousand leaned forward and pushed the paper across the table towards da Costa. 'Mr da Costa. This woman. This is the job.'

He leant back, put his head on one side and furrowed his brow.

'I don't understand you,' he said.

'I think you do. And you can do this. Can I be plainer? This woman has done terrible things. I want you to remove her for me. Remove her altogether.'

He held his hands wide. 'Crazy! You are crazy woman. I know this person and what she do. So is it revenge? Is this revenge for what she does to Simon's friend? Then go and speak with her. Not for me. San Antonio da Costa is not for revenge. He is businessman.'

'No, Mr da Costa. This is not revenge. This is business for you and me. Normal business.'

'Normal? This is normal? I am businessman. Only that.'

She breathed in fully and then out again slowly.

'I have come here,' she began, 'because I know you can do this. In your world such things are not unusual. I have worked in Washington too long not to know that. Now please, tell me how much it will be. I can pay.'

Da Costa did not speak.

'I can pay,' she said again. 'I say one million dollars. Any currency. Any bank. Dry.'

He shrugged and looked up at Raõl.

'Very well,' she said. 'Two. I won't go higher.'

He sat forward. 'You and I Miss Nocta, or should I say Major Nocta? We have not done business before. I do not know you. Only from Buddy and Simon. The first time we see each other is last week when it was not good. And now you ask me for this. I think not. I think you trick.'

'You have my word. No trick.'

'An American's word? We talk about this before I think.'

'Then Simon's word again too. I am speaking for him. This is for him.'

'Simoon? Then he can speak to me.'

'No. He sent me. Tell me how much.'

Da Costa shrugged and put his hands on his knees again.

'Four,' he said.

'Two five.'

'Three.'

'OK.' Da Costa picked up the photograph and looked at it closely. 'Americans,' he said, 'are not easy to understand for me, Major. Not easy at all.'

She stood up to go. Suddenly feeling physically sick at what she had done.

'Today,' she said. 'The money is already in a Dry Account. I will send you the authorisation. I will call myself to confirm that your part of the work is done. Then I will do my part.'

'Very good, Major. Business it is. I look forward to more with you. Will you be doing the work of Colonel Marlin? Perhaps they will promote you?'

She began to walk towards the door and turned as she reached for the handle. 'By tomorrow you will understand why I am asking this of you. As a businessman you will understand. Thank you.'

When she had gone, da Costa passed the photograph to Raõl. 'Today, Raõl. The lady said today.'

'Yes. Today.'

Thousand felt faint in the lift back to the basement car park and had to grip the side rail very tight to control her nausea.

Her car was parked near the door into the lifts. As she arrived at the bay, she felt another wave of nausea. She leant over with one hand on the roof of the car and retched onto the concrete at her feet. She opened the door and slid in behind the wheel. It was not a cold evening but she was shivering so much she could hardly put the keys in the ignition.

Chapter Fourteen

By nine o'clock that morning, Simon was sitting in his shorts waiting for Cable News to come on television in the chalet at the Turtle Beach Hotel. The window and door were open onto the beach and a warm breeze was just moving the curtains. He could smell the sea.

He was chewing absently on the core of a fresh pineapple when the commercials finished and a woman newsreader came on sitting in front of a large picture of the White House.

'Dateline Washington. Helen Greenhowe here. The world of the foreign exchange markets is in chaos this morning following a major communication satellite failure last night. The malfunction happened at close of trading on Wall Street, midnight East Coast Time. Details are still coming in as we speak but the Dollar, the Deutschmark and the Yen are all two percentage points down against a basket of nine second rank currencies including the Saudi Rial and Australian Dollar. Over now to Federal Bank Headquarters in Washington to our reporter Frederick

Stokes who has the latest news for us.'

The picture changed to a young man standing in front of some wide steps. 'Well, Helen, it seems that there was a power shut-down shortly before midnight last night as the day's accounts were being reconciled. The shut-down continued until after the midnight deadline for trading and the price setting for the following session. The breakdown could not have come at a worse time because it meant that the new exchange prices could not be set and, for the first hour of trading this morning, the dealers were essentially flying blind. They were uncertain whether to use the prices at shut-down or to anticipate the blackout the crash would precipitate. A few minutes ago I spoke to Herman Bradley, an acting Vice-President at the Federal Bank and this is what he had to say . . .'

The picture switched to Bradley in front of a plain grey wall.

He began, 'I can confirm that the eight satellites used for inter-bank transfers were out of operation for a short period due to a failure in an out-sourced power sequencer and a number of banking transactions were compromised.'

'Mr Bradley,' the reporter interrupted, 'there are rumours already circulating on Wall Street that there was unauthorised user access to the dealing computers and that the power was deliberately withdrawn from the system to minimise Forex and bank losses.'

'Negative to that,' replied Bradley, as if rehearsed. 'The system is fully secure and fully backed up. It would not be possible for any person or persons to gain ingress to the dealing system as only authorised Forex traders have the access sequence codes to initiate the dealing transactions.'

'Thank you, Herman,' continued the reporter, 'but could you put a figure on the losses sustained and assure our audience that those losses are the responsibility of the Federal Bank who owns the errant satellites.'

Bradley continued, 'We will have further details on that after a meeting with the heads of the banks at ten o'clock this morning. A full statement will be made available at that time to the media. But I can say that there were contingency plans in operation against even such an unlikely scenario as we have experienced today. All transactions proven to be lost at the time of the power-out will be fully made good.'

The girl sitting in front of the studio picture of the White House came on again. 'That was Herman Bradley of the Federal Bank,' she began. 'We will of course continue to bring you details of that story as it develops throughout the day and we will bring you the press conference live at around ten thirty. Now, other news and sport.'

Simon pressed the off switch on the remote control. He put it down next to the telephone on the table next to him and picked up the receiver to check it was still working. He listened to the reassuring dialling tone and put the telephone down again.

She had not called.

He stood up and walked slowly out of the chalet door onto the white beach.

The sand was pleasantly warm under his bare feet as he began walking down the gentle slope to the water about fifty yards away.

He waded in up to his knees and felt the soft sand between his toes. He put his hand up to shield his eyes against the brightness and looked out over the bay. A group of six windsurfers were crossing from the headland towards the spread of the beach and palm trees to his left. The vivid red and yellow sails contrasted with the blue of the horizon and the dark tropical green of the headland.

He sat down in the shallow water and leaned back until he was floating with just his hands touching the sand beneath him. He put his head back further and felt the cool water run through his hair and over his face. The salt taste brought back sudden memories of childhood holidays at the seaside with his parents. And then later with Ellen when Lewes was still a baby. It seemed a long time ago. He opened his eyes and looked up into the cloudless blue of the sky.

After about five minutes he sat up and leant back on his arms looking out to sea. He turned his head and looked over his shoulder at the beach. A row of five wooden fishing boats was pulled high up on the sand. His footprints made a line over the wet sand towards where he sat in the shallow water.

She had said she would come.

The sky back in Washington was not so clear. An autumn haze took the edge off the autumn colours as Maddie drove out of the garage under Buddy's house at Great Falls. She was glad to be leaving the house. She had not been there for some years and had been shocked at how run down it had become since Susan had left. Now that Buddy was gone too it had seemed completely lifeless.

The evening before she had made a start of going through his things for Susan and the children but had abandoned her task after only an hour and had settled down with one of the several half-empty whisky bottles she had come across hidden about the house.

Maddie had slept badly and had been about to begin her sorting out when a call came from Warkowski's office that she should go in for a meeting at ten. They had not told her what the meeting was about. Perhaps her taking Buddy's things? It scarcely mattered to her. There was no expression on her face or in her eyes as she pulled the car left down the Leesburg road towards the river.

On another day she might have noticed the black car with the tinted windows that pulled up to three cars behind her as she passed Swinks Mill. It remained three cars behind all the way until she was opposite Georgetown and about to go on Key Bridge. She did not see it until it came up level with her halfway over the bridge. If it had not come so close she might not even have noticed it then. As it was she glanced over when it was only about two feet from her side of the car and was met by the stare of a man looking directly at her. He had wound his window down and seemed to be waving at her. Did she know him? Did he want her to pull over? But then he wasn't waving. He was pointing. What was it he was pointing?

Two shots and it was over. Her car suddenly veered across and hit the central barrier. Then it slewed back across the lanes and cars banged into one another behind her as her own came to rest against the side of the bridge. Horns began to blare out and traffic built up in a solid block behind her.

Half her head was blown away and her body was knocked sideways over the front seat. Her right eye was staring sightlessly upwards with no more or less life than had been in it five minutes ago. The windscreen and the side window were covered with the contents of her head. Red and grey ran down the glass in streaks. Her blonde hair was wet with blood as it lay over the seat. The colours of autumn.

The black car pulled away into the Washington traffic. Windows up.

At midnight Simon climbed out of bed and walked to the open window of the chalet. The stars shone down from a clear tropical sky and made dancing reflections on the quiet waters of Grand Cayman Bay. In the distance he could see the winking lights of the fishing boats out for the night's catch.

He went over to his suitcase and took out a small hollow copper ball. There were star shapes cut into it all around the sides and in the middle was a small candle. He lit it and placed it by the open window.

He watched as star shapes from the light of the candle danced on the walls and ceiling of the room. He turned to look out to the real stars again, wondering which constellations were above him tonight. What they meant.

Then he looked down again at the candle burning in the holder. He smiled.

He turned, went quietly across the room again and climbed back into the bed. Gently, so as not to wake her.

Pasiphae

William Smethurst

PASIPHAE is the most advanced military communications satellite ever built. But strange signals are penetrating its security system – signals that appear to emanate from the fourteenth century. And as chaos strikes the world's communications systems from Paris to Tokyo, it becomes obvious that the enigmatic messages are full of murderous passion.

The key lies in the mind of a young archaeologist in Herefordshire who finds herself drawn to the tomb of a Franklin, dead for five hundred years. Night after night, she feels herself compelled to lie by his effigy, haunted by dreams of love and betrayal. Lizzie Draude has become a carrier, a transmitter between the time of Richard II and the present-day world. But can the flow of signals be stopped before horrendous forces are unleashed, destroying more than Lizzie herself?

'Enthralling' *The Times*

0 7472 4817 6

HEADLINE
FEATURE

The Night Crew

John Sandford

Anna Batory is a scavenger. Roaming the streets of
LA by night, her video news crew hunt for
sensational stories to sell to the TV networks. And
Anna knows just where to dig to find the stories
people want to see.

When they film an attack on the UCLA Medical
Center by animal rights activists, Anna's not
convinced the networks will go for it. Later the
same night, however, they get the scoop they've
been hoping for – a teenager jumps from a five-
storey hotel window to his death and all of it's on
tape.

For Anna it's the beginning of a dizzying freefall
into madness, obsession and murder. Soon,
disturbing connections between herself and the
dead teenager start coming to light. And then she
finds she is being stalked by someone who claims
to know her better than she knows herself . . .

'John Sandford is a brilliant writer' *Guardian*

'In a crowded market, Sandford shines at the
quality end' *Daily Telegraph*

0 7472 5621 7

If you enjoyed this book here is a selection of other bestselling titles from Headline

CAT AND MOUSE	James Patterson	£5.99 ☐
CLOSER	Kit Craig	£5.99 ☐
WITHOUT PREJUDICE	Nicola Williams	£5.99 ☐
CLOSE QUARTERS	Jeff Gulvin	£5.99 ☐
INHERITANCE	Keith Baker	£5.99 ☐
SERPENT'S TOOTH	Faye Kellerman	£5.99 ☐
UNDONE	Michael Kimball	£5.99 ☐
GUILT	John Lescroart	£5.99 ☐
A DESPERATE SILENCE	Sarah Lovett	£5.99 ☐
THE LIST	Steve Martini	£5.99 ☐
FOOLPROOF	Dianne Pugh	£5.99 ☐
DUE DILIGENCE	Grant Sutherland	£5.99 ☐

Headline books are available at your local bookshop or newsagent. Alternatively, books can be ordered direct from the publisher. Just tick the titles you want and fill in the form below. Prices and availability subject to change without notice.

Buy four books from the selection above and get free postage and packaging and delivery within 48 hours. Just send a cheque or postal order made payable to Bookpoint Ltd to the value of the total cover price of the four books. Alternatively, if you wish to buy fewer than four books the following postage and packaging applies:

UK and BFPO £4.30 for one book; £6.30 for two books; £8.30 for three books.

Overseas and Eire: £4.80 for one book; £7.10 for 2 or 3 books (surface mail).

Please enclose a cheque or postal order made payable to *Bookpoint Limited*, and send to: Headline Publishing Ltd, 39 Milton Park, Abingdon, OXON OX14 4TD, UK.
Email Address: orders@bookpoint.co.uk

If you would prefer to pay by credit card, our call team would be delighted to take your order by telephone. Our direct line is 01235 400 414 (lines open 9.00 am–6.00 pm Monday to Saturday 24 hour message answering service). Alternatively you can send a fax on 01235 400 454.

Name   ....

Address ....

....

....

If you would prefer to pay by credit card, please complete:
Please debit my Visa/Access/Diner's Card/American Express (delete as applicable) card number:

Signature .... Expiry Date..............